ESCAPE

from

SAIGON

ESCAPE
from
SAIGON

A NOVEL

Michael Morris &
Dick Pirozzolo

Skyhorse Publishing

Skyhorse Publishing books may be purchased in bulk at special discounts for sales promotion, corporate gifts, fund-raising, or educational purposes. Special editions can also be created to specifications. For details, contact the Special Sales Department, Skyhorse Publishing, 307 West 36th Street, 11th Floor, New York, NY 10018 or info@skyhorse-publishing.com.

Skyhorse® and Skyhorse Publishing® are registered trademarks of Skyhorse Publishing, Inc.®, a Delaware corporation.

Visit our website at www.skyhorsepublishing.com.

10 9 8 7 6 5 4 3 2 1

Library of Congress Cataloging-in-Publication Data is available on file.

Cover design by Laura Klynstra

Print ISBN: 978-1-5107-0298-1
Ebook ISBN: 978-1-5107-0299-8

Printed in the United States of America

This book is dedicated to our wives, Karen and Jane, who have steadfastly encouraged and supported us through the years.

And to all who have sacrificed for their country, then and now.

Escape from Saigon is based on true events. Although the situations and characters have been dramatized, the story was inspired by real people and actions that occurred at the time.

Foreword

Keep quiet! Don't shout!
The Ambassador won't leave till
Everyone's out
The choppers are on their way
There's room for you all
They're climbing over the wall!
Get back!
Tell you, don't shout!
The Ambassador won't leave till
Everyone's out
The Ambassador just sent an order to
Freeze
That's it!
No more Vietnamese!

(From "The Fall of Saigon," *Miss Saigon*)

Tuesday, April 1, 1975

Tan Son Nhut Air Base, South Vietnam

THE GROUND CREW GUIDED THE MAMMOTH C-141 Starlifter into place between two tall, protective steel revetments. The jet's tailgate ramp lowered even before it rolled to a stop and the plane's crew chief hopped down, waving the waiting jeeps forward. Bags followed down the ramp, each carried by a soldier dressed in tan tropical-weight khakis, followed by a tall man in U.S. Army olive-drab jungle fatigues. Unlike the soldiers waiting on the tarmac, the man's fatigues were new, impeccably clean, and freshly starched. Four black stars were embroidered on each lapel.

One of the ground crew snapped to attention as he recognized the officer—General Weyand, the U.S. Army Chief of Staff. The soldier began to raise his arm, but before he could salute, the officer cut him off.

"At ease, soldier!" the general barked. "You don't salute your officers in a combat zone, so don't do it for me! You might as well paint a big red bull's-eye on my backside!"

"Yes sir!" the soldier stammered. "Your chopper's waiting for you, sir. It's the one over by the C&C shed, this way." He pointed across the field to a low tan corrugated metal building. A single-rotor UH-1D helicopter—a Huey—sat in front, its blades slowly beginning to turn.

As he looked at the chopper, the general reflected on the fact that, when he was stationed here, every aircraft on the field would have carried a U.S. Army insignia. Now, Air America—the CIA's covert air operation—was painted on both sides of this bird. And something else had changed since the war. Like the general's uniform, it was new and clean. The general nodded to the soldier, then waved his aides toward the first jeep and hopped in the front seat.

"Let's get moving! I don't want to keep the ambassador waiting!"

* * *

The chopper's blades were spinning furiously and its turbine roar had peaked to a deafening level by the time the Vietnamese base workers loaded the general's gear into the Huey and the officers strapped themselves into the sling seats behind the pilots. When the starboard-side machine gunner could see that all were aboard and ready he spoke into his helmet mic, letting the pilots know they were good to go. A sudden upward lurch was followed by a steep tilt forward as the chopper lifted off and rapidly gained altitude.

"Sir," the gunner shouted to the general over the din, "our flight plan is to reach altitude till we're beyond the base. The North Viets have brought up some heavy weapons in the past weeks and they've been picking off aircraft between here and the city. Once we're on our way we'll drop down to the deck where we're not such an easy target for antiaircraft. There's always the threat of small arms, but we'll be movin' right smart—it'd take a mighty quick gunner to even draw a bead on us."

The general nodded in agreement, then sat back and, like the others, welcomed the cooler air that came with the altitude. Their uniforms were already soaked through with sweat from the few minutes they had been on the ground. Vietnam was still as hot as he remembered. *Too damn hot!*

* * *

As the Vietnamese ground crew turned away from the cyclone of dust and sand thrown up by the Huey's rotor blades, one of the men pulled a cloth from his pocket to cover his face. It was a Western-style bandanna, bright red with a white paisley decorative pattern, the kind of bandanna the cowboys in American movies—like Clint Eastwood, his favorite—wore around their necks. The man had asked one of his GI friends to buy it for him at the Base Exchange.

No one among the workers noticed as the man shook the cloth vigorously, as though attempting to shake out the dust and sweat he had wiped from his face. No one except the teenager lying in the tall grass beyond the air base fence. This man was dressed in typical Vietnamese black pajamas, but he had carefully camouflaged himself head to foot with freshly cut leafy branches, and his exposed face and hands were smeared with dark mud. He had lain motionless in the grass for three days, waiting for this moment. When he saw the waving red bandanna, he crawled from his position toward a shallow ravine with a small stream at its bottom, discarded his camouflage and washed off the mud, then followed the watercourse away from the air base.

* * *

The Huey rose until it reached its cruising altitude some twelve hundred feet above the sprawling air base. It traced a half-circle across the sky, then banked toward the distant city and, within seconds, was a distant speck against the clouds.

The man in the grass soon reached his military unit, the encampment concealed in a bamboo grove less than a mile from the air base perimeter.

"Comrades!" he shouted. "A high-ranking American officer has arrived and is en route to Saigon. His helicopter will be over our forward defenses in moments! Contact them now to be ready to intercept them!"

A young woman wearing a commo headset and dressed in dark green military garb—the uniform of the People's Army of Viet Nam, or PAVN to her southern enemies—immediately began keying her radio handset, alerting similar units hidden farther to the west.

Deep in a patch of jungle scrub that offered a direct line of sight to the highway leading to the city, the signal was received and other PAVN soldiers hurried to their prearranged firing positions. They pulled camouflage tarps away from the big twin barrel anti-aircraft gun that had served them so well in their march south. A week earlier they had used it to shoot down an attacking A-1E Skyraider, a low-flying fighter-bomber used by the South Vietnam Air Force. It was a major accomplishment that had cheered and emboldened their comrades. Now, with a helicopter approaching their position, they had a chance to strike another blow that would bring them one step closer to victory.

"When you hear the helicopter coming, set your sights on the highway at treetop level," ordered their captain, a man whose hatred of both the Americans and the Saigon regime was legendary among his troops. Though born in the south, he took obvious pleasure in destroying the local forces whenever they clashed. He allowed no mercy, no prisoners, and no surrender, each time demanding that they wipe out the enemy down to the last man, and anyone who failed to follow his orders faced scathing retribution.

The rapid, heavy drumbeat of rotors—an unmistakable sound that characterized all Hueys—began to grow louder from far off in the east. "Ready your weapons!" the captain hissed. "Be prepared to fire on my command!"

Flying at maximum airspeed, the dark form of the Huey took shape and quickly grew in their sights. Nose pitched slightly down, moving at well over one hundred knots, it jinked and swerved to follow the twisting roadway, no more than twenty feet over the heads of startled pedestrians and bicyclists. A formidable target, but one the waiting soldiers could not miss at this range.

"Get ready!" the captain ordered as the sound grew to a roar and the chopper flew toward their field of fire.

At the very last moment, another voice directly behind the gunners yelled, *"Stand down! Do not fire your weapons! Do not fire!"*

Startled and confused, the soldiers turned and looked from their officer to the man who now stepped up to their gun position. This officer commanded the tank troop that had been attached to their company since the battle for Ban Me Thuot days earlier. Because he outranked their captain, the soldiers had no choice but to comply. They lowered their rifles and the antiaircraft gunner released his grip on the firing handles.

A moment later, the Huey blasted past their position unscathed, scattering peasants' hats and leaving a dust-choked whirlwind in its wake as it flew off toward the heart of the city.

* * *

General Weyand's aides held tight to anything they could lock their hands on and sat ashen-faced as their Huey skimmed the treetops, banking and swerving scant feet above the highway, flying at maximum speed on its way toward Saigon. Unlike his aides, the general was enjoying the ride, grinning like a schoolboy with each sudden maneuver, a soldier once again in his element.

They never saw the enemy antiaircraft emplacement hidden in the bamboo grove as they flew past.

Deep within the grove, Captain Vo Giang seethed as he watched the helicopter—within seconds already far beyond their gun sights—clatter off toward Saigon.

"You let them get away!" he said, barely able to keep his anger in check. The officer who ordered them to hold their fire, Colonel Binh Anh Le, commander of the People's Army Fifth Tank Regiment, outranked Vo and was in charge of his unit. Vo could not countermand or question a senior officer. But he also could not help showing his displeasure that the colonel had let such a prize escape. "Our watchers told us there were important American military officers onboard! We had them in our sights!"

"Yes, Captain Vo. That is why I ordered your men to let them pass! Do you want a resumption of the American war now that we are so close to victory over the South? Do you want their jets and troops to return to kill more of our people? Shooting down a helicopter carrying their emissaries would be a grave mistake—one that would only prolong this bloodshed and delay the inevitable."

"But they have killed so many of our comrades! Caused us years of suffering! They deserve to die!"

"Perhaps so, Captain. But now we must be careful not to repeat the past. We must be strategic in our thinking—and our actions."

"And what if they are here to help the Southern forces repulse our advance? What if they are already plotting to return with their troops?"

"That is a chance we have to take. Remember, we have watchers in many places—in the government offices in Saigon, and in Paris where the diplomats are also fighting our war. You may not know this, but they have told us to be patient now, to allow the events to unfold as they are. The South is defeated—they do not yet accept it. We have overrun their forces on the battlefield and taken the entire country. Now we have completely surrounded their last holdout, Saigon. The Americans know this, and they know they have no other option than to allow the government to collapse."

"Then we should attack quickly and hasten their fall!"

"Be patient, Captain. My superiors have told me that we must give them time—a grace period to let the cowards run away, like cockroaches fleeing from the light. The Americans are already evacuating their people. Their aircraft land and take away hundreds with every flight. We can afford to let the cockroaches leave with them. We have no need for traitors or those who might try to undo the victory we are about to achieve."

Hearing this, Vo's fury only increased. "Let traitors go? They should be made to pay for the years of suffering they have inflicted on us!"

"As we have done to them, *Dai uy*. We need to wait a little longer."

"How much longer?"

"The birth date of our comrade leader Ho Chi Minh is less than one month from now, and May Day is within weeks. So we will invade and claim our victory no later than the first of May. Until then we must keep our forces in check! Our sappers and combat units are already infiltrating the city. We can harass our Southern brothers—those who are still willing to fight—destroy their remaining defenses and let them feel our might, and lay the groundwork for our takeover when the signal is given. There may be fighting in the streets when that happens, so prepare your men. You may yet have an opportunity to shed blood for Saigon, Captain Vo. Let us both hope it is theirs, and not yours."

* * *

Le P'tit Bistrot, Saigon

"The artillery. Listen. It's stopped," Jean Paul Pellerin commented absentmindedly as he polished glasses behind the long cypress bar at Le P'tit Bistrot.

"Yeah, just enough shelling for the North to let us know they're knocking on the door, but not enough to piss off the Seventh Fleet," Sam Esposito said as he took up his usual spot at the far end of the bar. "They never take out the runways, though. The last thing they want is for the *New Jersey* to come back with its sixteen-inch guns."

Le P'tit was the unofficial headquarters for the four-hundred or so credentialed news correspondents, local and foreign cameramen and photographers whose press passes got them on board the Hueys and unfettered access to the fighting. There were at least twice as many hangers-on—mostly reporters from the Saigon papers and freelancers who came to the war zone because it seemed cool and hoped to get a job at a major newspaper or TV bureau.

Army and Air Force press relations officers could always be counted on to be there to rub elbows with the press. Now and then an author like Jamie Sullivan would show up. After two weeks in-country, he thought he knew everything he needed to know about the war and the GIs who fought and died in it. He wrote *Yellow Fire, Red Heat*, a book that became a best seller, often quoted by naïve congressmen during foreign policy speeches.

Le P'tit afforded Sam the two things he needed—a steady stream of Hennessy, which he drank straight up in a rocks glass, and a telephone that worked most of the time. If Sam wasn't at the *Washington Legend* office—which was conveniently located across the broad Nguyen Hue Boulevard just outside the door—everyone knew they could find him at Le P'tit.

"On the house, Sam," Jean Paul said as he poured out an inch of cognac and slid the glass across the bar. Jean Paul always made sure that Sam got the seat next to the house phone and the stack of overseas newspapers and magazines that he kept for his customers. If a newcomer who didn't know the ropes sat in Sam's seat, Jean Paul would politely mention that Sam was expected any minute and would be needing the phone, "So why don't you sit here where you don't have to move, and what can I get for you today?" he would say, so smoothly that there was never a protest.

"What's the occasion, Jean Paul?" Sam asked.

"It's April first. All Fools' Day. And since we are both here, that makes two fools—a good excuse to celebrate, maybe with two drinks." Jean Paul poured himself a Hennessy as he spoke.

* * *

Cholon District, Saigon

Vinh Anh Nguyen woke to the sound of rain and thunder. As he listened to Thu quietly breathing beside him, he could feel the heat from the sunrise and he realized he must have been dreaming of rain. The distant thunder was real enough, however—it continued to rattle the rattan sunshades at the windows and echo across the broad rice paddies beyond the city. But he was mistaken about this, too. It wasn't thunder but the sound of artillery pounding away in a steady, staccato rumble.

Every day now, the sound of artillery and exploding bombs were heard around Saigon. And the attacks were getting closer, now no more than a few kilometers from the city's outskirts. It had become so commonplace that people in the street didn't even look up when an especially loud barrage struck somewhere off in the distance. They simply shrugged and continued about their business. *Our army will hold them back*, they would say, but with little conviction. Or, *the Americans will have no choice but to return to help us now*. Again, with little conviction.

Without U.S. soldiers to help them, the South's army was steadily losing the war. Thu worked for the few hundred Americans that still remained in the city, at the U.S. Embassy and other government buildings in and around Saigon. But the soldiers with their helicopters and jets and ships were all gone, almost three years now. They had been an inescapable presence throughout Thu's life, and now the entire country, and Saigon especially, seemed empty and less vibrant. Empty and afraid.

Vinh felt a pang of grief and homesickness as he thought about his older brothers, both lost forever fighting Ho Chi Minh's communists, and about their once-beautiful ancestral home in Quang Ngai along the coast, destroyed by the war, and about the rest of his family, his mother and father. All gone now.

But he had Thu. Beautiful Thu. When they were young she was the most desirable girl in their village—in the entire province—the girl the heroes of the war thought they would win for their own, but she had chosen him instead. She had married Vinh over the objections of her father. Vinh knew this hurt her deeply, yet she never showed regret. And she chose him despite his handicap.

The polio that almost crippled him and left him with a withered leg and an enduring limp was "a blessing," she said, "because it kept him out of the war." As always, she was right. She was as smart as she was beautiful, and she loved him. That was his real blessing.

"The bombs are definitely closer," Thu said softly, her face half-buried in the pillow.

"Yes. Are you going into work today? We need to think about what we will do when the inevitable comes."

"As long as the embassy is open, I will go to work. It's my job. I'm part of the embassy staff now, and that will protect us when the time comes. Some evacuations have already begun, and we will go when *our* time comes."

"America has bigger problems than to worry about my little country girl. Your embassy friends will not protect you. Not only will the communists know you worked for the Americans, they will know we are Catholics, too, and they hate our religion. They will not be kind. You will be tortured until you give them information. We may both be killed. I know how they work."

"If our army can't stop the North, we will have to leave, I know that. There will be nothing left for us here. But I have been loyal to the United States. The Americans will stand by us. We will go to America and raise our children in a new world, where there is no war."

"But we have to have a plan—"

"Here is my plan. You go out and get *pho* for our breakfast and I will get dressed. After that, I'll go to the embassy and you can decide what will fit into one suitcase for each of us. We have saved some U.S. dollars—that will help. When I get to my office I will talk to Carwood. He will tell me about the evacuation plans and where we are on the list. My job is important, and I am sure we will be among the last to go, but we will be evacuated when the time comes. We have to be ready. And brave."

"You are the brave one. I am the worrier."

Thu jumped from the bed, lithe and alert, and struck a martial arts pose.

"You can be the worrier! I am a warrior—a warrior goddess!" she said, laughing. "Now go—and buy some *pho* for breakfast while I dress. We need to be strong."

* * *

"Big Dog, this is Glorybird Star One-Six inbound! Mark your position!"

The Huey's pilot gradually reduced airspeed as they approached Saigon. When they reached the streets where the buildings were taller, the chopper then ascended from its on-the-deck flight path above the highway and continued at rooftop level toward the center of the city.

"Smoke popped, Star One-Six," came the reply.

A plume of bright green smoke appeared on one of the rooftops in the distance. It expanded rapidly in the still morning air, and then slowly began to dissipate.

"I see green smoke, Big Dog."

"That's affirmative, Star One-Six, and I have eyes on you at five hundred meters. I'll be guiding you in."

"I read you Lima Charlie, Big Dog—loud and clear. I am on visual approach."

The Huey banked toward the man standing with upraised arms on the flat roof of the U.S. Embassy, a low, sprawling, white-brick building located in what appeared from the air to be a park-like estate. A similar building stood across from it, separated by tennis courts and a swimming pool. As the chopper closed on the embassy's rooftop helipad, the pilot could see armed Marine guards positioned at the gates and around the estate perimeter.

The pilot headed straight toward the tiny landing zone, pitching the chopper's nose up as he flared at the last second and dropped to the roof. The rotor blades created an instant maelstrom of wind and flying debris that pasted the clothing against the man with the upraised arms.

It was McWhorter, the ambassador's chief of staff, who fought to hold his ground against the buffeting wind. Roaring ferociously, the Huey swooped in and touched down in front of him, the ship's nose inches from his chest. McWhorter knew these Air America pilots—young hot dogs, all of them, who loved nothing more than to scare the crap out of shirt-and-tie embassy types like himself. Their little game of chicken didn't scare him. They were damn good pilots and he knew they wouldn't hit him. Or so he hoped. He didn't flinch.

Squinting against the hurricane, he could see the two pilots inside the now-stationary but still roaring Huey grinning broadly beneath their visors. Grinning back, McWhorter flipped them the bird, followed by a quick salute, then ran around to the side to help the passengers offload.

"Welcome to Saigon, General!" he shouted above the turbine roar.

As the last officer stepped down from the Huey, McWhorter backed away and gave a thumbs-up to the pilot. The chopper lifted straight up, ascending far out of reach in seconds, then banked sharply to the left and zoomed away in a wide arc over the city's rooftops.

"This way, General," McWhorter said as the aircraft's roar subsided, guiding Weyand and his aides through the rooftop door to the internal stairs. "Ambassador Martin is waiting for you. I'm sure he'll be happy to see you again."

"That remains to be seen," the general replied. "It always depends on whether the news is good or bad, doesn't it?"

* * *

"No, I don't think I need to be introduced, young lady. The ambassador is expecting me."

General Frederick Weyand, with his two aides trailing in his wake, didn't break stride as he bounded down the stairs leading to the ambassador's office suite, marching quickly past the flustered receptionist and through the doors to the inner office.

"General! How good to see you!" Ambassador Graham Martin rose from his desk. He didn't extend his hand, instead waving the officers to seats at his conference table.

"The damn ARVN is falling apart—disappearing as fast as they can run. Pretty much what we expected," Weyand growled. "Our intel says the South has lost 150,000 troops in the past three weeks alone! Lost them! What we didn't expect was that General Giap and his army would be so quick on the uptake. Hue is gone, Da Nang was overrun on Sunday, and Quang Ngai will be next. Meanwhile, Hanoi's got Lord knows how many men and a couple of tank brigades pushing through the Central Highlands like shit through a goose! If the ARVNs give up Kontum and Pleiku without a fight, Ban Me Thuot doesn't have the defenses to hold them. Then the only cities standing between the NVA and Saigon will be Phan Rang and Xuan Loc."

"I've seen the reports," Martin said, taking his seat at the head of the table. "President Thieu wants us to use our B-52s to slow the advance, give them time to regroup."

"Regroup! Christ on a cracker, Martin! There are no damn ARVN troops left between here and the DMZ *to* regroup! And we've already got Arc Lights"—Weyand used the military code word for the heavy B-52 Stratofortress bombing sorties—"working round the clock just to keep the NVA's heads down! It may slow them but it won't stop their advance. If Thieu can't pull a military miracle out of his ass, and we seriously doubt he will, it's all over— for him, for Saigon, and for South Vietnam."

Martin said nothing for a moment, letting the general's words hang in the air. Then, "Thieu wants more than bombers. He wants us back in the fight—use the Seventh Fleet to provide air cover and offshore bombardment while we insert our troops into strategic locations to shore up the South's forces. He believes the North won't engage us for fear that we'll restart our war with them, and this would block their plans to capture the country once and for all."

"What!? There's no way the U.S. can get back into this fight without creating a political shit storm back home—not like the president isn't dealing with that already!"

"Nevertheless, Thieu may be right. Hanoi can't afford a second round with us. We had them on the ropes before and they won't want to risk it again."

"You tell Thieu there's no fucking way—no, I'll tell him myself! It's time he understands that we have the power but our people back home no longer have the stomach to fight South Vietnam's battles. It's game over for us. And if Thieu can't muster his people to stand up to the North Vietnamese Army, it's over for him as well!"

"We're scheduled to meet with President Thieu in a half hour. Is that really what you—what we—are going to tell him?"

"Don't forget that I am a soldier, Martin," Weyand said, softening his tone. "I didn't fly the hell out here from Washington without some kind of a plan." He nodded to one of his aides, who pulled several maps from a briefcase and spread them on the table.

"We know that Saigon is Giap's target, and as you know there are three major land routes into and out of the city—Highway One along the coast, Highway Four between here and Cambodia, and the overland trade corridor heading south from Phan Rang. Unless the North Vietnamese want to wade all the way here through rice paddies along the coast or hack their way down through the jungle . . ."

"I would think they've done enough of that coming down the Ho Chi Minh Trail," Martin interjected.

"Yes, well then they have no choice but to use these routes to advance on Saigon," Weyand continued. "The coastal and Cambodia highways are choke points—even the damn ARVN should be able to hold them there long enough for Thieu to call up reinforcements, if he can find any. As for the central route,

Phan Rang is almost four hundred klicks north of here, and it's defensible. The ARVN can stop them there long enough to let our B-52s—yes, Thieu will get his wish—carpet bomb the shit out of any forces that mass against them."

"And after that . . . ?"

"Who knows? We go back to the table in Paris? Try to negotiate a settlement that will satisfy the North and let the South Vietnamese government hold on to whatever it can? That's not up to me and it's not up to you. Right now our job is to keep the South—or what's left of it—intact, which means keeping the NVA out of Saigon. After that, it's Washington's problem."

Wednesday, April 2

UNLIKE THE HUNDREDS OF NEWS CORRESPONDENTS who converged on South Vietnam when the American Marines first came ashore in the early 1960s, Lisette Vo immediately stood out from the pack. Her name and features were Vietnamese, but she was taller, which made her look more American. She spoke the language perfectly in an upper-class style that revealed her boarding school upbringing. This was a tribute to her Vietnamese father, who came to Washington as an executive with the French oil conglomerate Total and married Lisette's mother, an American of French descent and daughter of an H Street lobbyist.

She arrived in 1963, right after graduating from Georgetown University, and found her way to the NBS News bureau on the eleventh floor of the Caravelle Hotel. It took the bureau chief no more than five minutes to decide to hire her. He needed something to distinguish NBS—the North American Broadcast System— from the competition. Lisette Vo was perfect. He saw her as a rising star covering the Vietnam War, America's first television war.

Since then, Lisette had earned a couple of Peabody awards and become a ratings hit back in the States. Against the advice of her parents, she used a big chunk of her first year's salary to buy a new blue-and-cream-colored Citroën DS. Whenever she pulled up in front of Le P'tit, everyone noticed. "Lisette's here," was often heard throughout the bistrot.

She fell in with the routine of life as a war correspondent—morning coffee and a pastry at Givral's, find a chopper to take her out on a mission so she had something to cover for the day, then get her film out of the country that afternoon. Whenever there was a lull in the fighting and she needed to feed the TV news maw, Lisette covered the daily press briefing conducted by the Joint United States Public Affairs Office, or JUSPAO.

In no time at all, the Saigon press corps sardonically nicknamed the briefings the Five O'clock Follies and the name stuck. Even the folks at JUSPAO used the term, shortening it to "the Follies."

Over time, the Follies devolved into a cacophony of government briefers speaking in officialese while jaded American and other foreign correspondents and local Vietnamese journalists—including the communist press—shouted out questions and made snide comments. In addition to the official program, Army and Air Force PR types worked the room, pitching story ideas about their respective branches of service to any reporters who would listen. The mix included suspected undercover VC operatives, who watched from the sidelines, hoping to gather intelligence on troop movements.

The Follies were both work and a daily social event for journalists, military people, and civilian government employees. Everyone met their friends there and decided where to go drinking that night—the Rex Hotel's rooftop bar, the veranda of the Hotel Continental, or Le P'tit Bistrot, a piano bar tucked into the first floor of the Caravelle Hotel, where Lisette counted on running into the *Washington Legend*'s Sam Esposito—the correspondent she'd met the day she arrived in Saigon.

Lisette and Sam had become nearly inseparable. Sam liked driving around with Lisette in her Citroën with the windows open, watching her long black hair blow in the wind. Her hair had a slight wave to it that she inherited from her mother. Though she'd heard Sam's corny pun a hundred times, Lisette laughed whenever Sam said, "Let's make ice cream," as he pressed the *essuie glace* button on the dashboard, making the wipers slap back and forth over the dusty windshield.

As Sam and Lisette drove to a news conference at Tan Son Nhut, the car windows were rolled up tight. Today's rumor mill said there were North Vietnamese sappers in the city riding on bicycles, pulling alongside foreigners' cars, and then tossing hand grenades into the backseats.

While she drove, Sam reminded Lisette, "Ten years ago—hell, a year ago—you wouldn't see half the correspondents in South Vietnam rushing to attend an embassy news conference. We'd be out on patrol with the Army. When we wanted to get to a battle, see things for ourselves, the chopper pilots were more than willing to take us. We could always hop on a Huey. We'd ride out with the troops and report what we saw with our own eyes. Remember, we didn't learn about My Lai because some information weenie told us about it at the Follies!"

Sam never tired of reminding Lisette and anyone else within earshot how it was when Americans were running the war. Access was easier then. The Pentagon ordered every field commander to make sure correspondents had complete freedom to go wherever they pleased—including into the field with the troops. The brass wanted the press and the American public to see lots of pictures on TV and in the newspapers of Army helicopters taking U.S. servicemen to the fight. They wanted the public, and of course Congress, to see how quickly our choppers could move soldiers into and out of battle.

While Sam rambled on, Lisette noticed how empty the streets had become. Every shop's security gates were down. A few were guarded by teenagers armed with antiquated rifles.

"Sam, look," she said. "Where is everyone? This looks pretty ominous. Maybe they know something we don't."

Where dozens of pedicab drivers normally hung out in front of the Continental, there were now none. The local police had rounded up all the pedicabs—or cyclos—and corralled them behind concertina wire at the old Brinks Hotel, the Visiting Officers Quarters for Americans that had been abandoned since 1973. The cops feared that the cyclo drivers, who were mostly destitute, would be easy prey for Northern infiltrators, who would turn them into saboteurs for a few piasters.

Farther up the road, they saw a teenager siphoning gasoline from a Renault taxi, whose wheels were gone and windscreen shattered. At a makeshift tire-patch stand, its owner sat on a plastic stool hoping a passing vehicle would have a blowout. He also sold gasoline, which he stored in one-liter glass bottles next to the open charcoal fire he used to vulcanize the tire patches.

Nearing the civilian side of Tan Son Nhut, traffic slowed to a walk. The roadway was packed with bikes, Hondas, a group of children carrying suitcases, and mothers with their daughters dressed in silk *ao dai*. An elderly couple wearing peasant pajamas shuffled along in the middle of the roadway. On the shaded esplanade in front of the terminal a man, who looked to be in his eighties, was sleeping in a pushcart between cardboard suitcases and using a burlap sack as a pillow. A dozen nuns in gray and white habits were arguing with two Air Force sergeants at a table that had been set up in front of the terminal. Like everyone else, the nuns crowded the sergeants' table, desperate to get on a refugee flight and flee South Vietnam—the sooner the better.

As Lisette inched forward, a Honda with a man and two toddlers sitting astride the gas tank sputtered past the Citroën. A young woman sat sidesaddle behind the man, her *ao dai* tunic blowing in the wind. She carried an open parasol to shade her face from the sun.

Sam gestured toward the overloaded motorbike. "Appearances still matter here. I bet she thinks if her complexion is too dark she'll look like a Montagnard and they won't let her on the plane."

"Café au lait is not so popular in the U.S.," Lisette quipped.

"Well, I hope she gets out, I hope they all do," Sam remarked. "And I hope we'll learn something that I can use for the next edition. The embassy has been stonewalling until now. Maybe something *is* going on. They wouldn't call us all out here for nothing."

"Sam, the word I got was that there had been a big meeting yesterday with Thieu, Martin, and someone sent out from Washington. No matter what, I can get some footage."

* * *

As they broke through the crowd and headed to the military side of the air base, Sam asked, "Are you going to film this yourself? We didn't pick up Tuan. Where's Tuan and your camera gear? In the ten years that I've known you, I've never seen you cover a story without him."

"He told me he would go out to the base to set up ahead of time. He has been going off on his own lately, always with some excuse about a sick aunt, or sister who got in a moped accident, or some other excuse. But if there's a story, don't worry, he'll show," Lisette told Sam. The guard at the gate, who had seen Lisette and her Citroën come and go numerous times, waved them on to the flight line to where the news conference would take place.

* * *

General Weyand gazed down at the streets from his Visiting Officers Quarters suite on the top floor of the U.S. Embassy. He checked his watch. The news conference was less than an hour away. Below, the local Vietnamese embassy workers were queuing up at the front gate, ready to show their IDs to the Marine guards so they could to be let through. Off to one side, another group of Vietnamese, clutching papers, clamored for the guards' attention. After brief conversations, all of them were turned away.

Weyand shaved and brought the spit shine back to his boots with a couple of quick swipes with his handkerchief. He dressed in freshly-pressed tropical fatigues. Weyand thought about the message he wanted to convey to the press, and especially to the South Vietnamese Army. He wanted to tell them that *America believes South Vietnam is strong and will never abandon its friends in Asia.*

As he was going over it in his mind, a Marine sergeant knocked at his door.

"Your chopper's coming in now, General. Can I take your gear up to the helipad?"

As Weyand climbed the steel stairs to the roof and emerged into the sunlight, Martin and Weyand's South Vietnamese Army counterpart, General Cao Van Vien, were already boarding the Huey.

Returning the Marine's salute, Weyand boarded the chopper and, within seconds, the Huey rose and turned toward Tan Son Nhut. Weyand moved easily between the worlds of politics, foreign affairs, and the military. A Berkeley graduate and a veteran of three wars, he had risen to become Army Chief of Staff despite his lack of a West Point pedigree. He was at once a dedicated soldier and an intellectual. He had no trouble telling three presidents and members of Congress that the Vietnam War lacked a clear mission. Throughout America's involvement, no president had ever sent a command letter to the general staff stating the desired outcome. The war was a rudderless ship without a destination.

Despite his criticism over the lack of civilian guidance, Weyand was trusted and respected for his candor. After the briefing he would board a Military Airlift Command C-141 Starlifter and head directly to Washington, where he would brief President Ford and Secretary of State Henry Kissinger with his assessment of conditions on the ground. That was the easy part. Ford and Kissinger were eager to give Thieu as much money as needed to keep the North out of Saigon, money needed to make the NVA pay for every inch they advanced with their soldiers' lives and force a negotiated end to fighting. After that, Weyand would meet with Congressional leaders and testify before a recalcitrant Congress.

Weyand had already made up his mind to hit them hard. He was determined to get every dollar the South needed to push the North back to the DMZ and shove their asses into Haiphong Harbor. He wasn't going to lose South Vietnam. Not after twenty years. Not on his watch.

* * *

By the time Weyand's chopper landed, the embassy staffers had already brought in the podium and attached the Seal of the United States to it, and had put out more than enough folding chairs for the press.

Looking over the setup, Sam nudged Lisette. "Look," he said, "they placed the podium so the airport runway will be directly behind the big muckety-mucks. When you're filming, you'll get the flights taking off and landing like its LaGuardia. Everyone back in the States will see it and think, 'Just business as usual here at Tan Son Nhut, folks. It's perfectly safe, no North Vietnamese Army in sight.' Outstanding!"

The embassy was eager to project an impression of normalcy, but it had set up the conference between two tall steel revetments that protected parked fighter jets from enemy bombardment. Only a highly unlikely direct hit could take out the ambassador, the generals, and their entourage.

Weyand was resolute as he stood at the podium beside Martin and General Vien. He again went over his objective in his mind. He needed to get it through their heads—South Vietnam's army is up to the task, and we don't abandon our friends.

The number of press people he needed to convince of America's stalwart support had dwindled by now. Most of the accredited correspondents had left for jobs back in their home countries or in another hotspot, if a boring stateside assignment was not in their psychological makeup. Peter Arnett and George Esper were both hanging on, reporting for the Associated Press. Fox Butterfield, whose coverage of the Pentagon Papers had won him a Pulitzer, was there from the *New York Times*. Butterfield had plopped himself into a folding chair in the first row, the only place with enough room to accommodate his long legs and size-twelve feet.

Sam sat in the back row to pick up bits of conversation between Lisette and the local Vietnamese journalists whose sympathies shifted with the wind. Lisette never minded translating a few juicy tidbits for him.

As much as Ambassador Martin wanted to ignore it, he began by acknowledging just how grim the situation was. If he expected to have any credibility with the press, he needed to admit that Thieu had already abandoned the northern part of South Vietnam. City after city was falling to the NVA.

"It's obvious to all that the situation here in South Vietnam is precarious," Martin began. "But, after consulting with General Weyand and our diplomatic staff on the ground"—embassy speak for the CIA—"we are assured that Saigon will hold."

When Weyand walked up to the podium to stand next to Martin, he remained silent for several moments. On the taxiway behind the dais, a long row of aircraft—C-130s and C-47s, an occasional commercial airline flight, and some small private aircraft, were clearly visible. They were waiting their turn to take off, having to squeeze between the continual stream of aircraft that were landing on the distant runway.

It looked like the comings and goings of any busy airport, save for the fact that the planes leaving were packed with refugees and the arriving flights were bringing in munitions and supplies for South Vietnam's army. The planes would land, dump their cargo of weapons and ammunition, refuel, and load up with more South Vietnamese heading for refugee camps in Guam, the Philippines, and Thailand. Unfortunately, the South Vietnamese Army was in such disarray that most of the war materiel eventually wound up in the hands of the enemy.

Shouting above the noise of planes running up their engines before takeoff, Weyand told the handful of journalists, "There have been many, *many* instances of great and heroic fighting by the South Vietnamese. I am confident that, given our support, they will fight just as those soldiers have fought in the past."

Gesturing toward General Vien, Weyand continued, "I leave here with great affection and respect for the people of South Vietnam, and I will do all in my power to be of assistance to them. I want to express the strong personal support of President Ford and his personal determination to help the South defend itself against an invasion by North Vietnam."

Weyand looked directly at General Vien to make sure he got the message.

Martin then leaned into the microphone and added, "I have every assurance from the president of the United States and Congress that we will continue to support our ally in the fight against this communist takeover of Southeast Asia. The president will go before Congress to seek additional aid, and we," he covered the mic and coughed before continuing, "we . . . we believe that the United States will continue to assist South Vietnam, militarily and economically."

As he looked up, every hand shot into the air.

"General Weyand, how long . . ."

"General Weyand, will American armed forces return . . ."

"General, what is the current status of forces in-country . . ."

Weyand scanned the seats looking for a reporter he could trust. He wanted a question that would enable him to reinforce the message one last time. *Tell them what you are going to say, say it, then tell them what you said* was the Army way, and it had stood by him for over three decades.

He noticed Esposito in the back row. Weyand met Sam when he commanded the U.S. Army in Vietnam during the communists' Lunar New Year Tet Offensive of 1968. That January, the Viet Cong emerged from their tunnels and other hiding places around Saigon to fight the South Vietnamese in the streets. After the fighting died down, correspondents in Vietnam romanticized the Viet

Cong and lauded them for their determination, cleverness, and success. In reality, Weyand's soldiers crushed the attackers and the VC never recovered from their defeat. Esposito was the only reporter who got it right and, in Weyand's view, reported on the enemy rout accurately. Sam's story ran front page in the *Legend*—the paper every Congressman reads over morning coffee—and won him a Pulitzer. The victory won Weyand an additional star.

"Sam, you have a question?" Weyand asked. He expected a softball question from Esposito, the easy opening he needed to reinforce his message about stopping the spread of communism in Southeast Asia and forcing a negotiated peace.

But Sam would have none of it. His response was more like a shot than a question. It would have been impetuous in private, but this was in the presence of the U.S. Ambassador, the chief of the South Vietnam Army, and reporters from the U.S., Japan, France, Germany, Australia, as well as the local communist press.

"General, are you now willing to admit that America has abandoned South Vietnam?" Sam asked.

"*Motherfucker!*" Weyand muttered under his breath. No one could hear him, but one didn't have to be a lip-reader to get the gist—and Tuan certainly got it on film for the evening news.

Weyand could not have been angrier if Sam had burned the American flag in front of him. The veins in his neck pulsed and his face turned red. Despite his anger, his demeanor remained calm.

"Thank you for that question, Sam," he replied. "The South Vietnamese have been trained and equipped by the finest military organization in the world—the United States Army! Our support, America's support, is unflagging. Saigon is safe. South Vietnam is safe. Next question? . . . The lady in the back row. State your name, please."

"Lisette Vo, NBS News. General Weyand, there are four aircraft carriers moving into the South China Sea. Another dozen warships are on their way, and an Air Force Tactical Air Command squadron is right over the border at Udon Air Base, as are our B-52s at

U-Tapao, Thailand. That's a lot of firepower. If the NVA attempts to invade Saigon, will the United States re-enter the war? Can the South Vietnamese count on U.S. air and ground support to defend their country?"

"Lisette, both you and I know that Hanoi fears an aerial assault by our Navy fighter squadrons. And they do not want to risk renewed shore bombardment from our battleships. That's not counting the return of our Army and Marine ground forces. Hanoi won't take that chance. Not with the Seventh Fleet offshore. If the North ever reaches Saigon—and it's still questionable whether they can—they'll stand down outside the city. They will *not* provoke the United States of America."

Peter Arnett, who wrote his notes on scraps of paper, chimed in with a question about whether the NVA would simply drive down Highway One to attack Saigon in a bid to cut off the city and starve its people.

"We don't plan the enemy's strategy for them," Weyand answered.

Esper didn't ask any questions at all. He preferred to work the room—find a naïve junior officer and flatter his ego by assigning the man more authority than he actually possessed. "So tell me, Lieutenant Phillips," he would casually ask in his disarming way, glancing at the soldier's name badge, "Are we pulling out *all* the Vietnamese SEALs operating undercover up North?" Esper knew that at least a dozen South Vietnamese sailors and soldiers had been trained alongside the U.S. Navy SEALs on Lake Michigan. It didn't take much to figure out why, or what they might be up to.

"George . . . you must have me confused with someone else," the lieutenant sighed.

"What do you mean?"

"I'm FIGMO, I've been assigned to Hickham Air Force Base, Hon-o-lu-lu, and I'm leaving on the general's plane. Yup, goin' back to the world. Nothing but sun, surf, and Spam for me."

FIGMO was universal Army slang. It meant *Fuck it I Got My Orders* and applied to those who were moving on to their next duty assignment and could care less about their present situation.

Back at the podium, the general was anxious to wrap it up. Before anyone could ask another question, he nodded to his aide, who twirled a hand in the air, signaling the pilots in the Starlifter cockpit. On cue, the inboard engines came to life as the general ducked away from the podium and hustled toward the tailgate ramp. Within seconds the outboard engines began spooling up. The embassy staff hurried the reporters out of harm's way as the massive cargo plane turned onto the taxiway. The jet wash blew over chairs and shook the embassy seal from the podium, sending it rolling into a ditch.

"Sam, let's go," Lisette urged. "I've got Tuan's footage. Now I need to get the film out on the next flight to New York. And you need to get back to your bureau to Telex your story to the *Legend*."

"Some story! Here's the headline: *Ford Sends U.S. Army Chief of Staff to Saigon; Fails to Mention City Is Surrounded. Ambassador Urges Calm!* Yeah, another American SNAFU—situation normal, all fucked up."

When Lisette returned to her car, she dumped the raw film into an orange onion sack with NBS NEWS stenciled on it. She tossed the bag into the backseat as Sam sat next to her, going over his notes.

Starting her Citroën, she sped to the base operations building where she asked the duty officer to hold the next plane going out. He radioed the pilot of a C-130 that was getting ready to taxi and told him to "hold in place," saying that a film sack was on its way. Lisette jumped back into her car and raced to the plane. The pilot slid open the cockpit window, gave Lisette a wave, and dropped a kite string to the ground. Lisette tied the sack to the string and he reeled it in. In a few hours, the C-130 would be met in Hong Kong, where the film would be processed and sent on its way to New York.

As they passed the now-slumbering sentries on their way out of the main gate, Lisette glanced in the rearview mirror and saw the C-130 lift off the runway behind them, heading toward the South China Sea. She said to herself, "I want this on the *Evening News*, dammit!"

Thursday, April 3

THE AIR CONDITIONER IN RIORDAN'S OFFICE blew a continuous stream of cold air at his face, but all he could feel was the clammy sweat suddenly soaking the back of his shirt.

"Boss, I can't burn everything!" he said into the telephone, now slippery against his palm. "How do I sort out what's important from what's not in one day? I couldn't do that in a week!"

As usual, the landline connection to the bank's headquarters in New York—over wires that stretched eight thousand miles via undersea cable and another three thousand miles across the continent—was filled with static, making conversation difficult. But Riordan had no trouble hearing Harmon, his manager, throwing a fit on the other end.

"We chartered a plane for you! You need to get yourself and your staff on it and throw everything in the furnace before you leave!" Harmon yelled. "It's a hundred-plus degrees in Saigon every fucking day—why else do you think your shithole office even has a furnace?!" He was through arguing with Riordan. The head office had given him an order, pointedly reminding him that there were thirty-four American employees in Riordan's branch and if they fell into the hands of the North Vietnamese Army it was Harmon—not Riordan—who would be held responsible.

"What about my plan to get everyone else out—all the SVN nationals working here? The VC know they work for us and will slaughter them when the NVA take the city!" *Not if*, Riordan thought. *When.*

"If your people—*your people*, not the goddamn South Vietnamese who have been living so good off the American dollars we pay them—aren't out of there tonight I will fire your ass and leave *you* behind to deal with the North Vietnamese!"

The line went dead. Riordan knew that Harmon would make good on his threat if he wasn't on that plane. But Harmon didn't work with them—with Mrs. Em Bah, who had been Riordan's interpreter and unofficial liaison to the Vietnamese community for the past three years, or with Cao, who drove him everywhere, or Vinh, who had a bad limp but was happy to run messages for them all over the city. There were over a hundred South Vietnamese employed by the branch in one way or another. Riordan knew he couldn't have kept the office open without them. And *he* was responsible for them, not Harmon.

"Well, screw you, Harmon," he muttered to himself.

"Sally," he said to his secretary, "I need you to arrange for a bus—a big one, full-size—to be here on Friday. And round up all the SVNs, tell them I want to meet with them here tomorrow. Everyone needs to be here. What I have to tell them is important."

Sally had watched Riordan on the phone and had heard Harmon screaming on the other end of the line. She was worried then. Now she was frightened. "Are we closing the branch?" she said.

"Yes," said Riordan. "And you and the rest of the staff—only the Americans and third-country nationals—have to pack quickly and be on a charter flight that's coming in to Tan Son Nhut tonight. You're being relocated to Hong Kong temporarily, until this gets sorted out. I know it's short notice, but we've all seen this coming. Now you've got to go, and hopefully you'll be able to come back once things settle down."

"You're not coming with us?"

"Not right away. I've got to get the rest of the people who work with us out of Saigon, before the North Vietnamese roll in. The ARVNs can't stop them. You've seen the news—it could be as soon as a week or a matter of days, but the NVA will take Saigon, and after that no one knows what will happen."

He looked at the calendar on his desk. Three pretty Vietnamese girls in flowing *ao dais*—the elegant, high-collared white tunics, slit to the waist and worn over colorful silken pants, that were the traditional dress for Vietnamese women—smiled back at him from the photo.

The date was April third. Riordan wondered how much time they really had left.

Friday, April 4

THE SPEEDOMETER WAS PUSHING EIGHTY KILOMETERS per hour as Lisette dodged the mud-filled bomb craters that pockmarked the dirt road. The potholes could be six feet deep, for all she knew. If she hit one the wrong way, the transmission would drop right out of the car.

Lisette downshifted and navigated her prized Citroën around the obstacles. This was the only route leading to the plume of black smoke and orange-red flames rising above the trees. After passing some nasty-looking craters, she floored the gas pedal and sped toward the crash site, a few kilometers east of the air base.

Despite the Citroën's vaunted pneumatic shock absorbers, it kept bottoming out in the deep ruts, and she briefly worried about the brand-new CP-16 sound camera that her network recently issued to all the news crews. It was bouncing around on the backseat and looked like it would get dumped on the floor together with the canvas bag full of film magazines, microphones, gaffer tape, and the ever-present twenty dollar bill needed to bribe officials whenever they claimed they needed to "inspect" a bag and threatened to confiscate the "unauthorized" equipment.

I wish Tuan were here to film. Where the hell is he? Lisette thought as she watched the flames shooting into the air. She then gripped

32

the steering wheel tighter, hit the gas, and kept going as she glanced back to make sure her camera didn't hit the floor. *No camera, no story,* she thought.

Lisette had made a sign out of gaffer tape for the passenger side of the windshield. The foot-high letters spelled out BAO CHI, Vietnamese for PRESS.

She figured the BAO CHI sign would get her through any South Vietnamese Army roadblocks. Or she hoped it would. Since the press was reporting on their defeats north of Saigon every day and portraying their army as being in disarray, *bao chi* was increasingly coming to mean *persona non grata.*

"Damn, I wish Tuan were with me," she said aloud. Tuan was a great camera and sound man, but more importantly, he was her fixer. Tuan could talk his way into and out of any situation. Without him, Lisette had only herself to rely on—that and her government-issued press pass, which showed she worked for the American broadcaster NBS.

As Lisette drew closer to the crash site, the smoke thickened and grew more acrid. She could barely make out the gray carcass of the mammoth C-5 Galaxy transport plane that had fallen to earth less than an hour ago, cutting a mile-long swath of burning jet fuel through the rice paddies and grass before coming to a halt half-buried in the mud. A few peasants and what looked like several Western civilians—embassy staffers or journalists, perhaps—wandered among the pieces of ripped aluminum panels, smoldering seats cushions, and hundreds of suitcases burst open from the impact. The burning jet fuel stung her eyes, but it wasn't the only smell in the air. The North Vietnamese Army had shelled this area the previous night, and the distinct odor of cordite from the artillery mingled with the smoke.

As she pressed closer, two South Vietnamese soldiers from the Army of the Republic of Vietnam, or ARVN, who were guarding the road hopped from their jeep. Both looked like teenagers. The younger of the two raised his hand, signaling her to stop.

"What are you doing here? You have no business, no business here!" the soldier challenged in English.

Lisette stopped the car and got out, but instead of answering the soldier, she reached into the backseat for the camera, popped in a four-hundred-foot film magazine, hoisted it to her shoulder, and walked toward the jeep. In perfect Vietnamese, she told him, "I am a journalist with the American TV network NBS and it's my job to be here, corporal. If I can't drive any closer, I'll roll up my pants and walk across the paddies. Please let me pass."

The soldiers didn't know what to make of this vaguely Asian-American looking woman, who spoke Vietnamese like a native, but didn't really look Vietnamese. She was too tall and she didn't wear pajamas like the peasants, or an *ao dai* like a proper Vietnamese lady. "I got my mother's ass. No way am I even trying on one of those," she liked to tell her friends.

When the soldiers didn't respond, Lisette tried a more aggressive tack, again in perfect Vietnamese. "I need to get closer. I need film for TV," she said, patting the camera. The *Bao Chi* press pass she wore on a lanyard around her neck had their attention now, she realized, most likely because it emphasized her tits.

"*Bao Chi,*" she insisted, lifting the pass by its lanyard and waving it in front of the soldier's face.

"*Bao Chi,*" she repeated.

"Soldier!" the corporal countered, slapping the magazine on the M-16 he held across his chest.

As the argument grew, it attracted a small crowd of onlookers. Within moments, a crowd of journalists had gathered around her and began bombarding the ARVN soldiers with questions and demands to let them through.

Finally, after some discussion with the soldier, Lisette agreed to leave the car and walk toward the wreckage. The downed jet transport had been flying mercy flights code-named "Operation Babylift" that were aimed at getting orphaned children of mixed American and Vietnamese heritage out of the country.

Wreckage was strewn everywhere—blackened metal aircraft parts, huge shredded tires embedded in the mud, suitcases that had burst open and scattered clothing and the personal items of the hundreds of people onboard. And corpses, dozens of them, including many, many tiny bodies that looked too small to be real, like toy dolls cast about the field. As she stood in the ankle-deep mud and surveyed the scene, she didn't know what was more pitiful, the tiny bodies or the stunned survivors wandering around, searching for the children who had been in their care. Their faces were blank. They showed about as much emotion as one does when looking for a quarter dropped in the street. That is until they found a loved one, then the pain became unbearable, the wailing so horrid, that Lisette, without realizing it, covered her ears with her hands to block the sound.

Lisette then threw up and wiped her face with a Kleenex. *Okay, get it together,* she told herself, then began filming the wreckage and the faces of the survivors as they walked past. She tried to get one or two to talk, but got little response.

After logging some footage, she asked an ARVN soldier, one of several who had arrived and were now guarding the site, to help her film her standup. He didn't show much interest until she pulled out the twenty, which was far preferable to Vietnamese piasters. As soon as he saw the American greenback, the soldier broke into a smile and immediately reached out to hold the camera for her.

"When I say 'press here,'" she said, showing him the red button, "you press and hold it. And when I say 'cut' you let it go. Okay?" The soldier looked mystified, but he dutifully accepted the camera and aimed it toward Lisette.

"One take and I get the hell out of here," Lisette told herself, tapping the mic for a sound check. Then she smoothed her mud-spattered jacket, straightened her shoulders, and looked straight into the camera.

"This was Operation Babylift, a last-ditch effort by the United States to remove . . ."

Not right, damn it.

"Okay, cut! Let's start again. . . . Behind me is the wreckage of an Air Force C-5 Galaxy that was flying missions as part of Operation Babylift. The operation is a last-ditch effort to *rescue* the many children—orphans mostly, fathered by American soldiers—from the North Vietnamese advance on Saigon, and today it has gone horribly wrong. This huge C-5 transport plane—the largest ship in the U.S. Air Force arsenal—took off from Tan Son Nhut air base this morning carrying those children and over three hundred Americans fearing the worst if North Vietnam's army overruns the city. All we know at this time is that there was an explosion on board and the pilots tried to return to the runway. No one knows if it was equipment failure, sabotage, or possibly enemy fire. We understand the pilot and co-pilot survived along with several crewmembers and passengers. We are awaiting an official briefing that we hope will provide additional information. Lisette Vo, NBS News, Saigon."

Lisette dropped the mic to her waist. "Okay . . . cut, stop filming . . . stop, cut." After a moment, the soldier got the message and released the *Record Button.*

Lisette took the movie camera from the soldier and trudged back to her car. Of the many bad days and hundreds of tragic reports she had aired since arriving in-country, this was the worst. She threw her equipment into the backseat, jumped in, and, as she drove back to Saigon, turned up the volume on her radio as far as it would go.

"Damn this war! It's never going to stop," she screamed, "Never! Not today, not tomorrow, not next month, not next year. Fucking never!"

* * *

"You look like crap," Sam exclaimed the minute he turned toward Lisette, who had taken the bar stool next to him. She usually affected a calm, perfectly composed demeanor off camera as she did when she was doing a standup for NBS. But now her blouse was filthy, her hair was sweaty, her shoes caked with mud; she didn't even look like the Lisette he had known since he met her over ten years ago.

"You really know how to put on the charm," Lisette responded halfheartedly.

Sam looked at her again, "Yeah, but you still look like crap . . . So what's wrong?"

"I can't talk about it right now."

"Okay," Sam said as he turned slightly away and went back to sipping his drink.

"Sam, it was horrible."

"This sounds like talking about it," Sam interjected.

"I mean, I've seen dead soldiers but not this, Sam, the dead babies from the crash. They were strewn about the rice paddies like they'd been discarded. The loadmasters strapped them into the lower level in these little cardboard carton bassinettes. Then the plane bellied in. The embassy put the count at seventy-eight. Seventy-eight babies died in the crash, Sam! They never stood a chance."

Jean Paul placed Lisette's gin and tonic in front of her. "Something stronger, Jean Paul," Sam asked. Jean Paul returned with two shots of Jim Beam and slid them over to Sam and Lisette.

"Sam, there were three hundred people on that plane. Those kids are dead now. They were orphans, mostly children of GIs and their Vietnamese girlfriends. They were all mixed race, they never had a chance before the crash, and they wouldn't have had any kind of life in Vietnam. And now this! Plus the embassy people—my God, we saw some of those people every day. They were our friends. And the eleven crew members. All dead. Dead, Sam! Fucking dead."

"And the survivors?"

"Huh?"

"Survivors? Were . . . there . . . any . . . survivors?"

"Yes, Sam. There were survivors. You're the one who always looks at the dark side of everything that happens in this country. Now you want to switch and see something positive in all this? Okay, two hundred people survived. They're flying the orphans to the Philippines. They'll make it to American or Australia. They'll be adopted. They'll have lives . . ."

"You survived, didn't you?"

While Sam's version of a pep talk didn't help much, the tear he wiped from Lisette's cheek did. For the first time in a long while Lisette had shown some vulnerability. Sam liked it, but he didn't linger in the moment.

"Come on, let's take a walk by the river, you can see the stars from there. It always makes me feel better," Sam said, touching Lisette's shoulder. As he motioned her toward the exit, she turned toward him and kissed him.

"I don't need the stars, Sam. I need you."

Lisette grabbed Sam by the hand and dragged him down the hallway to the Caravelle lobby, where an elevator was waiting. As soon as the door closed and the elevator reached the third floor, she flipped the switch to *Out-of-Service*. Lisette wanted Sam inside her now. She wanted to feel alive, connected, and she wanted to be rid of all the death she had seen that morning. She wanted it out of her, out in a single burst of passion. They made love, deep and hard, keeping their moans to a whisper.

Sam held Lisette close to him, looked into her face, and kissed her. She held him tight, savoring the moment, until someone from the gathering crowd in the lobby yelled, "Hey, who's holding up the elevator?"

Lisette pushed Sam away, hiked up her black lace panties, and pulled her bra down to cover her breasts. She buttoned her blouse and fluffed up her hair.

"I need to get to my floor!" chimed in another from the lobby below.

"Send the car down!"

Sam, who never even took off his glasses, composed himself and flipped the switch to *In-Service*. The elevator groaned back to life and descended to the lobby. As soon as the door opened, a half dozen people squeezed into the waiting car, barely giving Lisette and Sam a chance to get out.

Sam spoke first. "What was that, Lise? Emergency sex?"

"Yes, Sam, it was emergency sex. That's all it was, nothing more," she said, as she turned her back on him and walked away, muttering under her breath, "Sam, you are such an asshole."

Saturday, April 5

Sam Esposito had been in South Vietnam for thirteen years, arriving in 1963 with the same red Olivetti portable he used to type his term papers at Yale. At the time he showed up there were 3,200 American military advisors in-country under the newly organized Military Assistance Command—Vietnam, or MAC-V, which would remain in charge of a war that started out as a humanitarian effort with limited military involvement. As the government explained in a mimeographed press release: "The MAC-V mission in South Vietnam is to secure over ten thousand villages and hamlets in the country. As part of that mission the U.S. Army will build schools, provide water and other needed services to ward against insurgents and the spread of Communism in Asia."

This supposedly altruistic plan did not last long. The South Vietnamese forces, under an oppressive "democratic" regime, proved too weak and inept to withstand their determined North Vietnamese enemies. Before long, the number of American soldiers in Vietnam grew into the hundreds of thousands as U.S. forces gradually took on the task of fighting a communist takeover.

In one of Sam's earlier dispatches for the *Legend*, he wrote: "The danger is being presented here and in Washington as a domino effect, with military advisors claiming that if South Vietnam falls to the communists, so falls Laos, Cambodia, and Thailand to Communist rule."

By 1967 a half million American servicemen were in Vietnam. As fighting intensified and many of those soldiers died, protests against the war increased at home. Ultimately, the war was viewed as a failed mission, unwinnable by American military power. The U.S. reversed course and started reducing its involvement. Every year fewer solders were sent to Vietnam. In 1973, the war was officially turned over to the South Vietnamese in a process called "Vietnamization." With American boys no longer being sent to Vietnam, the home-front protests also stopped. Politicians declared the war over and Vietnamization a huge success, and said the world had been saved from the communist tide.

Two years after the official end of America's involvement, Sam wrote a piece for the *Legend*'s *Sunday Week in Review*:

"Though Pentagon officials put the number of U.S. military in Vietnam at fifty, he wrote, there is not a single correspondent in the country who believes the number is anywhere near that low. For that matter, neither do the North Vietnamese, who claim there are *thousands* of Americans still fighting in Vietnam and are demanding they leave before they will even talk about a negotiated peace. Since I counted fifty U.S. servicemen at Le P'tit last Friday night, I'm guessing there are a few more American soldiers somewhere in-country. Perhaps they are on KP peeling onions at a secret mess hall."

April 1975 was a sharp contrast to the war that began while Sam was at Yale in the 1960s. Back then there was no doubt—come up with an alternative or be drafted and sent to fight in Vietnam right after graduation. Sam, who was to graduate in 1962, was caught in that wave. He even wrote articles for the campus newspaper about how students weighed the options: "Enlist for two years and get it over with? Join the National Health Service? Defect to Canada? Poke out an eye? Act crazy? Get a deferment as a Conscientious Objector? These are all considered acceptable options by my fellow students. No one passed judgment on how to deal with—or dodge—the draft. Guys who volunteered for the Marines remain friends with classmates who fled to Canada or became conscientious objectors."

Sam thought about going to graduate school, then maybe work on a doctorate, hoping by that time the war would be over. But he never got around to applying. He liked the idea of flying, but since he had 20/200 eyesight, it was a sure bet he could not avoid the draft by becoming a fighter pilot like the Naval Reserve Officer Training students on campus. He simply left things to chance.

Graduation day was gloriously sunny in New Haven. Sam's parents drove from Norwalk to see him receive his diploma. President John F. Kennedy delivered the commencement address. After the ceremony, Sam and his parents got to shake hands with the president. Then, Sam's mother, who had promised his father not to mar Sam's day, couldn't hold it in any longer: "Sam, I'm sorry," she said tearfully as she handed him a letter that had arrived from the local draft board that morning.

The decision had been made for him, so Sam resigned himself to a two-year stint in the Army. He dutifully appeared for his physical exam, where he was asked, "Did anyone ever tell you that you have a heart murmur?" Sam was reclassified 1-Y, which meant he could be called to fight only in a national emergency. The Army was out. Flying was out. Since he'd written a few articles for the school paper, Sam figured news writing was something he could do. So he went down to the UPI office in New Haven, where the bureau chief, Parker Reines III, offered him a job as a reporter for seventy-five dollars a week.

* * *

Reines wore bow ties and walked with a walrus tusk-handled cane. He had been bureau chief since 1955. Reines criticized Sam mercilessly. "Too many adjectives," he would say. "You buried your lead. Percent is one word, not hyphenated. It's police, not THE police."

When Sam got a break from reporting, he read the news copy that came by Telex over the international wire. Increasingly the news was about Vietnam. On June 2, the South was winning. On June 3, South Vietnam was losing a key battle over some peninsula he couldn't pronounce. A week later it looked like the war was spreading to Laos. He had to check the atlas to find out where Laos was.

He learned that South Vietnam reports of minor victories were doctored. In one case, sixty captured North Vietnamese Army regulars turned out to be women and children. During that time Viet Cong became a new term in his vocabulary, synonymous with assassinations, killing rampages, and torture. Twelve thousand American military advisors were being sent to help the South Vietnamese fight them.

"Advisors my ass," Reines would sneer when he saw the reports. "They're kids who still need advice from their mothers, and they're going to get killed."

* * *

A few days before Thanksgiving in 1963, Sam ran into Billy Freda, a kid from his neighborhood. Billy was home after a one-year tour in Vietnam and Sam wanted to know what it was really like over there.

"Come on," he said to Billy. "Let's take a drive over to Temple Street. We'll hit Mory's for a couple of beers then maybe Pepe's for a slice later."

While they sat and drank at one of the old carved-up wood tables in Mory's, all Billy wanted to do was reminisce about the time Norwalk beat West Haven by one point in the biggest game of his high school basketball career. But after a few beers he opened up and began to talk about his time in Vietnam.

"I've never seen anything like it, Sam," he said. "We got these 'Ricans in our unit. I mean *had* them in our unit. They're all KIA now. Anyway, because they're built small, Sarge sends them down into these tunnels where we think the gooks are hiding." Billy's eyes widened as he went on, "Then the Viet Cong sets booby traps all over the place. They bury sharpened bamboo stakes in a pit—punji sticks, they call them—and cover the pit with a burlap bag and dead leaves. One of my buddies fell into one on patrol. They had to amputate both his legs. It wasn't the wound—they could have fixed that. It was the infection. Those little fuckers coated the stakes with their own shit."

Sam let Billy ramble on, recounting one war story after another.

"So let me see if I've got this right," Sam said. "They've got guys in pajamas fighting us on the ground with sharpened sticks straight out of the Stone Age, while the Russians are giving their pals—the North Vietnamese—radar-controlled surface-to-air missiles and MiG-15s. On top of this, the North Vietnamese Army is invading through Laos and Cambodia, carrying weapons on bicycles and elephants." The incongruity was lost on Billy.

"Here's how I see it, Sam. Do we want to fight them over *there* or fight them over *here*? I say over there is better and I'm going back for a second tour. I'll be fighting to save your ass from the commies. So this round's on you, Sam!"

"Sure. Beer's on me. And if I see the Western Union guy on our street, let's hope he's not visiting your mom."

"Sam, I gotta go back. I have to. I feel like shit in the States. All my friends are gone. When I'm there, man, I feel right. Like how I felt when we beat West Haven by one point with one second on the clock. And Billy Freda scores the winning point."

* * *

Two days later—at precisely 1:30 in the afternoon on November 22, 1963—the office walls shook as every Teletype machine in the UPI bureau sprang to life simultaneously. First, the machines' alarm bells alarm went off, warning everyone something big was coming. Then the machines started typing, rhythmically beating out news reports faster than any human could type, churning through the rolls of copy paper that hung above each machine.

Sam ripped the copy out of the nearest machine. It read:

"Dallas, Texas . . . President John F. Kennedy has been shot during a motorcade near Dealey Plaza . . ."

Then every phone in the bureau began to ring. Newspaper editors who relied on UPI for their international news demanded to know: "Is it true?" One editor called to say he was holding the front page for confirmation.

Minute by minute the calls came in. A half hour passed. Then one of the machines typed out: "Kennedy pronounced dead by doctors at the Memorial Hospital . . ."

Kennedy's assassination, seeing Billy, and listening to Reines natter on about police versus *the* police hit Sam all at once. He blurted: "I am going to die if I don't get the fuck out of here!"

That day, Sam bought a one-way airline ticket to Saigon.

* * *

Word of Sam's arrival in Vietnam preceded him. To Sam's surprise, Reines didn't hold his abrupt departure against him. Reines secretly admired and envied Sam and took it upon himself to cable the UPI bureau chief in Saigon, saying, "Keep an eye peeled for a skinny young man with horn-rimmed glasses. He's a little green but he's a damn good writer. He should be—I taught him!"

The cable worked. Sam got a job as a UPI stringer earning eighty bucks a story, "More if we run one of your pictures," he was told.

Sam Esposito's byline started appearing weekly, then a few times a week, then daily. He was a rising star among a growing number of in-country correspondents. As an accredited correspondent, he was issued a MAC-V press pass, which enabled him to hop on any Huey helicopter any time and go anywhere with the army. He never hung back. He saw Vietnam being scorched with napalm. He watched as the Air Force sprayed miles upon square miles with the defoliant Agent Orange. He rode out on missions with scared kids, and rode back with blood-spattered soldiers—some of them in body bags.

It didn't take long for Sam's skepticism to grow. In one of his dispatches he wrote: "Here's how I view the war at this point. South Vietnam's government is corrupt. The Viet Cong are vicious murderers—a street gang with a devotion to Ho Chi Minh that rivals religious fanaticism. North Vietnam's Army seems to thrive on punishment—no matter how many bombs the B-52s drop on them, no matter how often U.S. soldiers defeat them in battle or how high the body count, they just keep coming. Meanwhile, our military releases unrealistic body-count numbers claiming hundreds of enemy killed every day. All this while the diplomats sit around in Paris talking and wringing their hands."

* * *

In time, Sam made a name for himself among the Saigon press corps for calling out the military on their exaggerated body counts and official action reports that turned out to be bullshit. Meanwhile, as more American boys died in Vietnam, college students back home were chanting "Hell no, I won't go!" By 1966, the *Washington Legend* decided it needed a seasoned correspondent in Vietnam to dig beneath the daily press briefings and Pentagon blather. The paper sought out Sam and made him its Saigon bureau chief.

With this new responsibility, he reported with even greater vigor. Though his coverage included mentions of VC and North Vietnamese atrocities, he focused more on excesses by the U.S. military, on their inability to win over the "hearts and minds" of Vietnam's population, and on the fact that they could demonstrate no clear measure of victory. His reporting won Sam the intense ire of the president.

Once, while sitting in Le P'tit, Sam ran into a former White House newspaper correspondent who had arrived in-country the previous day and was assigned to cover the deteriorating situation in Vietnam. He described how Sam's columns were getting a lot of attention in the Oval Office.

"Man, are you pissing off Nixon!" he said. "He calls your stories 'Esposito *neg-atorials*.'"

"I like that," Sam responded. "*Negatorial* has a nice ring."

"Wait, it gets better. So I'm interviewing Nixon and right away he says something like 'I can't wait to get that bastard Yalie fuckin' cocksucker reporter friend of yours. Even George Bush can't rein that fucker in, and he practically owns Yale and could probably get Esposito fired from half the newspapers in the country. But not the *Legend*. Who's running that rag now? Charlie Waverly's widow? Who the fuck does she think she is?' he says. 'Who the fuck does Esposito think he is?'

"Then right in front of me—because he knows I'm going to Vietnam and will play this back to you—he turns to his chief of staff—his buddy Haldeman—and says, 'I want a dossier on Esposito. Give me everything you can get on that prick! Everything!'"

"I've heard that he's not too happy," Sam smiled.

"Yeah, well, watch your back, Sam. Nixon never forgets an enemy. He'll get you if you're not careful."

But the angrier Nixon got at Sam, the more Sam investigated, the more his stories appeared on page one, above the fold, and the more Americans became disenchanted with a war that had by this point dragged on longer than any war in the nation's history.

Fortunately for Sam, the *Legend's* biggest competitor, the *Washington Post*, exposed a seemingly small-time burglary at an apartment and office complex called the Watergate that eventually implicated the Nixon Administration for its political dirty tricks. Two years later, on August 9, 1974, Richard M. Nixon was forced to resign, becoming the only president in U.S. history to have done so.

Gerald Ford was sworn in as president. Now all eyes were on him to end the Vietnam War.

Sunday, April 6

The White House, Washington, D.C.

IN OFFICE LESS THAN EIGHT MONTHS following the humiliation and
resignation of his predecessor Richard Nixon, President Gerald
R. Ford sat in pensive silence, his hands absentmindedly caressing
the polished surface of the desk before him. *This was Kennedy's
desk,* he thought. *This is where the war began, when Kennedy ordered
advisors to Vietnam.*

With him were Secretary of Defense James Schlesinger
and Secretary of State Henry Kissinger, who also served as the
President's National Security Advisor. Kissinger waited several
uncomfortable minutes before speaking. "Is there anything else we
need to discuss before General Weyand arrives, Mr. President?"

"You know, this damn war has chewed up three United States
presidents already," Ford murmured, half aloud. "I'll be damned if
it's going to ruin me as well."

"We have already brought our troops home," Kissinger replied,
his voice equally subdued. "Perhaps it's time to sever the last of our
support to the current regime. Thieu is increasingly unstable. If he
falls, we will be seen as culpable and fall with him."

"And if we abandon him now we will look like cowards who let
an ally go down in defeat. Is that what we want?"

The intercom light on his desk blinked on as the voice of Ford's secretary interrupted them.

"Sir, General Weyand is here to see you."

"Send him in," ordered the President, leaning forward in his chair.

"Mr. President. Jim, Henry." General Weyand greeted them with a nod in each direction. Weyand wasn't a big man, but he carried himself with military bearing, a presence in any room, even the Oval Office.

"Good morning, General," said Ford. He neither liked nor disliked Weyand, but he appreciated the man's forthrightness and sense of duty. Weyand had always given him straight answers and the unvarnished truth, good or bad. Unfortunately, of late it had all been bad. "Get any rest on the ride home?"

"It is the other side of the planet, sir—in more ways than one. I'll catch up on my sleep when the jet lag catches up with me. My report couldn't wait."

"You're right, of course. So how is our friend Thieu faring? Can he hold on? More to the point, can his troops?"

"And does our ambassador still have confidence in him?" Kissinger added.

"It's not looking good, Mr. President. North Vietnam's got the full-court press on, with several of their infantry and armor divisions racing to see who can get to Saigon first. Hue's gone, overrun. Once Da Nang falls—and it won't be long, by the looks of it—the other northern and Central Highland cities will quickly follow. We all know the South Vietnamese Army is weak and North Vietnam's General Giap knows it, too. I think the only reason he's waited this long was to see what we'd do when push really came to shove. Now that he sees we're effectively standing down, he's turned loose the dogs."

Weyand turned toward Kissinger. He was used to strong men who used force to get their way. But Kissinger was a manipulator on a grand scale, a Machiavelli who had a hand in everything that was unfolding, and who had somehow managed to survive as counsel to this president as well as the last when all of the other architects of the war had gone down in disgrace. Weyand disliked him intensely.

"As to your question, Mr. Secretary," he said in a level voice, "the ambassador still thinks Thieu can pull it together, find the backbone to rally his troops and halt the advance. I have my doubts, but that's not my call."

"Did you present the plan we agreed on?" said Kissinger.

"Yes, sir, I did. And I think Ambassador Martin and I convinced President Thieu that it's his only chance to turn this around, to prevent a complete rout. It could work, but it would still be a holding action. The NVA smells blood in the water. They're not likely to back off now."

"I don't expect the media to back off, either," Ford interjected. "We watched your press conference on the news while you were en route home. I don't think they were convinced that Thieu or his forces can stand up to the NVA now. That bastard Esposito was especially pushy. But if we let the damn journalists dictate the outcome of this war before it's actually over we really will have lost it—lost it all—South Vietnam, the war, our involvement, all the sacrifices our soldiers have made over there, everything!"

As Ford spoke he became increasingly agitated, finally slamming his fist on the desk—the Kennedy desk—for emphasis.

"Is that it, General? Is that your complete assessment of the situation on the ground as things stand today? And I'd welcome your personal opinion—if Thieu can stop the NVA advance is there any chance for a negotiated solution, absent a military one?"

Weyand gathered himself to meet the president's gaze.

"Mister President, there's no way to dance around this," he replied. "The current military situation is critical. As for the probability of survival of South Vietnam as a truncated nation, I think that's marginal at best. The government of Vietnam is on the brink of military defeat. Given the speed at which events are moving, I believe the U.S. should plan now for a mass evacuation of some six thousand American citizens and tens of thousands of SVN and third-country nationals."

Ford sat stone silent for a full minute as he absorbed the general's comments.

"Henry," he said, finally. "We've got to get Congress to act! There's not much else this office can do alone. Let's get the House and Senate leaders in here, and include McGovern and Joe Biden—we need the Democrats on board. There are lives at stake here—thousands of them!"

Monday, April 7

"YOU BUY ME SAIGON TEA?" WHISPERED a sweet voice in Steve Carwood's ear. The pretty young woman sidled up close and draped a slender arm across his shoulder as he turned from the bar to face her.

Impossibly young was Carwood's first thought. *No doubt illegally young* was his second. After three years with the CIA in Saigon, Carwood knew this routine well enough. Like most of the bar girls in Saigon, she was a beauty, and oh-so-adept at manipulating any man who wandered in the door. Any man with cash in his pocket and lust in his heart.

Behind the bar on a raised platform, a trio of equally young women danced to a jukebox song. They wore high heels and very little else. The club was dark and packed at this hour with customers lined up shoulder to shoulder along the bar, all of them eyeing the girls, mesmerized as they watched their fantasies slowly gyrating to the music.

"I show you good time, no short time," the girl at Carwood's side said with an alluring smile. "I be your babysan you buy me one Saigon Tea."

"Not tonight, sweetheart," he said. "No babysan. No Saigon Tea."

"You numbah ten!" she said, giving him a gentle slap on the shoulder. "You play big joke on babysan!" She shifted closer, her breath warm on his neck, and placed one hand on his thigh. Slowly, her hand moved toward his crotch, which had grown increasingly tight. "I give you numbah one massage, two dollah. Boom-boom, six dollah!"

Carwood would have liked nothing more than to take her up on her offer. But not tonight. He was at the bar to meet an asset—a well-placed Vietnamese government official named Huan Dinh who lived a clandestine life as the CIA's top double agent in Saigon. For months now, the man had been passing Carwood secrets about VC activity in and around the city. And for all Carwood knew, he was probably selling CIA secrets back to the VC. It didn't matter, as long as the CIA got good information, actionable information, and didn't have to give up too much of importance in return.

Over the girl's shoulder, he spotted his man walk into the club. As Carwood stood to leave, the girl firmly grasped the bulge in his pants. "No, please not go," she insisted. "I want to see the miracle! You so big! Make babysan happy, cry with pleasure!"

He brushed the girl's hand away and turned aside, hoping his suddenly prominent pants bulge wasn't too noticeable. "Sorry, gotta go!" he said, detaching himself from her as he pulled his bar stool between them. She gave him a quizzical look, then immediately turned toward the next man at the bar.

"You buy babysan Saigon Tea?" he heard her say, as he moved off toward the darkened booths along the back wall, where his man had taken a seat. He didn't stop at the booth, but paused near it to light a cigarette, striking the match three times before it flared into life. It was their prearranged signal—one strike meant the meeting was canceled, two meant they were dangerously compromised, three the meeting was on and they were to rendezvous at the safe house the CIA maintained nearby.

Carwood left the club and hurried to their meeting place, a ground-floor flat with a private entrance at the rear of a large apartment building off Tu Do Street. He didn't have to wait long. Within minutes he heard a key rattle in the lock as the man, silhouetted from behind by a distant streetlamp, quietly entered the darkened room. Like Carwood, Huan Dinh made no attempt to turn on a light, instead moving with familiar ease to a chair across from where Carwood sat. He laid a pack of cigarettes on the table, struck a match, and quickly cupped the flame in his hands as he lit his smoke, then offered the flame to Carwood, who took one of the cigarettes and lit up.

"We haven't talked in a while, my friend," Carwood said. "I hope you are well."

"As well as can be expected in these difficult times," the man answered. "More difficult for you than for me, I think. Yes?"

"Business as usual," Carwood replied, trying to sound nonchalant. "Nothing has changed."

"Ah, but everything has changed. Soon you will leave Saigon, I think. Leave Vietnam." He paused to let his words sink in. "*If* the North Vietnamese allow you to leave."

"*If* that time ever comes, the embassy will decide whether to stay or to leave. We don't see it happening anytime soon."

"A pity you do not play chess, Mr. Carwood. You do not see the danger ahead because you do not look to the future. Unlike you, Hanoi is playing the long game, and what is happening today is the result of actions initiated some time ago."

"And what would that be?" Although the night was warm, Carwood felt a sudden chill. His man was rarely this chatty. Huan Dinh had something important to reveal. "What actions are you talking about?"

"Do you know what anniversary is coming soon—two anniversaries, actually? The first of May is the international communist workers' holiday, of course. This is an important date for North Vietnam. But May nineteen is even more special."

"Ho Chi Minh's birthday, right?"

"Very good! You know this date! But what you do not know is that Hanoi has decided that Saigon will be the most fitting present it can give to its people to honor their dear Uncle Ho's memory. My sources tell me that General Giap has ordered the North's army to take Saigon at any cost, with the invasion to be completed by May the first, in order to celebrate a great communist victory on that date."

Carwood took his time replying, lighting another cigarette for himself and one for his informant. If what Huan Dinh said was accurate, they really were in deep shit, despite what the ambassador kept insisting.

"South Vietnam is not about to give up," he said, finally, "and the U.S. is still ready to step in if push comes to shove. North Vietnam—"

Huan Dinh didn't let him finish. "North Vietnam has taken every city and province in the country by force and the United States has not even attempted to stop them. Hanoi has been testing you, watching these events carefully. Do you not see? Now their army has surrounded Saigon. There are no South Vietnamese forces left to stop them from invading the city and taking it, too."

"Then why haven't they? What's preventing them—other than knowing our military still has the capability to kill another million of them, if need be, or resume bombing every rice paddy and factory north of the DMZ until Hanoi crawls back to the table in Paris."

Huan Dinh's cigarette glowed as he took a long drag. "Hanoi doesn't want this, of course. They want you to leave. Just leave. The war is over, Mr. Carwood. If you go now it will end quietly, without unnecessary bloodshed. Hanoi does not care that many Vietnamese want to leave with you—they can go, with your help. Hanoi knows you are already evacuating people. But this will not go on indefinitely. There is a time when it must stop."

"May first—*if* what you say is true."

"You may choose to believe what you want to believe, Mr. Carwood," Huan Dinh said as he stood and turned toward the door. "The future is always right in front of us. It is up to you to recognize it and act accordingly. I wish you good luck, my friend. Perhaps we will meet again—before you and your people depart."

Tuesday, April 8

SAM JAMMED ANOTHER BLANK SHEET INTO his Olivetti and started typing. He'd get two or three lines into it and then tear out the paper, ball it up, and toss it into the wastebasket behind the bar.

"Sam, if this is where you do your best work, I'd like to see where you do your worst," Jean Paul joked as he slid a coffee cup toward Sam and added, "Maybe some caffeine will help."

"I guess I could use a break," Sam responded while Jean Paul picked through the discarded paper in the basket, straightening out one of the sheets that seemed to have the most copy and started reading it.

Vietnamizing Vietnam
By Samuel Esposito

Saigon Tuesday April 8—Captain Nguyen Thanh Trung is the poster boy for the Vietnamization of the war—yes, Vietnamization, the U.S. strategy of turning the war over to the people who should be fighting it instead of the Americans. The process began in the late 1960s and was declared a success by 1973—the year U.S. forces returned home. That was two years ago. Today, one would be hard-pressed to find an embassy official willing to even utter the word Vietnamization, as the South Vietnamese Army collapses in the face of advancing North Vietnamese armed forces.

One small part of the Vietnamization program was for the U.S. Air Force to send Captain Trung to Texas for a year for advanced fighter training on the F-5—the warbird version of the Air Force's supersonic trainer, the T-38 Talon, fitted out with bomb racks and rocket launchers.

Trung was perfect. He was a natural aviator with tremendous good looks and charm. He was on the fast track for a command position in the South Vietnam Air Force, and was expected to rise to General of the South Vietnamese Air Force while still in his forties. When anyone described Trung, the word most often used was "dashing." He even wore a white silk scarf to enhance the image.

As part of the U.S. propaganda effort, the previous ambassador to South Vietnam, Ellsworth Bunker, loved to show off Trung at embassy parties, including his Yale alumni events, to which this reporter was often invited. He called those parties Bulldog Bashes, and Bunker ran his bashes like frat house beer brawls. Bunker would gather his fellow alumni 'round the piano to sing, "From the tables down and Mory's to the place where Louie dwells, to the . . ."

Trung could be expected to sing his heart out for "the dear old Temple Bar," the venerable Yale College watering hole that he had never seen. Trung would join in with even more gusto to sing the Bulldog's fight song: "Boolah, boolah, boolah, boolah, boolah boolah, and do it again . . ."

Bunker once put his arm around Trung's shoulder and toasted him in front of a half-dozen Navy fighter jocks, calling Trung "one of us."

Today, that all changed. It is now safe to report that Trung was my "not for attribution" source for years. He seemed to have unusual access to North Vietnam's plans and strategies. He had enough information to be believable, but there were plenty of times his information was slightly off, so as to not arouse suspicion.

Trung was in fact a . . .

* * *

Jean Paul looked up from the crumpled sheet that had ended so abruptly. "Sam, I'm a bartender, not a famous journalist like you, but I see your problem."

"Yeah, this coffee could use a shot of bourbon. That's my problem."

"Coming right up," Jean Paul said and, while pouring a shot of Jim Beam into Sam's cup, he added, "Look, you're the great journalist. The Pulitzer Prize winner. The guy who was going to change the war with the words your little red Olivetti vomits. But this story? You cannot write it because you got fooled. Trung, how do you Americans say it, 'pulled the wool over your eyes.' He lied to you and you fell for it. And you are angry."

"Somehow you are not making me feel better," Sam acknowledged adding, "That sonofabitch! How fucking stupid was I? Trung fed me enough information to keep me on the hook, and readers back home convinced that South Vietnam's Air Force was failing." Sam was fuming.

"Why don't you tell the truth, Sam. Tell the truth. After all, four, maybe five of your presidents have been fooled by Vietnam's leaders. You will be in very good company. So tell the truth. Write it from here," Jean Paul added, pointing to his heart.

* * *

That morning, the same Captain Nguyen Thanh Trung had lined up on the runway with three other F-5s from his South Vietnamese Air Force squadron. Carrying their full load of five-hundred-pound bombs, the jets prepared to take off on a mission against the North Vietnamese troops advancing on Saigon.

During the engine run-up—the last check to make sure the single engine F-5s were "all systems go"—in the crucial moments before takeoff, the squadron maintained radio silence. Everything seemed routine until the last seconds when Trung, using hand signals, indicated to his squadron leader that his plane was experiencing a malfunction. The other pilot acknowledged, then he and the others taxied toward takeoff. If Trung had to abort and could not catch up at the predetermined rendezvous point, they would proceed toward their target without him, as planned.

But after his comrades had flown out of sight, Trung throttled up his no-longer "malfunctioning" engine and took off alone. Once airborne, instead of racing to catch up with his squadron, he made a steep turn low to the ground and headed off on a course in the opposite direction.

* * *

Tuesday, April 8, marked the fifth year of Steve Carwood's Far East assignment with the CIA and his third year in Saigon. Despite the latest bad news about the North Vietnamese advance up in Phan Rang, and despite what his snitch, Huan Dinh, had told him, the anniversary reminded him of how much he had accomplished in those years. It made him feel good for a change, almost buoyant, and the cool morning air prompted him to walk the few blocks to his meeting at the Presidential Palace.

He felt even better when he recalled that President Thieu wouldn't be at the meeting. They could do without him—Thieu was a mess, more hindrance than help these days. "A slight illness," his aide had said on the phone late last night. More like a case of nerves, Carwood decided.

When he reached the corner of the palace grounds, he stopped at a kiosk for the morning paper. Beyond the fence, surrounded by lawn at the end of a long circular drive, the palace sat serenely in its park-like surroundings. The gleaming white marble structure was impressive, but to Carwood it looked more like a postmodern mausoleum than a palace. However, he liked its airy, mahogany-lined corridors and high-ceilinged meeting rooms, and he didn't mind seeing Thieu's ministers here instead of in his cramped office at the embassy. Besides, the lunch they served was always better than anything dished out at the embassy mess.

As Carwood stepped from the curb, he heard a deafening roar from above and behind. Suddenly, a fighter jet appeared directly overhead, no more than forty feet over the treetops lining Nguyen Du Boulevard. It was an American-made F-5 with South Vietnamese Air Force markings, and it had two fat, black, five-hundred-pound bombs slung beneath its wings—so close Carwood could see the serial numbers stenciled on them. The jet flew straight for the palace.

With Carwood watching in disbelief, the jet released the bombs as its pilot simultaneously hit the afterburners and pitched the aircraft into a steep climb. Like a rocket, it screamed upward on a column of purple-white flame, and a sound louder than Carwood had ever heard made him recoil into the street. Tailfins snapped out from the rear of each bomb, slowing their flight. To Carwood they looked like a pair of enormous metal insects that slowly wobbled and floated on a graceful downward arc toward their destination.

Both bombs struck the roof of the palace. Flames and smoke and debris erupted with a tremendous blast, followed by a shock wave that slammed Carwood backward and whipped the leaves off the trees around him.

In the street, chaos erupted. Pedestrians screamed and ran. Cars and pedicabs collided. Carwood, thrown to the gutter by the blasts, got to his feet just as the jet reappeared from high above, now shrieking downward at a steep angle, its 20-millimeter wing cannons snarling like a chain saw. The high-explosive rounds showered the burning building with small explosions and tore into a limousine parked in the drive. The vehicle blew itself apart, adding to the flaming debris scattered across the lawn and drive.

Then, as quickly as the attack began, the jet was gone, roaring away beyond the rooftops, leaving a trail of flaming wreckage on the ground below.

Carwood could only stare, stupefied and numb, at the smoking palace. Slowly, the sounds of his surroundings increased as his hearing returned. His legs still shaking, he began to run toward the palace.

Only one thought occupied his mind: *What the FUCK just happened here!?*

* * *

Trung's F-5 made one more low-level turn, allowing him to survey the damage before he blasted north toward the landing strip that had been prearranged by his new North Vietnamese allies. Alone in the cockpit, he smiled as he considered what he had done.

Trung, the pride of the South Vietnam Air Force, the guy who sang the Yale fight song with gusto during Ambassador Bunker's annual picnic aboard the embassy yacht, had just defected in a twenty-five million dollar made-in-America fighter jet. And— while he was at it—had bombed South Vietnam's Presidential Palace.

* * *

After Jean Paul's pep talk and a couple of swigs of his bourbon-laced coffee, Sam inserted another sheet of copy paper into his typewriter and continued writing.

Vietnamizing Vietnam

-page 2- S. Esposito

Trung was a turncoat. He had fooled everyone in both the U.S. and South Vietnamese Air Force. To make matters worse, after his deceptions, he rubbed salt into the wounds of those who had trusted him.

He called a press conference in Hanoi that was covered by the BBC and heard around the world. "The scheme to steal an American fighter went off without a hitch because I have been planning this since I was eight. My father," Trung explained over the radio, "was Viet Cong and in the year he was killed by the American puppet President Diem's forces, I vowed revenge."

He continued, "I practiced and practiced, how I would steal the F-5 and plotted my course over the palace. My only regret is that I did not kill Thieu when I released my bombs over the building."

In a later interview, General George Brown, the 7th Air Force commander, who oversaw Vietnamization of the air war, could not contain his anger. "We flew that bastard all the way to Texas, taught him how to fly our F-5s in combat. He went up with our best aces. He learned every tactic and every command and control strategy we used to maintained air supremacy throughout the Vietnam War. Then he steals the aircraft right out from under our noses.

"Vietnamization my ass. I'll shoot him myself if I ever find him."
S.ESPOSITO—EVERGREEN

Wednesday, April 9

G ENERAL BROWN NEVER MANAGED TO FIND Trung, but Sam did.

After filing his story about Trung's deception, Sam cooled off. But he began pushing Jean Paul for a connection to Trung because he knew Jean Paul kept a Rolodex of North Vietnamese contacts in his brain.

"C'mon, Jean Paul, put out the word. I heard the BBC, I saw the Russian papers. Trung's picture is on the front page. He's a big hero in Moscow and in the ARVN for trying to assassinate Thieu. Jean Paul, I want to talk to him. It still pisses me off that he gave the story to the BBC and Isvestia and not me. So much for loyal sources."

"Face it, Sam. He used everyone." Jean Paul poured another Hennessy into the glass in front of him and casually remarked, "Now that you have your typewriter here, you don't have to spend much time at the *Legend* office."

"The publisher's called everyone in the bureau home. All that's left there are a bunch of steel desks and a Telex. So I go over there only to file my stories. That's it," Sam answered.

After his second Hennessey, Sam asked, almost as casually as if he were asking for directions to the washroom, "Jean Paul, you will get a message to Trung for me, won't you? Whenever I want a source up North, you always seem to have a way to get through."

"It's late in the game, Sam. Don't you get what's happening here?"

"He wasn't just a source. Trung and I were friends, I think that still counts. I have to get hold of the guy. I know you can do it."

"For what?" Jean Paul demanded. "Why now? No one in America cares anymore. Your *Legend* doesn't care." He threw a week-old copy of the *Legend* on the bar. "Look. Do you see Sam Esposito on page one? Do you see Sam Esposito on page two? How about page twelve?" He turned to a page filled with lingerie ads. "Oh, what a surprise, you are not there either. All the news you see about Vietnam is from reporters in Washington. People would rather hear about what is happening at home, and you should too."

Jean Paul kept flipping through the pages, "There, page twenty. I see a story about Saigon by Sam Esposito. One more story isn't going to make a difference. When I left the North with my family, when they closed the border in 1954, journalists like you wrote stories for their papers, too. No one cared. Not in France. Not in the States. Not anywhere. It's been twenty years, the same thing is happening here now. Get out while you can, Sam. Go!"

Sam wasn't about to give up. He needed Jean Paul's help. "If I can score an interview with Trung and that's the last story I file from Vietnam, then so be it," he told his friend. "I want the story. I know you can help me if you want to."

* * *

The minute Sam sat down at his usual seat next to the house phone, Jean Paul said in a low voice, "I had nothing to do with this. Nothing, you hear me. But . . . someone called and said Captain Trung has a message for you. He said Trung cannot say anything over the phone. He wants to talk to you. It was about an hour ago. He said it's important. Here is his number." Jean Paul handed Sam the receiver and the phone number written on a bar slip.

"No shit? Trung!" Sam said, grabbing the receiver from Jean Paul. *If Trung has a message for me it's really big*, Sam thought as he picked up the receiver and started dialing.

Someone picked up the phone on the other end and said nothing.

"Hello, anybody there?" Sam asked.

"Don't say anything. I want you to meet me," said the voice.

"Who are you?"

"A friend of our mutual friend. You have to meet me. We can't talk over the phone."

"Okay. Where?"

"Where you said good-bye to an old friend. Do you know the place?"

"Yeah." Sam was catching on.

The last place he saw Trung was at the cyclodrome, where teenagers raced two-cycle motorcycles around a track to entertain people with nothing better to do on Sunday afternoons.

"Be there," the voice said. "Ten tomorrow morning."

Click.

As Sam replaced the handset in its cradle, a voice behind him said, "Buy a girl a drink, sailor?" It was Lisette. "What are you hiding, Sam? You look guilty," she said.

Sam crumpled the phone message, trying to appear nonchalant.

But it was too late. Lisette spotted the note in his hand. After ordering a drink, she shifted to a more seductive voice. "You've got something, Sam. Come on, give. You've got a real scoop. I know you do." she begged, trying to unfold his hand. He held the note like a child hiding a prize marble.

"It's a source. He wants to talk to me. Alone."

"How long have we known each other, Sam." It wasn't a question.

"I don't know. When was TV invented?"

"Very funny."

"You trying to tell me something?"

"No, just thinking. The devil is at the door and I honestly don't know what I'm going to do. See this face? Even though I'm as American as you are, my eyes make me a target for the North.

Okay, Sam, for the first time, well maybe fourth time, I'm scared. Really scared. I don't know what there is for me in the States. What are you going to do?"

Sam shifted on his bar stool. "I figure the *Legend* will be there for me. They'll throw a big welcome home party for me in the newsroom with cake—the kind the publisher's assistant sends his secretary out to buy five minutes before the event. Then a couple of speeches, 'Blah, blah blah . . . we're keeping you here, nice and safe in D.C. . . . no more war zones for you . . . thanks for your contribution to the *Legend*, above and beyond . . .' That sort of thing. Then they pay me for the rest of my life. I file a couple of stories a week. A column would be nice. It would be enough dough to support myself while I write my memoirs."

"Christ, Sam, you make it sound so exciting. I can hardly wait," Lisette replied.

Sam didn't miss a beat. "Maybe I'll even get married. Find a senator's daughter. Or I could always go into PR."

Lisette nearly choked on her drink. "Yeah, and maybe I'll do the weather in Boise."

* * *

For Sam, covering Vietnam became just a job. He was there four years before the embassy was completed in late 1967, three months before the Tet Offensive. This gave the U.S. a big building, so what to do with it? Fill it with CIA agents, Vietnamese office workers, and Ambassador Ellsworth Bunker's staff of Ivy League graduates who fancied themselves professional diplomats. The embassy staff expanded so quickly that within a year, the State Department began renting additional office space all over Saigon, including the Armed Forces Radio station at 9 Hong Thap Tu Street, several blocks from the embassy. The CIA used the broadcasts as an overt means of sending covert messages to the dwindling number of American soldiers, Marines, and diplomats left in the country.

With no real strategy to defeat the enemy, by the 1970s the U.S. government needed something to show that America was still winning. So the Pentagon came up with a scorecard—body counts. Every day the Pentagon released data that exaggerated the number of North Vietnamese killed while downplaying the number of American and South Vietnamese deaths. The war was stuck in the muck like stalks of rice planted in the Mekong Delta paddies.

As the war devolved into a vague, amorphous guessing game, correspondents found ways to break their boredom. Every reporter had a girlfriend. "We ate, we drank, we fucked, and when we could we wrote," was how one of them described it.

Some correspondents created a uniform of their own—the Saigon suit. It was probably the first leisure suit. Local tailors made them in seersucker, gabardine, and baby blue pinstripes. A few of the big names—the AP's Esper and Arnett, the *Times*' Halberstam and the *Legend*'s Sam Esposito—would have none of it. They developed their own style. Esper looked like he belonged with MAC-V—he wore olive-drab mostly and rolled up his shirtsleeves to the elbow in the MAC-V Headquarters style. He blended in, spoke barely above a whisper, and made friends of the brass and everyone else.

Halberstam, on the other hand, berated the generals any chance he got, along with the senators and congressmen who flew in for a quick look. He was especially rancorous toward Nixon, to the point where the president wanted to know, "Who the hell does this guy think he is?" and looked for ways to, as he once said, "bang Halberstam's and Esposito's heads together on TV."

Sam simply went about his business. His mode of operation was simply to make sure no one really noticed him until he scooped them all with his reporting on the Tet Offensive. After Sam's story was published he slipped back into his own world.

"Sam! Snap out of it!" Lisette said, jolting him out of his trip down memory lane. Sitting next to him at Le P'tit, she added,

"You know, Sam, maybe the least of my worries is getting a job in the States with the network. Maybe I should make sure I stay alive."

Sam came out of his reverie and looked at Lisette as though for the first time. He wanted her alive, too.

* * *

The roar of the two-cycle engines was deafening and the cloud of burned oil and gasoline that rose above the cyclodrome stung Sam's eyes. It was only the first motorcycle race of the day, and although the track was outdoors, the air was already filled with blue fumes.

Sam watched the racers go around and around the track until he got bored. He found a park bench and lit a cigarette with his Zippo lighter. He waited for over two hours for his contact to show up. Then as he was about to leave, he heard a voice from behind.

"Do you know how to get to the Statue of Liberty?" a voice said. "Don't turn around. Look toward the motorcycles. Don't look at me."

"*Chao ong,*" Sam greeted the voice.

"Captain Trung has a surprise for you. It is a story you will want for your newspaper. You will be contacted again. I promise, April 28 will be a very special day."

"That's it?" Sam replied, puzzled. When he turned around, whoever had given him the message had already melted into the crowd.

Thursday, April 10

From the Congressional Record

April 10, 1975, President Gerald R. Ford addresses
a joint session of Congress:

I have received a full report from General Weyand, whom I sent
to Vietnam to assess the situation. He advises that the current
military situation is very critical, but that South Vietnam is continuing to defend itself with the resources available. However, he
feels that if there is to be any chance of success for their defense
plan, South Vietnam urgently needs an additional $722 million in
very specific military supplies from the United States.

In my judgment, a stabilization of the military situation offers
the best opportunity for a political solution.

I must, of course, as I think each of you would, consider the safety
of nearly six thousand Americans who remain in South Vietnam
and tens of thousands of South Vietnamese employees of the
United States Government, of news agencies, of contractors, and
businesses whose lives, with their dependents, are in grave peril.

There are tens of thousands of other South Vietnamese intellectuals, professors, teachers, editors, and opinion leaders who

have supported the South Vietnamese cause and the alliance with the United States to whom we have a profound moral obligation.

And I also ask prompt revision of the law to cover those Vietnamese to whom we have a very, very special obligation and whose lives may be endangered should the worst come to pass.

I hope that this authority will never have to be used, but if it is needed, there will be no time for Congressional debate. Because of the gravity of the situation, I ask the Congress to complete action on all of these measures not later than April 19.

Saturday, April 12

It often seemed to Pham Thi Quanh—or "Pam" now, to her new neighbors and friends in San Diego—that the peaceful, sun-warmed, laid-back routine that had become her life in Southern California was everything she had ever wanted. The small suburban Craftsman-style home she and Matt had moved into after they married was quiet, calm, and spotlessly clean. People washed their cars in the driveway here. The streets were clean. Everything looked bright and new. She felt safe.

Pham also loved her life before California. After graduating from secondary school in Saigon, she had found a job at World Travel Services. Smart and ambitious, she quickly worked her way up to manager. At the height of the war, World Travel helped organize the commercial airline flights that brought American soldiers into the country. On one of the flights that she happened to be aboard, she met Matt. By chance they met again while he was on in-country R&R in Vung Tao, the seaside resort south of Saigon. Despite his return to the boonies and a nearly yearlong separation, they managed to stay in touch. At the end of his tour, they married in the Notre Dame Catholic Basilica in Saigon among her family and childhood friends.

Now Pham wanted her life to be like this always. The world she left behind, a world she once loved, was fraught with chaos and fear. The fond memories she had of growing up in her parents' green-shuttered stucco home off Rue de Pasteur slipped further away as each day passed.

But not today. Today the news in the papers and on the television was all about her homeland, Vietnam, and about the war that grew increasingly grim as the armies of the North and South clashed and the people trapped between them died. People she knew. Her entire family was there, her mother and father, her sisters and aunts and cousins and second, third, and fourth cousins. While Pham had managed to get away and make a life in a new world, they had stayed behind, out of inertia but also as a matter of choice and a desire to cling to the old order and traditions, and to the land that had belonged to them for a thousand years.

If what the television news was saying was true, all of that was about to be ripped away.

"Matt, please come in here, you need to see this!" Pham called to the other room as she focused on the television. The TV, an extravagantly large Sony Trinitron, along with all their furniture, his Nikon cameras, their western clothing, and two oversize decorative ceramic elephants standing by the front door which Matt bought them at the PX in Saigon when he was discharged from the Marines five years ago. Now the memories of that life, and of her ancestral home in Vietnam, came back in a rush as scenes of war and destruction swept across the TV screen.

Matt Moran emerged from the bathroom wrapped in a towel. "Honey, I'm shaving, what's up."

"You shaved last year, *babysan*, get in here," It was their little joke. Despite his two tours on the DMZ, one of which had earned him a Purple Heart, Matt still looked like a high school sophomore. Pham liked the way he looked, especially now. He had gained back most of the weight he lost as a grunt living and fighting in the jungle, and he was fit and muscular and tan as a surfer—his favorite pastime when he wasn't studying for his economics degree or working part time at Wax My Mama, a surf shop south of the San Diego State campus.

Matt pulled on a cutoff sweatshirt and stood beside Pham, as the two of them stared wordlessly at the television. He wrapped his arms around her to feel her warmth. Pham welcomed the embrace and used the remote control to turn up the volume.

The newsman in the broadcast was reporting from a helicopter landing zone somewhere in Vietnam, describing events as they were happening around him.

". . . Flush with victory, the North Vietnamese Army with their Soviet-made tanks has now captured both Hue and Da Nang, two major population centers American soldiers and Marines defended for more than a decade and key defensive strongholds that South Vietnam's President Thieu had vowed to hold . . .

". . . The South's remaining divisions still control positions in the Central Highlands and along the South-Central coast, but observers now wonder if they have the resolve to stop the NVA advance and keep them from barreling straight to Saigon, which would strike a fatal blow to the heart of this beleaguered nation . . ."

Matt gave a low groan. "This isn't good," he muttered. "Not good at all."

". . . In other action, North Vietnam infiltrators have reportedly begun attacking Tan Son Nhut, the huge airfield near Saigon that now serves as this country's main commercial air hub as well as its military air force base . . .

". . . Although sources tell me the airfield and city are not in danger of being overrun any time soon, this entire turn of events could be the precursor to the end many people inside and outside the government have feared. This is Lisette Vo, NBS News, reporting from a firebase outside Phan Rang, South Vietnam . . ."

"We have to do something," Pham said, turning to face Matt. She repeated it with emphasis. "We have to do something *now*."

"Jesus, Pham. All those chances we could have had to bring your family to the States . . . what can we do now? If they're shelling Tan Son Nhut we may not get them out at all. We were stupid not to do it when we could."

After the American military pulled out of Vietnam two years earlier, Pham and Matt had discussed getting visas for her parents and sisters and relocating them to the States. But her parents resisted, unwilling to leave their home and life in Saigon. It didn't seem like a burning issue at the time. Like most people in South Vietnam and in the U.S., they believed the fighting would eventually reach a standoff and Vietnam would remain a divided nation, like North and South Korea. The U.S. government still supported South Vietnam, so the communists in the North were unlikely to press their luck and attempt a total takeover. Or so they had thought.

"I'll go," said Matt. "Even if the NVA head for Saigon, we may still have time to get them out."

"You're crazy! *Dinky dao, GI!*" Pham said, tapping his forehead with a slender finger. "You can't just fly in there now if the fighting is so close! We should go to the State Department office in L.A. first and see what they can do."

"They won't do anything—there must be a million nationals who want to *dee-dee* the hell out of Saigon now, along with all their relations here in the States who'll be trying to get them out. It's too late for that. If I can get in, I'll find a way to take them out with me. You still have contacts there who might be able to help—you know people at the airline and I've stayed in touch with a couple of Marine buddies at the Defense Attaché Office. Let's just hope we're not too late."

"Okay, okay. Let me see if I can get through to my friends in the Saigon office," said Pham. "Pan Am is a military contractor—my guess is they'll still be flying into Saigon right up until the day the city falls. Maybe I can find out what's going on, and see if they can get word to my parents and sisters and get them on a flight out. It's worth a try."

"And what if your parents still won't budge?" Matt countered. "One of us has to go to convince them to leave. You're South Vietnamese, even if you're married to me and an American citizen now. If the NVA do invade, you'll be in danger. I'm the one to go. You get on the phone and see if you can wrangle me onto a flight. I'll pack."

"Okay, cowboy," Pham said. She thought for a moment and added, "We'll wrangle you an airplane."

April 13, 1975,

My Beloved Margaret,

I know I should have written before, but this is the
first time I have had a spare ten minutes.

I spent my last two weeks in Vietnam in a trailer on
the flight line at TSN. I sleep in my fatigues and,
yes I am wearing my flak jacket.

We hear the daily shelling but it is off in the distance, so not to worry. It goes around the clock, as
do the American C-141 jet transports. We're flying in
and literally dumping military supplies on the tarmac for the South Vietnamese troops. Unfortunately,
most of the supplies end up in the hands of the
invading North Vietnamese Army.

Then we board the refugees, probably twice the maximum passenger load—but the passengers are mostly
children—children of GIs, abandoned girlfriends
and wives and U.S. government and NGO workers.

Two weeks nonstop. And you know what? For some reason I'm not tired. Just incredibly sad.

Give my love to Peg, Bill, and Harry, Jr. Kiss them
for me.

With my love and devotion,

Lawrence

Monday, April 14

WEARING THE BLACK PAJAMAS OF PEASANT workers and a conical bamboo hat pulled down far over his eyes, the elderly-looking man quickly flashed his ID as he shuffled through the main gate and past the guard shack at Pleiku Air Base. He was among the local workers who swept the sidewalks, cooked the meals, washed the fine china from the officers' mess, and otherwise kept Pleiku Air Base clean, tidy, and running smoothly for the VNAF—the South Vietnamese Air Force, which had taken over from the Americans with the Vietnamization of the war.

Even without coloring his teeth with boot black to look like he was addicted to chewing betel nut—a habit among Vietnam's villagers that produced a mild high and turned one's teeth black as coal—no one could have imagined it was Trung. Trung, the darling of the United States Air Force, South Vietnam's dashing hero aviator, the shoo-in to become the Supreme High Commander of South Vietnam's Air Force, had shuffled past the main gate sentries in a pair of mud-caked sandals cut from an old jeep tire.

Once inside the fence, Nguyen Thanh Trung busied himself by sweeping the pathway to the HQ building, keeping his head down, affecting a limp so as not betray the presence of a twelve-inch bayonet stuck in his pants leg. By nightfall, when all the other local workers shuffled out, Trung, who had staked out the sentry post long enough to know the guards would not do a head count, remained behind. He waited for the darkness he needed to put his plan into action.

From a hilltop in the nearby jungle, Trung had been observing the comings and goings of the officers who flew the A-37 fighter jets and the mechanics who kept them running. Because of its bulbous cockpit and long, thin fuselage, the A-37 was aptly named "the Dragonfly."

Every USAF pilot had affection for the A-37. The trainer version was the first jet each pilot flew after transitioning from a civilian Cessna 172. It was fast but not supersonic, fully aerobatic, and pilots sat side by side as they would in a civilian plane. This made training a lot easier than with tandem seating—especially when there is a language barrier. If a trainee got himself into a death spiral and wouldn't let go of the stick, a punch to the arm by his right-seat trainer would get him to let go.

When the U.S. decided to turn the air war over to the Vietnamese, converting this diminutive jet trainer, which stood only waist high, into an armed Vietnamese Air Force fighter was an easy choice. The U.S. equipped the plane to carry four five-hundred-pound bombs and a 7.62 millimeter Gatling-style machine gun mounted in the nose—enough of a weapon system to provide close air support. But even with wingtip-mounted fuel tanks, which added weight and limited its destructive payload, it could not carry enough fuel to drop bombs north of the DMZ and return. Notwithstanding, the Dragonfly did not have the electronic countermeasures needed to penetrate the North's radar defenses. The U.S. wanted it that way, fearing a South Vietnam group commander would go rogue and attempt an attack deep inside North Vietnam that would end any diplomatic solution to the war.

Trung, now hiding by the chain link security fence, chuckled and said to himself, "If we pull this off, what fun to see the faces of the South Vietnam Air Force pilots when they wake up to find the planes gone and a truckload of spare parts stripped from the maintenance hangar. Even more fun when we turn their own weapon against them—striking a blow against both the South and the United States."

Trung's hijacking of a USAF F-5 fighter from Tan Son Nhut and bombing the Presidential Palace had won him accolades from his superiors. The story grew more bold and daring as Trung's gambit was told and retold throughout the North Vietnamese Air Force.

His daring caught the attention of the North's Air Force General Van Tien Dung, who summoned Trung to his office. "You have a new mission, Comrade Trung. We are putting together a select band of fighter pilots. You will be in command. Your mission is to infiltrate Pleiku Air Base and steal the Dragonflies right out from under the noses of the South Vietnamese Air Force." The general added with a thin smile," Of course, this is voluntary, Captain."

Trung was speechless. He could only utter, "General, I accept the mission."

"Good, your comrades are waiting for you. Six good pilots. All of them have combat experience. They trained in Russia as MiG-15 fighter pilots. You have six days to turn them into A-37 pilots."

* * *

"Comrades," Trung began as he addressed his assembled aviators, "you have been selected to serve in an elite squadron and join me in a dangerous mission. You've earned your place because of your bravery, your loyalty, and your skill as fighter pilots.

"I remind you," Trung went on, "this is a voluntary mission. Before we go one minute further, I must caution you. It is one thing to strafe a truck convoy from five hundred feet or provide close air support when you know you are protecting your brothers in arms on the ground. But if you cannot sneak up behind one of our countrymen from the South—someone whose mother looks like your mother—pull his head back and slit his throat, you may leave the squadron right now. No one will think less of you." Trung waited a full minute, making eye contact each of his pilots. Not one of them seemed to even blink.

With that, Trung introduced the pilots to their two training officers. They had been pilots with the South who were captured when the North overran Da Nang and immediately capitulated by taking a loyalty oath to North Vietnam. In addition to their skills as pilots, they both spoke and read English and were able to translate a stolen A-37 flight manual into Vietnamese.

None of its members had ever been in the cockpit of an A-37. Their training officers drilled them using cardboard cutouts with the instrument panel and controls drawn on them. The second their students sat in an A-37, they wanted the pilots to be comfortable enough with the controls to get the planes off the ground and fly them northward to a secret runway. Once there, they could practice their attack.

"You learned enough Russian to fly a MiG, and now you will learn enough English to fly the Dragonfly. As they say in Texas, it's gonna be a piece o' cake! *Yee-ha, doggies!*"

The six squadron members sat dumfounded, looking at one another. If they knew any English at all, it certainly was not Texas English.

But Trung, who had spent plenty of time in the Lone Star state, got the gag immediately and chimed in, "Okay boys, rodeo time!" For the first time, Trung cracked a smile, giving the entire squadron permission to laugh over a joke they didn't understand at all.

* * *

As night fell and the South Vietnamese airmen retired to their quarters, the base lights came on dimly. Since there were no night missions planned, the air traffic control tower was unmanned. The main gate was secured by a young corporal who hadn't even been born when Vietnam liberated the country from the French. A hundred yards or so from the gate sat another soldier, a sergeant, in a low wood tower that had been erected to protect the flight line from a sapper attack. He sleepily manned a .50-caliber machine gun and was the last obstacle before anyone could reach the neat rows of Dragonflies, resting between corrugated steel revetments. The rest of the defenses were left up to a single patrol that drove inside the double perimeter fence and concertina wire that encircled the base. The trip around the base, inspecting for breaches, took a half hour at least—that is, if the soldiers on patrol didn't stop to take a nap.

"Why sneak under the fence like chickens?" Trung reasoned, when he came up with the idea for the heist. *No, we are going to come through the main gate, like soldiers,* Trung thought as he walked, or rather staggered up to the sentry who was sitting on a low plastic chair outside the guard shack. Trung dropped the half-empty bottle of Jim Beam on the ground to be sure the clink of glass hitting the pavement got his attention.

"Hey! Who's there?"

Nothing. Trung ambled closer to the guard who began to approach him.

"Hey old man, what are you doing here? The base closed hours ago. You should have left with the other papa-sans." He shook his head in disgust at the spectacle of a drunken old man. "Come on. Let me help you find your way out," he said as he walked toward the stranger, who staggered a little more now. This forced the guard to prop him up.

"I'll point you toward home," he told him and as he grabbed him by his elbow, and walked him toward the main gate. After one, or maybe two steps, Trung whirled; a quick uppercut to his solar plexus dropped the guard to the ground instantly.

Trung quickly dragged him off the pavement, where he tied his hands and ankles and gagged him. Soon, a South Vietnam Army truck—or at least that is what it was painted to look like—pulled up to the gate. Trung, who now manned the guard shack, got out holding a clipboard he had found inside. "Don't rush it. Don't panic. This is just another routine delivery," he told himself as he pressed the button to open the gate and let the truck pass. *Remember to stop at the guard shack, in case anyone is watching. This has to look normal,* he thought, hoping the driver would remember the plot and not rush past him.

The driver stopped. He was sweating in sheets and had wet his pants. But he remembered to stop. He was driving a very special cargo, six pilots right onto an enemy base, along with a handful of soldiers who would clean out the maintenance hangar of any spare parts they can get their hands on. "Stay calm. We are almost there. One wrong move and we fail," Trung told the driver, as he pretended to check off something on his clipboard. He beckoned him to pass.

Trung turned to wave to the machine gunner, giving him a thumbs-up sign to let the truck drive onto the tarmac. The truck made a quick turn right, then left to the maintenance hangar, which was unguarded and cloaked in darkness.

One by one, the pilots climbed down from the truck. They proceeded toward the planes, from the rear away from the dimly lit flight line. There were only three guards, and the steel walls that protected the planes would prove to be their undoing. They could not see one another, so they could not join forces to repel their attackers, nor could they tell whether the arriving pilots were friend or foe until it was too late. The guards were dead in seconds.

Meanwhile, the truck entered the maintenance hangar and the soldiers pulled equipment and parts from the shelves. "Take the electronic equipment," Trung had told them during their planning sessions. They packed the truck with anything that even remotely looked electronic: gauges, radios, and a couple of boxes marked TACAN RECEIVER. They ignored aluminum parts that were bulky and could be fabricated by their own maintenance people if need be.

After packing the truck, they drove unhurriedly to the sentry shack, where one of the soldiers crept inside, and pressed the red button to open the main gate. The truck drove through the open gate, while the soldier, pressing the button to close the gate, ran as fast as he could before the gate clunked shut and got back inside the truck.

By now the six planes, with Trung in the lead, followed each other closely down the taxiway toward the end of the three-thousand-meter runway. Though it was not in the plan, though they were supposed to launch in complete darkness, Trung decided, at that instant, to put on a show for his enemy. For airstrips without control towers or for those with towers that are only manned during daylight hours, pilots can turn on the runway lights from the cockpit. They simply click the mic five times in three seconds so they can light the runway and take off or land safely—especially handy in an emergency.

Trung couldn't resist the temptation. "Should I do it?" he shouted in the cockpit. "Hell, yeah! Yee-ha!"

Click. Click. Click, click, click.

With one big snap, the entire runway—all three thousand meters—lit up on both sides with ribbons of brilliant white lights all the way to the outer marker.

That will get their attention, Trung thought, as he turned onto the runway and eased his Dragonfly into the wind. After making the turn he held fast, his feet hard on the brakes. He pushed the throttle to the firewall, revving the engine to thirty percent power, then sixty, then ninety. The engines screamed. He watched the gauge, waiting for the needle to hit ninety-eight percent. "Wait for it . . . Wait for it." It felt like every rivet would shake loose from the wings.

As the engine power reached ninety-eight percent, then ninety-nine percent, Trung released the brakes and the plane, straining at the thrust of its twin turbines, lunged forward and blasted its way into the sky in less than one thousand meters.

The glow of the jet engines shone like a comet against the black sky, guiding his fellow aviators, who followed in quick succession and disappeared into the starlit night.

Monday, April 14

ON THEIR WAY TO THE AIRPORT, Pham stopped at the bank so Matt could withdraw the cash he would need when he landed in Saigon. She had to call in favors from her airline friends, but she managed to get him booked on the next flight out from San Diego. While he was in the bank, she searched up and down the radio dial for news out of Saigon. What she heard wasn't good.

"You look like a bank robber with your wife driving the getaway car," she said as Matt hurried back to the car.

"Thirty-six hundred was all I could get," he said. "The rent is paid and we've got a hundred or so left in cash hidden in the freezer. That's everything. It will have to do."

* * *

Matt took one look around as he boarded his plane and realized it was not a typical flight filled with vacationers and Vietnamese ex-pats visiting relatives. There were only a few passengers, all men in their early twenties and thirties. Some were dressed in fatigue shirts and pants—the "boonie suits" they wore when they served in Vietnam. Many of them sported shoulder-length hair and beards. All were aboard for the same reason. They needed to get to Saigon, collect the people they left behind, and get out fast.

After the usual seat belt briefing and advice on water landings, the captain announced, "Welcome aboard Pan American Flight 842. Our final destination is Tan Son Nhut International Airport Saigon, South Vietnam." The pilot left the cockpit door open.

Pan Am had scheduled the flight with one goal in mind. The airline was not going to abandon its employees in South Vietnam if the North invaded Saigon. The office managers there had been instructed to round up every employee and their family members and get them ready to depart the country. Some had been sleeping at the office for days, waiting for the flight to arrive. Flight 842 was now on its way to collect them.

"Folks, this is your captain," the pilot announced. "Air Traffic Control is telling me we may not be able to land at TSN." The captain spoke with an easygoing Oklahoma drawl and made this news sound as routine as a weather report. It was anything but.

"Seems there were a few artillery rounds aimed at the airfield during the night. They tell me this kind of harassment has been going on awhile, but only overnight when there are no landings or takeoffs. So we should have nothing to worry about. But the upshot of all this is that our flight time and final destination will depend on whether the runway is still there for our arrival."

Matt absentmindedly fidgeted with the backpack he held on his lap during the announcement and then closed his eyes. He was dozing off when a female voice woke him. It was one of Pham's stewardess friends.

"Matt! Pham told me you'd be on this flight. Where is she?"

"She wanted to come, but I figured I could move a lot quicker solo. Besides, there are five in her family and me—that makes six— that we have to get to the airport—we can all fit on a Honda." Matt was joking, but then he turned serious. "I'm going to Saigon to get her family out while there's still time."

"Let me see if the captain can get a message to Pan Am on the ground in Saigon. Our office is still officially running, but I don't know for how long. It's a mess. Maybe someone there can get word to Pham's parents, let them know you're coming and have them come to the office before it gets worse."

"Great! Pham is working on getting a message through herself. One way or another we'll reach them," Matt added hopefully.

"This is the captain again. We've gotten word that the situation on the ground has deteriorated. Washington has also designated us a DOD flight, which means we're now flying under orders of the Secretary of Defense. Officially, no commercial passengers can ride on my bus. That means we're all in the army now, fellas," he joked.

A few minutes later came the bad news: "We have been ordered to divert to Bangkok where you'll be met by gate agents to arrange return flights for you."

The passengers erupted.

"Are you nuts?"

"Hey, captain," a passenger shouted. "Give us a break!"

"I didn't fly twenty-seven hours here for nothing!"

"Hey, Captain! How about I kick your ass outta the left seat and take over? This would be a piece of cake after flying C-130s in-country."

"Hey, need a navigator? I flew '52s over 'Nam. I think I can find TSN."

The passengers began gathering in the aisles in groups, trying to figure out whether force or diplomacy was the right approach to convincing the pilot that it was Saigon or nothing. A few passengers started talking about hijacking the plane and forcing the pilot to take them to Saigon.

In an effort to quell the anger, the captain made another announcement: "Hey, fellas, I'm only here to drive this bus. Even if we land in Saigon, DOD won't let Pan Am take on commercial passengers, whoever you came in to pull out won't be going on this flight. You are going to have to rely on refugee flights out of the Air Force side of TSN. That's assuming the runway will still be open."

The captain's words didn't help, but Matt's soft-spoken manner and youthful looks did. People never felt threatened by him, so joining the hijack group that seemed to be the most volatile, Matt said, "Let's at least get the captain to radio Washington. DOD can't let a bunch of GIs—Vietnam vets—come halfway around the world for nothing. It's worth a try."

Pham's stewardess friend walked Matt to the flight deck and told the captain, "This is Matt Moran, Pham's husband—you might remember her, she's a travel agent in San Diego. Anyway, he's family."

"I'm sorry, but it's out of my hands. I can't violate ATC procedure, much less DOD. They'll pull my ticket. And I'm too close to retirement for that."

"I'm not asking you to do anything illegal," Matt interrupted. "But come on—you can push back on DOD. You can make them reverse their decision. I'm sure the Secretary of Defense doesn't want to hold a news conference about how American war veterans had to abandon little babies in a war zone because of DOD 'policy.'"

"Okay, okay. I'll try," the captain agreed, if only to get the persistent former Marine off his back.

Then Matt poured it on, "Think about how this will look in the newspapers: 'Vietnam Vets Hijack Pan Am Flight to Rescue Loved Ones after U.S. Says Leave 'em Behind.' Oh, and wait until these guys—and their wives—all start writing to their Congressmen . . .'"

"All right, you can knock off the violins. I said I would give it another go. No promises though."

After twenty minutes or so, Matt emerged from the flight deck flashing a thumbs-up sign to the passengers, and the captain announced, "We're going to Saigon, boys. We've got enough seats for four hundred return passengers. Make that four-oh-one with one in the jump seat. Nah, make that four-sixty if we have children sitting in laps, four-sixty-six if we use the toilets for seats!"

The passengers high-fived Matt all the way back to his seat.

Tuesday, April 15

PRESIDENT FORD READ THE MEMO HIS chief of staff had handed to him. Ever since he took office, the Congress—still fuming over the Watergate debacle—had stymied everything his administration tried to do. Now the Democrat-controlled Senate Armed Services Committee had rejected his emergency aid request for South Vietnam.

He knew what it meant. Without the help they needed, the nationalist government could not hold on much longer. This spelled the end—the end of South Vietnam as a nation and the end to the war that they and the U.S. had poured so much money and so many lives into over the past decade.

There was nothing he could do now. By taking revenge on him, the Democrats had sealed Vietnam's doom.

"Those bastards!" he yelled aloud to his empty office.

* * *

As the 747 crossed into South Vietnam airspace and proceeded to Tan Son Nhut, the captain announced, "We will be on the ground for two hours. Repeat two hours, not a second more. So I suggest you round up anyone who wants to ride with me and get back here on the double. We're not waiting. Two hours. No more."

* * *

As soon as the 747 landed, the captain taxied to a parking spot away from the terminal and runways. He was well aware that TSN currently held the top spot on the FAA's "Hazardous Airports" advisory bulletins, and parking too close to those targets would put the plane at risk during a shelling or ground assault.

The CIA was assigned responsibility for the safety of the 747 while it was in-country. Steve Carwood reassured the airline manager in Saigon with a hand-delivered message: "According to DOD and CIA intel, the North might bust up the runway or shell the military side of Tan Son Nhut. But risk damaging a U.S. Department of Defense-designated 747? Not a chance."

When the State Department later asked Carwood to assess the situation, he responded directly to the secretary with an uncoded message. It stated, "An attack on the plane would be extremely unlikely. If it does happen, the Seventh Fleet will strike the North with a fearsome vengeance and furious anger."

Five minutes later the CIA intercepted a one-word, uncoded message from Hanoi to its field commanders near Saigon.

"*Hiểu.*"

Translation: "Understood."

* * *

As Matt climbed down the stairs of the 747 and walked to the terminal, he saw two of Pham's sisters standing outside, anxiously waving to him.

"The officials are questioning Kim!" said Phuoc, pointing to their youngest sister, who was surrounded by uniformed men. One of the officials kept pointing to the girl's paperwork.

"You do not have the exit tax stamp here and here," the official said. "You need to go back and get it. You cannot leave the country until this matter is corrected."

Before Matt could react, the stewardess he met on the flight approached him.

"I have an idea," she said. She looked over at Kim and, with a slight wave, caught her attention, motioning toward the ladies room with a tilt of her head.

Kim picked up the hint. "I have to use the bathroom," she said to the official.

"It's on the other side of the gate," he curtly replied. "Someone will have to escort you. You have to wait."

"But I need to go now! *Please!*"

The official looked around. There were no female inspectors available to accompany her and the line was building up behind him. He shrugged and motioned her toward the gate.

"Go!"

Once inside the restroom, the stewardesses surrounded Kim.

"Take off your clothes," one of them said as she began unbuttoning her own uniform jacket, revealing an identical jacket underneath. "Here—put this on."

The other stewardess pulled down her uniform skirt revealing a second one underneath. Kim put it on as they tossed her clothes in the trash. Together, they left the room and walked her through the terminal—a phalanx of powder-blue uniforms with Matt and the sisters following a few yards behind.

They made it to the top of the stairs. Across the threshold they would be safe. No one would challenge crew members of a commercial flight—especially a flight with a U.S. Department of Defense designation.

Soon four busloads of Pan Am employees and their families arrived directly at planeside, skipping the terminal entirely. Matt and Pham's sisters surveyed the sea of people getting off the buses and heading up the stairs. There was no sign of Pham's parents.

"Kim, what happened to your parents? Where are they?"

"They kept trying to get here, but they were stopped and ordered to return home. They told us to wait until dark and go without them, so the three of us got on my Honda and made it. We slept in the terminal hoping they could follow us here today on one of the Pan Am buses."

"I'll get them here. I need your motorbike," Matt said. Kim handed him the keys and told him where he could find it.

By this time the 747 was overloaded by a dozen passengers. The captain couldn't wait any longer and began the preflight checklist. Pham's sisters and Matt boarded and, as the girls took their seats, he grabbed his backpack. As he passed the cockpit door on his way back out, he looked in at the captain and said, "I guess I'm staying in Saigon, so now you have room for one more."

"Your call, son. Good luck."

As Matt walked from the plane, he realized that it was probably the last U.S. commercial flight out. After that, the only option for Pham's relatives would be the C-130 refugee flights that the Air Force was running from the military side of TSN.

He headed off to the Quanhs' house, hoping he could get them out as well.

* * *

It was after dark when Matt finally found the house, which appeared to be abandoned. He pushed open the door. It was unlatched. The house was dark. All the shutters were closed. He heard a sound, and two people cautiously emerged to greet him. Then two more. Then another. Children come out from under a bed. Before long the house was swarming with children, teenagers, elderly people, and two familiar faces; Pham's parents. In all there were twenty-three people.

Matt breathed a sigh of relief. He had found them. Now, all he had to do was persuade them to come with him so he could put them on a refugee flight out of Vietnam.

Wednesday, April 16

Article published in the *Washington Legend*, 16 April 1975

England has its pubs, the U.S. its corner tavern, but in Saigon, piano bars rule.

by Sam Esposito

When Vietnam was partitioned in 1954, the Viet Minh took over the North while the governing body of the South was known as the State of Vietnam. French expatriates living in Hanoi were given a choice. If going back to France was not possible, they could stay behind with the hope that Hanoi would remain the quietly genteel city it had always been, though under communist rule. Or they could head to South Vietnam and hope to recreate the life to which they had grown accustomed in Hanoi.

Those who moved to South Vietnam got jobs at oil companies, managed hotels, or ran private clubs like the snooty Cercle Sportif.

And a number of them opened piano bars—Vietnam's version of the British pub or the American corner tavern. At last count there were some 260 piano bars in Saigon. One of them, Le P'tit Bistrot, is run by Jean Paul Pellerin. "I arrived in Saigon with my family, took the gold sewn into the hems of our clothes, and used it to rent a street-level space at the Caravelle Hotel building and open Le P'tit Bistrot."

Then he added, "With the money I had left after stocking the bar, I went over to the Rex. They were buying a new piano for the ballroom so I bought their old Steinway baby grand. What a bargain, and what stories that piano could tell if it could talk."

Pellerin then painted one wall white, and left markers on the tables so patrons could express themselves with thoughts about Vietnam and anyplace else that was not Vietnam, the place American GIs referred to as "The World."

When Jean Paul opened the doors to his new café, he banned "the rock and roll and bar girls. This is a place for cool jazz and great conversation," he told everyone who came in. Fortunately, when he left Hanoi, the one thing of value he brought with him, besides the gold, was his father's jazz collection, some of which were on 78-rpm records. "They weighed a ton," Jean Paul recalled. But it was worth the trouble. Le P'tit was always filled with the sounds of Duke Ellington, Thelonious Monk, Charlie Parker, Nina Simone, Billie Holliday, and Sarah Vaughn.

"You won't hear any renditions of 'Proud Mary' by Filipino vocalists. Not in my place. Never."

Fortunately a DJ from AFRTs, Armed Forces Radio and Television, affectionately known as A-FARTS, transferred all of Jean Paul's old records onto reel-to-reel recording tape that could be played continuously from the TEAC tape deck that enjoyed a place of honor on the back shelves of the bar—next to the Hennessy, Jim Beam, Glenfiddich and, when he could get hold of it, Pernod and sake.

Since the Caravelle was also the unofficial headquarters and lodging for the foreign press corps, Jean Paul's Le P'tit soon became the daily hangout for foreign reporters, Army and Air Force PR types, and their Vietnamese girlfriends. Whenever young American GIs showed up, they usually took one look, did an about-face, and headed for the bars and massage parlors on Tu

Do Street. Those who stayed got to rub shoulders with famous journalists. NBS's new on-air sensation Lisette Vo was a favorite everyone wanted to get to know.

Though Jean Paul opened Le P'tit in 1954, "The idea really started in 1927. That was when my parents left France and headed for Vietnam on a steamer. My father had been promised a job managing the Metropole Hotel in Hanoi, which he did all through the '30s and then during World War II when Japan occupied the country," Jean Paul recalled.

He added, "I remember the occupation. It was hard. But the Japanese needed lodging, and my father kept the Metropole functioning throughout the occupation. My father was also able to hide some gold in what he referred to as 'my shoebox,' which I used to start this new place in Saigon."

After the war in the Pacific ended and the Japanese where kicked out, the French retook their old positions as if nothing at all had happened.

It was then that Jean Paul's father opened a small piano bar overlooking Hoan Kiem Lake in central Hanoi. "As a kid I hung out there after school, and eventually took over running the place. My father still came in most nights to play piano." Though Jean Paul had never been to France he knew of Paris and the jazz scene there from stories his father told. "I became as much a fan of *the* American Jazz as my father. So, when Dien Bien Phu fell, I realized it was time to leave Hanoi for the last time—the music was about to stop."

Growing up as he did, Jean Paul acquired three things from his father: how to run a bar, how to play jazz piano, and how to disarm people with grace and charm. "I can read people instantly and figure out what they want or what they need even if they do not know it themselves. I keep a mental scorecard of favors granted and favors received."

He recounted, "I kept track of the Viet Minh elite who scorned their French overlords during the day, but did not mind skimming profits from their rubber plantations and opium trade and could banter easily with them over drinks at the hotel bar at night." Jean Paul knew which Viet Minh party leader had a French mistress and which French lieutenant was keeping a Vietnamese mistress in town, while living with his family in a villa on the outskirts of the city. "Information like that always paid off."

Along with starting a new life in the South, Jean Paul stayed in contact with the Vietnamese who remained in the North—especially the ones who populated the Metropole.

He eventually developed a reputation as a fixer. If you needed an export license, Jean Paul knew the civil servant you had to pay off to get it. Toward the end, when nothing was moving in or out of Hanoi, he even got a crate of Clicquot Club Champagne loaded onto a freighter in Marseille and delivered in time to celebrate New Year's Eve. That was December 31, 1953, and it was getting close to the time to go.

And in April 1954, Jean Paul did not wait for the grace period when ex-patriates could move freely between the North and South, nor did he put much stock in the fact that the partition of Vietnam was only temporary. Elections were to have been held in 1956 in a bid to unify the country.

He told his parents and his two younger brothers and sister that their journey had been prearranged. "We are all set," he assured them as they made their way to the harbor. "I'll go ahead and signal when it is time to come aboard."

Jean Paul did have the freighter all picked out and he knew the schedule. But he never bothered to make any arrangements. He'd watched the docks for weeks and knew the freighter would be fully loaded by now and ready to push off. That night, he waited near the gangway, knowing the harbor pilot would be boarding at any minute, ready to ease the freighter through the narrow mined channel and out into the open ocean. As the pilot got to the gangway, Jean Paul fell in behind him. "I still remember his look when I pulled back the hammer of my revolver and held it about a millimeter behind his ear. The message was clear. But just in case I said, 'Do what I say or you are dead. Now walk.'"

Jean Paul directed the pilot to a shed on the dock. "Give me your hat and shirt. Take them off right now," Jean Paul demanded. When the harbor pilot hesitated he dug the end of the barrel into his head. Within an instant the pilot was in his underwear and shivering.

Jean Paul then called to his brothers and sister, who were dumbfounded. "Tie him up. Gag him. We only need a few hours," he ordered, as he put on the pilot's uniform.

Then Jean Paul, cap down over his eyes, made his way to the bridge. As the captain turned to greet whom he thought was the Vietnamese ship's pilot, he realized that he was looking into a pair of blue eyes. "His brain tried to compute what was going on. But the pistol I shoved in his gut gave him the answer. 'You are the harbor pilot now, we're going to Saigon.'"

Jean Paul waved to his parents to come aboard and told the captain to order the crew to shove off. "Now, radio the pickup boat. Tell them the pilot didn't show up and you are taking the vessel through the channel. Tell them they are not needed." As they slid past, Jean Paul said, "Now, wave like everything is okay. Don't worry, you can have your ship back when we get to Saigon."

Eventually his family returned to France. South Vietnam, his father often said, "Does not have the quiet of the North. There is too much hustle and it is too noisy and harsh."

-30-

* * *

"Jean Paul, how long are you going to keep that framed copy of your life history on the wall?" asked Sam. "Everyone has to walk by it on their way to the toilet. Everyone has seen it a thousand times. Besides, I think I wrote it when Johnson was president. It's embarrassing."

Jean Paul often repeated the story of his escape from Hanoi, telling Sam or anyone who would listen about every detail over and over again. Now, with the North Vietnamese closing in on Saigon, Sam discovered that he had a newfound interest in stories of old lives rejected and new lives embraced.

"I keep it there to cover up something . . . something on the wall, that is."

* * *

Before she graduated from Georgetown University, Lisette Vo studied English literature and French history. Due in large part to her father's influence and the many stories he told her of French misdeeds in Cochin China, the nineteenth century French term for Southeast Asia, her indignation over big European countries dictating to small, weak countries was heightened. "The Chinese, the French, the Japanese, and now the Americans, what the hell are they all doing in Vietnam?" she asked anyone who would listen, challenging her classmates and professors alike.

As the war intensified, she watched reporters on TV reporting from Saigon every night. It didn't take long before Lisette convinced herself that she should be reporting from a country she felt was at least partly her home. So she took the money she got for graduation, bought a ticket to Saigon, and two days later landed at Tan Son Nhut. She had some cash and the address of an aunt she had never met.

She also brought with her a quality that made people want to get to know her. She came across as sophisticated but not snobby, which made her approachable. Her unconventional good looks made her even more attractive—darker than most Vietnamese but definitely not a Montagnard, the aboriginal people of Vietnam's remote highland provinces.

That was 1963. The networks, newspapers, and magazines were all scrambling for people, and journalism school graduates from

America and Europe were swarming the press bureaus, willing to cover the war of their generation—even if they were put on as stringers, the industry term for freelancers. They would be paid eighty dollars for a story and an extra fifteen dollars if a bureau chief moved one of their pictures on the wire.

Unless someone wanted to be a reporter in Idaho and hope to work his or her way into the *New York Times* or the *Washington Post*, or get onto one of the networks after slogging around Des Moines covering snowstorms, Vietnam was the career track. No matter what it took or how dangerous it was or how poorly it paid, dozens of young would-be reporters streamed into South Vietnam looking for their big break.

Lisette also knew that if she wanted to meet journalists and get herself hired, the first order of business would be to find out where they drank. It did not take long for her to discover Le P'tit. The first time she walked in, every eye turned toward her and sized her up. She didn't look like a bar girl, but there was enough of a murmur to let her know that every guy in the place wanted her—all they needed was enough courage to strike up a conversation.

That was also her first encounter with hotshot reporter Sam Esposito, who was fresh out Yale and on a mission to expose the truth about the war in Vietnam. Sam soon became a big thorn in Lyndon Johnson's side. Johnson talked about "escalation," Sam put a human face on it with stories about boys from Albuquerque, or the Bronx, who were dying to protect hamlets that were no more than a few grass huts, a buffalo, and a water well.

"Hi, I'm Sam. What's your name?" Esposito asked as he filled the seat next to Lisette at the bar. "Oh, and while we're getting to know each other, can I buy you a drink?"

"It's Lisette, and yes, gin and tonic."

"You don't look Vietnamese," Sam countered, as if to ask what the hell are you doing here and who the hell are you really?

"What do you think?"

"Chinese?"

"Nope—maybe I'm Malaysian," she responded putting the emphasis on *mal*, as if she meant *bad*. No sooner were the words out of her mouth that she realized she was coming on way too strong. So she cooled it down with, "And what are you? You don't look Vietnamese, either."

"I'm an American."

"And what do you do, Sam?"

"I tell stories and once in a great while, maybe once a year, I break a decent story that actually means something."

"You sound cynical. Like you hate the job. If you don't like being a reporter why did you become one?"

"'Cause it's a Venus fly trap. When you are standing on the outside it looks tempting, delicious in fact, so you dive in, you get stuck and eventually it consumes you. When I started in New Haven, I worked for Parker Reines III at UPI. He'd light a cigarette, shove a sheet of copy paper in his typewriter, and by the time he'd ground out five-hundred words, it was time to grind out the cigarette he was smoking. Day after day. But Reines had another life. The shelves behind his desk were lined with books he had written. Reines's *Parallel* was a critically acclaimed novel about the ennui of American and North Korean soldiers guarding the border between the two countries. *Molotov* was Reines's exposition of how the U.S. withheld support from anti-communist rebels during the Hungarian Revolution. The critics loved that one, too. When he wrote *Mercy* about the Berlin Airlift, he turned a little piece of history, a story about modern air traffic control really, into a critical success."

"So far so good. Is there a punch line coming? What am I missing?" Lisette wanted to know.

"There was another book on his shelf. I found a copy of *From Here to Eternity*. There's a salutation in it from James Jones and a reference to the summer Jones and Reines had spent at Lowney Handy's writer's colony. It said: *Parker, great having you in the next cabin, Lowney would be proud of you. You tell the truth. Warmly, Jimmy.*"

"Yeah?"

"So James Jones gets a blockbuster novel and a movie with Burt Lancaster and Deborah Kerr covered in sea foam in Honolulu, and now Jones lives in Hollywood and Reines is still punching out wire copy in a college town on Long Island Sound. See what I mean about a 'career in journalism'? It's a total crapshoot."

"No matter, Sam, I still want to cover the war. That's why I came here. I think I can do a good job. In fact, I think I'd be a good reporter. Look at this face. Can't you see this face on TV?" She continued, telling Sam about her Vietnamese roots and education and then thought, *Christ, I'm giving this guy my résumé and all he wants is to get into my pants.*

"There's a long line of wannabes just like you. They come here with these romantic notions about being a war correspondent, then they go out on an army chopper to get close to the action, get too close, and come back covered with blood—sometimes their own, sometimes from the soldier who was crouched down in the grass right next to them. Next thing you know, they're on a flight back to the world."

"I don't see you leaving," Lisette said, looking for a reaction.

"Look, if you think you've got what it takes, then get somebody—anybody—to hire you on as a stringer. My old boss Reines put in a good word for me and got me into UPI right off. If you're thinking TV, buy an old Bolex, they're cheap and there are plenty around since everyone's got all the new fancy sound-on-film stuff. Try stringing for one of the smaller networks that supply film to Africa and India. Show up with some decent footage and you're in. Besides, they might go for an on-air reporter chick."

"So, all I have to do is show up? That's it?"

"A good place to start is the Rex. Be there for the daily press briefings, wander around in the back of the room, keep your eyes open. See who asks the tough questions about what our president is doing to get us out of this mess and make nice. Somebody will take you on," Sam told her.

"Just like that?" Lisette responded in a low voice and touched his wrist in a way that got Sam's attention.

"Yeah, just like that. If nothing else you'll find out why we call it 'The Five O'clock Follies.' If you're lazy, you'll take the briefings at face value, file your stories, go drinking at night, and repeat the process the next day and the next after that."

"And I suppose there is an alternative?"

"An alternative? Sure. You can get on a Huey—the Army will take you anywhere on any mission—and do some real reporting. It's up to you. Just keep your head down." Sam paused for emphasis. "And wear your flak jacket."

He eyed her closely, sizing her up. A smart kid—and not bad looking either.

"You said your name was Lisette?"

"Yes. But you can call me Lise."

Thursday, April 17

LOOK, I'VE GOT MORE THAN A hundred SVN nationals camped at my villa in Cholon and I've told them I'll get them out, one way or another!" Riordan spoke in a hoarse half-whisper, leaning across Carwood's desk to make his point. "I tried finding a ship to take them but the port has already emptied out. You've got to get them on a plane! I know there are still military cargo planes coming into Tan Son Nhut—one of them can take the whole bunch on their way out."

Steve Carwood was the only guy Riordan knew at the embassy. They had met shortly after each first arrived in Saigon, and they occasionally went for drinks at the Caravelle after work. Now Carwood looked across the desk at his friend and shook his head.

"It's too late, Riordan. The embassy and the military are only evacuating Americans and their dependents now. There are too many South Vietnamese who want to get out of Saigon—we can't take them all."

"These people will be killed, you know that! Anyone who collaborated with us or worked for us will be targeted and murdered! I know them all, they've been with me for years—I can't let that happen!"

Carwood shrugged. "Try this. Take your family out to the airport and just process them through. It's a madhouse out there—you're an American, no one will notice or care who you claim."

Riordan looked at him incredulously. "You know I don't have family here. Or documents for any of the people I want to take out."

"So create a wife and children, no matter who they are, and go out there and sign the papers we're using for emergency egress of SVN dependents."

"You're saying I can do that—even if they're not my dependents?"

"Hey, you didn't hear it from me, okay? Look, here are the documents. Grab as many copies as you'll need, fill them out and take, I don't know, six or eight people at a time. Who'll know? Our planes will take anyone who gets through the South Vietnamese police at the gate, and the 'White Mice' are stamping any papers that look authentic. No one's left here to check anything."

Friday, April 18

MERDE! THE WHITE MICE! THEY'RE HEADING this way!" Jean Paul warned his patrons from behind the bar at Le P'tit.

White Mice was the derisive American slang for the officious Saigon police in their spanking white uniforms. The name stuck—even the Vietnamese translated it and called them *chuôt bach*, or *white mice*.

"They are always looking for 'suspicious activity,'" Jean Paul said, "which could be anything but it usually means they want a payoff. Or they could be sympathizers with the North. Either way, they are here to make trouble. Everybody, keep your mouths shut!"

Two White Mice strolled in, holding their batons in the crooks of their arms. Jean Paul put on an Ella Fitzgerald album and dropped the needle. The cops strolled around the bar, then one stopped at a table in the center of the room.

"Girlfriend?" The officer challenged Cameron Fletcher, a tall, well-built Australian pilot with stringy hair who was sitting with a young Vietnamese woman.

Fletcher flew for Air America, and had volunteered to help Jean Paul and any of his people out whenever he gave him the word. "The NVA will fight their way into Saigon. They'll blow up half of Nguyen Hue Boulevard. They'll blast their way into Le P'tit and when they get here we want to be sitting on a beach in Melbourne eating Vegemite sandwiches."

"What is her name?" the older of the two cops demanded, gesturing with his baton.

"Tina." It was the Australian's mother's name and the only name that popped into his head.

"Show me ID."

She obediently opened her purse and handed him her government card. "Vo Thi Ng Dung" was printed next to her name on the laminated card.

"Not Tina," said the officer.

The Aussie leaned over and tapped the ID with his index finger. "Lookie, mate. See, Thi Ng—same same Tee-na. Tina. That's her English name, Tina!"

Snickers broke out among the tables, then everyone at the bar started to chant:

"*Ti-na, Ti-na, Ti-na . . .*"

Humiliated, the White Mice turned and stormed out.

Sunday, April 20

McWHORTER WATCHED THE AMBASSADOR THROUGH THE half-open office door. The Old Man had worked through the night and he'd been in a nasty funk all morning. Sometime around midnight—midday Friday, Washington time—Kissinger had shot back a reply to Martin's angry Telex that he was being hung out to dry. Highly unusual for the Sec State to respond so quickly. Unusual that he had replied at all, the way relations between the ambassador and Washington had been lately. Now Martin sat facing the window, reading and rereading the reply.

"Mr. Ambassador?" McWhorter didn't bother to knock, but he waited a half-second before pushing open the door and entering. "This a good time to talk?"

"Come in, Philip, and close the door." The Old Man's hair was snow white and had been as long as McWhorter had known him, and he was definitely getting on in years, but this morning he looked even older than McWhorter remembered. "I need you to do something for me."

"Sure, boss, what's up?" He tried to sound cheerful. Not much of that around these days, what with the NVA knocking off one city after another and now bearing down on Saigon.

"Something has to be done about our friend President Thieu. He's unraveling. The whole damn country's falling down around him and he's making decisions based on his daily astrological chart! I want to ease him out—put Minh in and there's a chance the North will sue for peace."

McWhorter, like everyone else in the mission—like most of the people in Saigon—believed that was a fantasy. It took only three weeks for the North Vietnamese to take Hue, Da Nang, and Ban Me Tuot. The last-ditch defenses at Phan Rang and Xuan Loc couldn't hold much longer, and when they fell there would be nothing to stop the NVA from taking Saigon. Ball game over. But Martin refused to see it.

"Sir, maybe it's time we started evacuating some of our people and the people who've been working with us. There are thousands of South Vietnamese who are in real jeopardy from reprisals if the North gets its way. We've still got ships at the port that can take them all. If the NVA breaks through it will be too late."

Martin cut him short. "You forget there are still several ARVN divisions between here and the NVA—do you want to start the whole city panicking now? I'm not ready to throw in the towel and neither are the South Vietnamese—so I don't want to hear any more about evacuating! Not from you or anyone else in this embassy! Got it?"

"Yes sir. But we need to plan for every contingency."

"There's time enough if it comes to that, and I don't think it will. Neither does Washington. Kissinger wants us to hang on to Thieu awhile longer. He thinks he can use him as a bargaining chip—thinks the Soviets might see his resignation as a conciliatory gesture. Like the North, the Russians know we'll step back in to prevent the South from total collapse, and they don't want that to happen."

Martin glanced again at the cable in his hand. For his eyes only, dated yesterday, April 19. "My ass isn't covered," Kissinger had replied. "I can assure you I will be hanging several yards higher than you when this is all over."

When this is all over. It was clear to Martin that Kissinger was playing the endgame, throwing South Vietnam—and him, by inference—to the wolves in the North. *Well, I'm not ready to give up*, he thought.

"Thieu's got to tough it out, and so do we, for a little while longer," he said to McWhorter. "The North may have taken ground but we've still got cards to play. They're not here yet. In the meantime, I've got to meet with Thieu and prop him up—let him know that we'll stand by him and see this through. I want you to go to the palace and set a meeting for tomorrow morning."

"Yes sir. Anything else?"

"Oh, and cancel the press briefing for tomorrow—and the CIA briefings, all of them! I don't trust the damn spooks and I want to put a tight lid on the information that comes out of here for the time being. There's too much second-guessing going on, inside this embassy and out."

Martin wasn't about to tell McWhorter, or anyone else on the embassy staff, what else Kissinger had to say: "We are agreed that the number of Americans will be reduced by Tuesday to a size that can be evacuated by a single helicopter lift."

After McWhorter left, Martin reread the cable again:

0 19 1891Z APR 19
FM THE WHITE HOUSE
TO AMEMBASSY SAIGON
2XM

~~TOPSECRET~~ SENSITIVE EXCLUSIVELY EYES ONLY

DELIVER AT OPENING OF BUSINESS VIA MARTIN CHANNELS VH58728

APRIL 19, 1975
   1. THANKS FOR YOUR 0715.

2. MY ASS ISN'T COVERED. I CAN ASSURE YOU I WILL BE HANGING SEVERAL YARDS HIGHER THAN YOU WHEN THIS IS ALL OVER.

3. NOW THAT WE ARE AGREED THAT THE NUMBER OF AMERICANS WILL BE REDUCED BY TUESDAY TO A SIZE THAT CAN BE EVACUATED BY A SINGLE HELICOPTER LIFT, THE EXACT NUMBERS ARE UP TO YOU. THAT HAVING BEEN DECIDED, I WILL STOP BUGGING YOU ON NUMBERS, EXCEPT TO SAY THAT YOU SHOULD ENSURE THAT THE EMBASSY REMAINS ABLE TO FUNCTION EFFECTIVELY.

4. YOU SHOULD GO AHEAD WITH YOUR DISCUSSION WITH THIEU. IN YOUR SOUNDINGS RELATIVE TO HIS POSSIBLE RESIGNATION, HOWEVER, THE MATTER OF TIMING IS ALSO OF GREAT SIGNIFICANCE. IN ANY EVENT THE RESIGNATION SHOULD NOT TAKE PLACE PRECIPITATELY BUT SHOULD BE TIMED FOR LEVERAGE IN THE POLITICAL SITUATION. YOU SHOULD KNOW, ALTHOUGH YOU SHOULD NOT INTIMATE THIS TO THIEU, THAT WE THIS MORNING HAVE MADE AN APPROACH TO THE SOVIET UNION. WE SHOULD NOT BE SANGUINE ABOUT ANY RESULTS BUT, IF THERE ARE ANY, THEY COULD EASILY INVOLVE THIEU AS ONE OF THE BARGAINING POINTS.

5. YOU SHOULD ALSO KNOW THAT THE FRENCH HAVE APPROACHED US WITH THE IDEA OF RECONVENING THE PARIS CONFERENCE. WE TOLD THEM WE WERE OPPOSED AND FELT IT WOULD BE COUNTERPRODUCTIVE.

WARM REGARDS.

HK.

Evacuate all but essential staff by Tuesday?! Martin thought. *Damn Kissinger! Damn Congress and all of Washington! It's not over! There will be no evacuation while we can still pull this out of the fire!*

* * *

Because it was Sunday, Jack Star, the Saigon correspondent for the *Boston-Tribune*, decided to make it a day of rest. He needed a break, a time to think about his next story and whether he would stay or be part of the mass exodus of journalists leaving Vietnam each day.

He wandered over to Givral's Patisserie and ordered a Vietnamese coffee and a soft-boiled egg with a piece of a French baguette. The waitress brought the cup already half-filled with hot sweetened condensed milk. She placed a drip coffeemaker containing the fresh grounds over the mouth of the cup. As she poured a few ounces of hot water, he anticipated his first sip of the overly sweet hot brew. It would go perfectly with the French bread dunked in the gooey egg yolk. The whole experience reminded him of when he was a child, and his mother made him soft boiled eggs with toast cut into strips. She called them toast soldiers, toast soldiers with egg yolk helmets.

The day before, Star had covered the weekly briefing held by Saigon's Viet Cong military representative, Colonel Vo Phuong Dong. The briefings were a bizarre turn of events, bizarre even for this crazy war. During the American war years, the Viet Cong's underground political organization in South Vietnam was known as the People's Liberation Front, or PLF. But since the Paris treaty, the PLF had morphed into something now called the Provisional Revolutionary Government, or PRG. Presumably this lent an air of authority to what was once an "unofficial" body.

It also gave former Viet Cong guerillas and their North Vietnamese compatriots the right to hold their own press conferences. They were sequestered at Camp Davis, a neutral diplomatic compound set up at TSN where North and South Vietnamese, Americans, and the PRG attempted to end the war with the least amount of bloodshed. The compound was named for the first American killed in Vietnam, Specialist fourth class James T. Davis, who died in a Viet Cong ambush shortly before Christmas 1961.

This situation was fraught with complications. For the North Vietnamese, if they attacked the air base, they feared the Viet Cong at the compound would be taken as hostages or slaughtered by their ARVN guards. There was also some concern that the Viet Cong negotiators could suddenly demand political asylum and escape to the land of plenty.

Meanwhile, South Vietnamese troops patrolled outside the fence, occasionally sticking their gun barrels through the open chain links to threaten their hated enemies, while their adversaries calmly tended vegetable gardens and flower-bordered lanes on the opposite side. As for the South Vietnamese government, they worried that their soldiers would simply decide one day to shoot the VC and be done with them, which would potentially trigger the invasion of Saigon everyone hoped to avoid.

Star looked over his article, trying to figure out a follow-up story he could build onto it. Dong wanted Thieu to step down, and he demanded that all of the American military disguised as "civilians" leave the country. He also made it clear that the Viet Cong considered Ambassador Martin a military and political advisor. So he had to go, too.

Good luck with all that, Star thought, sipping his coffee.

Everyone was waiting to see what the American Congress would do, if they would continue to dump money and military assistance on what was beginning to look like a losing proposition. And then there was the question of whether the Russians would become involved—or perhaps even the Chinese, despite the lack of love between Beijing and Hanoi.

"Any chance of getting a cup of coffee?" Sam Esposito asked, as he pulled up a chair and sat down without waiting for an answer.

"Sure, why not?" Jack replied, gesturing for the waitress. "By the way, you missed a real opportunity, Sam. You should have come to the press conference yesterday. Colonel Dong was in rare form, licking his chops over the North's impending victory, making the usual demands—we can all have peace if only Thieu resigns, Martin leaves, all Americans get out of the country, blah, blah."

"Nothing new," Sam answered. He tried to sound casual but realized he had been scooped. "Did he say anything about us journalists? Anything?" He made a throat-slitting motion with a butter knife.

"He said the 'impartial' reporters could stay, but he doesn't approve of the ones who, as he put it, 'write harsh falsehoods about us.' That's a direct quote."

"Write harsh falsehoods! Now there's a description. Isn't that what they pay us for?"

* * *

It took some doing, but with help from the airline's office in Saigon, Matt managed to arrange for a bus and a driver willing to transport the family to the air base. When they arrived, they encountered an overworked Air Force staff sergeant who was processing people for evacuation.

"Name?"

"Moran, Matthew C."

"Citizenship"

"USA."

"Employer?"

"San Diego State. Teaching assistant."

"How many?"

"Twenty-three."

"You're only allowed to sponsor ten. You'll have to pick ten."

"Can't."

"Teaching assistant? Yea right. Look, you're a student. You can't take care of ten people, let alone twenty-three. See that line of people waiting their turn? I don't have time. Pick!"

"Well . . . this is my wife's mother and this is her father. The one standing next to her is her uncle and that's her uncle's wife and my wife's cousins and . . ." He pointed to each individual in turn, describing how all were related.

"You pick. I'll abide by whatever decision you make."

"I *can't* pick."

"Well, neither can I . . ."

Matt thought about it for a minute, then added, "Sergeant, you look a little busy here. I speak Vietnamese. I can help you process all these people a lot faster. How about this—I'll do the translating, and you let all of my people get on the plane."

"They go, you stay, right?"

"Yup."

"Deal."

A cheer went up as the sergeant motioned each relative up to the desk and filled out their exit visas. Matt shepherded the group onto the airfield, where they boarded a shuttle to a C-130 that would take them to a refugee camp in the Philippines.

At the plane, the last man in Matt's group, the oldest among them, hesitated when he stepped out. He looked at Matt and said, "We are still without one of our family."

"I thought we brought everyone here!" Matt replied. "Who's missing?"

"Pham's sister, Nuoc. She wanted to stay behind. She's in love with an officer, a helicopter pilot who is fighting now. She would not leave without him."

"Ong Quanh, there's no more time!" Matt said. "I've managed to get you all manifested. This could be the last flight out—you have to go."

"But you are not going. If you stay, you could find her, help her understand. She must join us before it is too late."

Matt couldn't believe what he was hearing. It was impossible. Find one woman in all of Saigon while it was falling apart and the North Vietnamese were knocking at the door . . . convince her to leave with him when everyone in her family couldn't do it . . . and then figure out how to get the hell out of the country—when, by that time, there might not be a way. . . .

"Sir, you must get on the plane!"

The man looked at him impassively, unmoving.

"Ong Quanh . . . okay, if you go ahead and board with the others, I'll do what I can to find her."

"And convince her to leave."

"I'll do my best."

"Then we will wait for you, and Nuoc, at our destination."

The man took both of Matt's hands in his and gave a slight bow, then turned and began to walk toward the plane. He paused and added, "You are a good man. Our Pham is fortunate to have found you. And I know you will find her sister and bring her to us, wherever we are."

* * *

By the time the last flight took off, it had grown dark and the air base terminal was quiet again.

Those unable to board a flight resigned themselves to having to wait until flights resumed the next day and began looking for places around the terminal to camp out.

The sergeants manning the desk were done for the day.

"Hey, you guys really helped us out," Matt said. "Can I buy you a drink?"

"Sure, by now I could use a beer," one sergeant replied. "And let us buy you one for handling the translations."

"Let's hit the Caravelle for a few *Ba Muoi Bas*," said Matt. "I've still got to round up one lost sheep, but right now, I need a night off."

Monday, April 21

THE ARTILLERY SHELLING HAD GONE ON all night in the outskirts of Saigon. The sound of explosions was by now part
of the rhythm of the city, like taxi drivers blowing their horns
and *pho* vendors clicking their paddles as they hawked their freshly
made soup for breakfast.

A particularly loud series of explosions rattled the masking-taped
windows at the NBS bureau almost to the point of shattering. But
Lisette paid less attention to the shock wave from the blast than to
the Official South Vietnamese Government press handout Tuan
dropped on her desk.

It was only two lines—brief and to the point:

*April 21, 1975 —President Nguyen van Thieu will deliver a significant
address to the credentialed press corps at 11 a.m. today, Presidential
Palace, Grand Ballroom.*

* * *

The press handout arrived a day after the People's Army had
finally overrun and captured Xuan Loc, some thirty miles north-
west of Saigon. The battle there raged for ten days. In the end the
North prevailed, leaving nothing left to protect Saigon from fifteen People's Army divisions supported by Russian-designed tanks

116

and artillery units. The only thing holding the commanders back from marching on the city were the reins being held by politicians and diplomats in Paris.

Now, not only was the last strategic city between the PAVN and Saigon defeated, but the fighting left the South Vietnamese Army demoralized and broken. Deserters discarded their uniforms, sought out villagers willing to exchange peasant clothes for their guns, and began walking to Saigon. There, they hoped to disappear into the crowds—obscurity being their last refuge.

"What do you think, Tuan? This has to be big this time? Right?"

Tuan stood in front of her desk. He already had their film camera hanging from his shoulder. He looked so anxious to get going that Lisette felt she was staring at a six-year-old boy who needed an immediate visit to the WC during an outing at the zoo.

They rode the creaky elevator down from the relative quiet and safety of the eleventh floor and headed outside. The street was packed with people. Chunks of masonry that had shaken loose from nearby buildings during last night's shelling were everywhere.

"There's no way we can get my car through the crowds," Lisette said, staring at the waves of people on bicycles, motorbikes, and on foot. Nearly everyone seemed to be carrying as much as they could possibly manage—burlap bundles tied with sisal rope, cheap brown suitcases, thin plastic bags. The *rat-a-tat-tat* of machine-gun fire in the distance punctuated their cries of fear and desperation.

"Wait here," Tuan said as he thrust his equipment into Lisette's hands and ran around the corner. Within minutes he returned on a Honda, spun it around and urged Lisette to climb on the back. He barely waited for her to get her balance before he twisted the gas full on and popped the clutch. Tuan shouted and blasted the horn to scare people out of the way, drove up on sidewalks, and zipped through alleys about as wide as the handlebars.

"Slow down, for crying out loud, Tuan; you'll kill someone, maybe even me!"

"Hang on. This announcement is going to be something big, very big, Lisette! I feel it," Tuan shouted as he gunned the machine up over a curb and down again to avoid hitting a pile of masonry in the street.

* * *

"You certainly have your ways of getting around town," Lisette said with a sarcastic shake of her head as their motorbike screeched to a stop in front of the Presidential Palace. They flashed their press passes and the gate guard told them to leave the motorbike, then he opened the tall wrought-iron gate just wide enough for them to enter the grounds on foot. Lisette had to run to keep up with Tuan, who was practically sprinting across the wide plaza toward the palace.

Inside the ballroom, the area where the bombs had nearly destroyed the building two weeks earlier was cordoned off. The mosaic floor was scuffed and dirty and there was no sign of any attempt to repair the damage. The deep maroon drapes with their gold piping and matching tassels were closed and drawn tight—a safety measure so that, if another explosion should occur, no one inside would be showered with flying glass.

Fearing they would be taken prisoner, or worse, if the North took over the country, few American reporters remained in Saigon. The room was packed with mostly Vietnamese and foreign journalists—called TCNs, or third-country nationals. They had already set up their cameras and mics in the space allotted to the press directly in front of the podium. The president's staff people stood off to the side, waiting.

Tuan set up next to a cameraman who worked for President Thieu's official biographer. He passed Tuan a cigarette, which Tuan tucked behind his ear to smoke later. Tuan whispered something to him. The man shrugged. Then they both started to laugh, catching themselves as Nguyen Van Thieu appeared.

President Thieu had come to power as part of a military junta and presided over South Vietnam after he was officially elected president in 1965. A powerful leader who had taken over a fractious government and galvanized the nation for a decade, he now walked hesitatingly as he ascended the two stair steps to a temporary raised platform. He stopped to shake hands and pat the arms of his closest military and civilian advisors as he made his way to the podium.

Then, quietly and without preamble Thieu began: "Why do I resign today? Because today is the day that the aid issue is undergoing debate and bargaining in the United States. The 722 million dollars promised by President Ford is not enough and the communists know this. All they need to do is escalate their attacks to gain military victory without the need of negotiating."

He went on, voice shaking, "The United States has not respected its promises. It is unfair. It is inhumane. It is not trustworthy. It is irresponsible. At the time of the 1973 peace agreement, the United States promised to replace equipment on a one-by-one basis, but the United States did not keep its word. . . . Is an American's word reliable these days?"

By now, a few reporters were running from the assembly hall on their way to their offices to Telex the news—hoping to scoop their competition.

Lisette and Tuan remained and continued filming. "We need the 722 million dollars plus the B-52s to return," Thieu went on. "The United States did not keep its promise to help us fight for freedom, and it was in the same fight that the United States lost fifty thousand of its young men."

A few reporters saw a tear in the president's eye, though his staffers argued he was wiping the sweat from his brow. No matter. By now Thieu had gone off script. What had started as a dignified resignation speech became a rant:

"Watergate undid American resolve in aiding Vietnam and Washington deserted its ally. . . . By the time Spiro Agnew visited Saigon he spoke coldly, referring only to Vietnamization of the war. He spoke of continuing military and economic aid but not of Nixon's promise to send American troops and B-52s if needed."

Finally, in an effort to underscore the paucity of military resources and U.S. assistance, Thieu reached the core of his message: "We could not hit a single hair of the North Vietnamese leg. I now put myself under the order of President Tran Van Huong."

On cue, Huong rose expecting to assume his place at the podium, but Theiu then rambled on. Indeed, he rambled for so long that, bit by bit, the cameramen detached their cameras from their tripods. Some of them walked right up to the podium and, within inches of Thieu's face, snatched their mics away, leaving tags of gaffer tape stuck to the dais. The diminishing respect for the president who had led South Vietnam through ten years of war was palpable. But Thieu seemed unfazed. Trancelike he vowed, "The South will fight on to defend the territory left to it. My army will defend the homeland against the communist aggressors."

After an hour and a half, Huong mercifully moved Thieu gently aside and took to the podium. He said only, "United we live, divided we die," and walked off as aides announced the conclusion of the press conference.

With that, Thieu's reign ended. He walked from the platform while Lisette tagged alongside of him. As he headed toward his private quarters, she stuck her microphone in his face and used her secret weapon—her impeccable Vietnamese. Hearing an American journalist speaking like a well-educated native got Thieu's attention.

"Ong Thieu," she called out, continuing in Vietnamese, "Do you blame Gerald Ford?"

Thieu stopped short. He looked incredulous. "Ford? You mean Kissinger! When Kissinger negotiated the ceasefire two years ago he accepted the presence of North Vietnamese troops in South Vietnam. Kissinger led the South Vietnamese people to our death!"

Thieu invited Lisette to walk with him. When they reached the ladies' WC, he pushed opened the door and, with a gesture somewhere between a gentle hand over her shoulder and a shove, Thieu forced Lisette into the lavatory with him.

"Now we can talk. You have covered my presidency for a long time. I have seen you many times and answered your questions. You are American, yes?"

"Well, Vietnamese and American. My father is Vietnamese."

As she spoke with Thieu, she kept her camera running to record his voice. Even though she would not have him on film, a private voice-over interview with the prime minister on the last day of his regime would be her biggest scoop yet.

"Why do you not have a Vietnamese name?"

"My name is La Anh Thi Vo. That's what is on my birth certificate. My parents called me Lisette in America because it sounds more Western and they wanted me to be accepted by the other children."

"Your father? Where is he?"

"In Washington, D.C. He works for Total, the French petroleum conglomerate."

"Will he return to Vietnam, or has he deserted us too?"

"He became a U.S. citizen last year."

"More abandonment. Ha!"

"I'm sorry." Lisette shrugged.

"Do you know Massachusetts? Is it very near Washington?"

"Yes, I know Massachusetts."

"And Harvard University. You know Harvard? I want to know about Harvard. I want my children to go to Harvard."

"I am sure your children will be welcomed at Harvard."

"I want to be very near there, too. Someone told me Newton, Massachusetts, is very near Harvard and very nice. Do you know it?"

"Only a little bit."

"Cold?"

"Yes, cold. In the winter. But pleasant the rest of the year. And warm."

"Very smart people live near Harvard, is that right?"

"Yes, I suppose." By now Lisette could hear a commotion outside as staffers anxiously searched for the former president, who seemed to have vanished.

"It is settled. I shall one day live in Newton, Massachusetts, and my children will go to Harvard. You will visit me and my family there." Thieu seemed more composed now, almost fatherly.

"Sir, good luck to you. I hope you will be safe. You did try. I know you tried. A lot of people in America know you tried."

Gesturing to her camera—Thieu knew she had been recording the conversation all along. He added, "Please tell them in America. Remind them that I tried. Thank you, La Anh. Good-bye."

Thieu held the door open for her. As she rushed out, she nearly collided with Tuan.

"Got it," Lisette told him, patting her camera. "Come on. We have to drive out to Tan Son Nhut and see if we can send your film with this interview today."

"Lisette, this is very good! Now the war will end soon!"

* * *

"You know, Sam," Jean Paul mused as he absentmindedly polished the bar and asked Sam to lift his elbows while he mopped up in front of him. "We always think the door is going to remain open for one more day. There will be the one more troop ship. Tomorrow, there will be the one more cargo plane waiting on the tarmac. Tomorrow. Then, tomorrow, you will make a dash for Tan Son Nhut. But no one ever tells you when that last plane leaves. Tomorrow, you will stand there on the tarmac. You will stand there for five minutes, maybe ten minutes, wishing it was yesterday."

"Oh, Christ. Knock it off. You are supposed to get depressed when you have a hangover. I haven't even started drinking. Here, let me buy you a Hennessy for a change," Sam offered, reaching into his pocket. "Besides, the more alcohol you have inside you, the less there will be for the RVN to drink when they show up here and plant their flag on top floor of the Caravelle Hotel."

The artillery shells continued to pound Tan Son Nhut Air Base rhythmically at first, and then the shells rained in so frequently there was no distinction between the blasts. The sky over the only airport in or out of Saigon glowed like a glorious sunrise. But it was noon. Rain was coming down in sheets. The sky was black.

It's happening again, Jean Paul thought. *I hope the masking tape I stuck to the windows will keep them from shattering.*

Then he announced, "Put away your money, Sam. Put away your money, everyone. Let's make a party tonight. Hey everyone, the drinks are on Jean Paul, step up, whatever is your poison."

As North Vietnam closed in on Saigon and most news report-ers were looking to get out, a few journalists returned to cover the latest developments. Among them was Carl DeCarlo, who had actually reported on-scene during the fall of Dien Bien Phu two decades earlier. In the years since, he had worked as an assignment editor for a New York television station. As other reporters were flying out on anything that would take them, he flew into Tan Son Nhut on an Air Force C-130 from Clark Air Base. DeCarlo's sta-tion wanted him to cover the evacuations and get the local angle if at all possible.

DeCarlo ordered a martini and then turned to Lisette. "Tell me, are you old enough to remember when Saigon was a sleepy colonial outpost in Asia?"

After telling him about her years in-country, DeCarlo said, "When I returned this time, the first thing I did was go to the Rex. I went inside and it is still there."

"What's still there?"

"The ballroom. This is the only city in Asia with a sprung dance floor. Back then, when I was here in the '50s, every Vietnamese boy and girl could waltz, foxtrot, samba, rhumba, and tango by the time they were fourteen. No matter what happened, we danced."

"We still do."

"Lisette, would you like to dance?"

Jean Paul put a waltz on the turntable and dropped the needle. "No, Jean Paul, not a waltz, a tango. Let's have a tango!" DeCarlo urged.

Lisette nodded and smiled. Carl, his hand firmly on her back, guided her through a few steps and then whispered, "You do realize we are dancing at a wake."

Sam watched, mesmerized by her moves, until Jean Paul jolted him out of his trance. "Hey, Don Juan. She's pretty, isn't she?"

"Huh?" Sam answered, realizing for that brief moment, only Lisette existed.

"Lisette. I like the way she moves," Jean Paul continued.

"I guess," Sam answered, trying to be nonchalant.

Pouring Sam a drink, Jean Paul went on, "I've known you and Lisette for a long time. It is like watching you in your own opera."

"An opera? What do you mean?"

"You take too long, you don't say what you mean, you have too many misunderstandings, and, in the end someone will get fucked—and not in a good way."

"I suppose." Sam shrugged.

"Or you might try telling her how you feel." Jean Paul smiled as the music ended and Lisette ambled toward Sam to take up her spot next to him.

* * *

Lisette eventually got around to putting together a reel—the TV news equivalent of a résumé. While news footage from Saigon aired, NBS New York would simultaneously film the broadcast off the TV screen using a machine known as a kinescope. This produced an exact 16-millimeter copy of the broadcast, called a *kine*, for short. The *kines* were then sent back to the bureaus so that reporters could see what of their work was airing and how it actually looked on TV.

Lisette charmed one of the Vietnamese film editors in the bureau to splice together a *kine* for her, producing the reel she needed to hunt for a job. "Life after Vietnam," she called it. While selecting film and handing the strips to the editor, she told him, "I've been here for ten years—my life after college, hah! And what do I do? I go out every day with one thing in mind; hoping I'll be discovered by the supreme high honcho of television news, Walter Cronkite, and you know what? Father Cronkite could not give a shit about me. I never even met Cronkite, and to think I spent a decade trying to get his attention with great footage of a war no one in America cares about anymore."

"Uh-huh," was all the enthusiasm the editor could muster. He had lost count of the number of reels he had put together for reporters looking for new jobs.

She went on, "After all I've done, will the network remember me and get my ass to the world when this whole thing falls apart? Do I get a cushy job in New York or at least at an NBS bureau in a nice warm city like LA? Or maybe Paris? Yes. Paris would be nice. You been to Paris?"

"Um. No, yes, I have been to Paris. Very nice city. How does this look," the editor cranked the Moviola forward then back, inviting Lisette to peer into the tiny screen so that she could watch herself on TV.

"I don't know. I guess it's okay."

Ever since the Americans and most of her journalist pals left in '73, Lisette found herself running over the same ramble, and if no one was there to listen she went over it in her mind at least once a day. "Start with New York, then LA, possibly D.C., even a smaller market like Miami would be okay," Lisette told the editor as he handed her the evidence of her ten years of work in Vietnam, all tightly wound inside a metal canister held together with a strip of black tape.

No matter what, I'll be out of here, and the sooner the better, she thought. Lisette dropped the reel in her desk drawer and looked in the assignment basket for press handouts. She needed something newsworthy to chase down tomorrow—presuming the ARVN could hold back the North Vietnamese invasion for one more day.

She found an item that looked promising and, walking toward the door, started to read it. When she opened the door to leave, Sam was right there. He had run up the stairs and was out of breath.

"Sam! What are you doing here?"

"Don't leave me. I need you. I'm in love with you."

"You are such an asshole," Lisette whispered as Sam grabbed her, held her to him, and softly kissed her lips.

Thieu Resigns, Calls U.S. Untrustworthy; Appoints Successor to Seek Negotiations; Evacuation of All Americans Considered - Headline *New York Times* April 22, 1975

Nguyen Van Thieu: ". . . the debates in Washington over aid were like bargaining over fish in the market . . . I could not afford to let other people bargain for the bodies of our soldiers."

Many Vietnamese repeated that comment and other pithy remarks with delight as they vented deep resentment over what they feel is betrayal by the United States. - Fox Butterfield, Special to the *New York Times*.

* * *

DEPARTMENT OF THE ARMY
HEADQUARTERS
3RD BATTALION, 10TH SPECIAL FORCES GROUP (AIRBORNE)
FORT CARSON, COLORADO 80913

CQ ALM, ANAC 1975: The House Armed Services Committee refused to authorize additional military aid for South Vietnam in a close vote April 22.

The House committee voted 21-17 to table a bill (HR 5929) that would have raised the fiscal 1975 military aid authorization for South Vietnam to $1.422-billion from $1-billion. The additional $422-million, combined with $300-million in previously authorized, but never appropriated, funds would have provided the $722-million requested.

The motion to table the bill was made by G.V. (Sonny) Montgomery (D-Miss.), a supporter of additional military assistance. Montgomery and many other aid supporters were said to fear that HR 5929 would have been defeated outright in a straight up or down committee vote.

Tuesday, April 22

SIR, XUAN LOC IS FINISHED. GONE. That was Saigon's last defense—now there's nothing between there and here to stop the North from taking the city."

Martin didn't want to hear it. Wouldn't hear it. Carwood sat hunched over, facing the ambassador but staring at the floor. He'd had no sleep since Thieu's resignation speech the day before. Hell, he couldn't recall when he'd had any sleep at all.

"The North Vietnamese won't invade—not while our Navy is sitting offshore," Martin said matter-of-factly. Always a chain-smoker, he shook another Caporal from the blue pack on his desk and lit it from the cigarette he had been smoking. His voice abruptly turned angry.

"Do you know what your boss at the CIA just told the president? *'South Vietnam faces total defeat, and soon.'* Soon, he said! It was all over the news, stateside. He might as well tell us to hand Saigon and the rest of the country over to General Giap and be done with it!"

"Sir, Director Colby was only repeating—"

"Colby's an ass! My contacts in Paris tell me the North is ready to negotiate! There will be no invasion of Saigon because they see the benefit in a power-sharing agreement as long as we're backing the South. They wanted Thieu out of the way and they got what

128

they wanted. He stepped down. But Hanoi won't be satisfied until they know he's out of the picture completely. Gone! So I want you to see to that—today! Get him the hell out. Fly him to Subic, or Taiwan, or all the way to California if you have to, but get him the hell out of Saigon and out of South Vietnam!"

* * *

Their plan was simple. Thieu was now vulnerable; he knew his life was in peril. It took him less than an hour to accept the ambassador's offer to spirit him to a safe haven out of the country. The Taiwanese had already agreed to take him in—hell, they were happy to, if for no other reason than to poke a thumb in China's eye. Despite their many differences, China and Hanoi were allies, and South Vietnam's defeat would be a communist victory that both could bask in.

Well, screw them, Carwood thought. They might get South Vietnam, but the U.S. wasn't giving them an opportunity to hang its former president. He would see to that.

He was sweating bullets as he drove to Thieu's villa. Thunder could be heard somewhere off in the darkness. The monsoon season was coming on and Saigon had become unbearably hot and humid. The flak jacket he wore only added to his discomfort. But it wasn't the weather or the heavy vest that made his shirt wet and his hands slippery on the Renault's steering wheel.

The North Vietnamese were not alone in wanting revenge on Thieu. There was no shortage of people now calling for his scalp. His former ministers, also stripped of power, were now equally vulnerable. Many others, inside as well as outside the government, were bitter because they felt Thieu had so easily capitulated to Hanoi's demands, or blamed him the way they were blaming the U.S. for caving in to the North. Carwood's sources said that even officials within Thieu's inner circle were demanding his head. And it wouldn't take much to put a hit on him, just another roadkill on the highway out of here.

The villa's lights were out and it looked deserted when Carwood, followed closely by a car carrying two U.S. Marines and a third car with two more men from his CIA contingent—all of them heavily armed—drove in through the gates. Carwood knew Thieu would be waiting for him, so he guessed that he and his bodyguards were sitting in the dark, guns ready, just in case any unwelcome visitors showed up. He reached across the seat and found the grip of his M-16. Just in case, he thought.

Carwood's group killed their headlights but kept the engines running. They didn't have to wait long. One of Thieu's men emerged from the house, toting an M-16 in his right hand, pistol style. With his other hand he dragged a heavy object, a duffel bag stuffed to capacity. For a moment Carwood wondered if it held Thieu's body. Then the former president himself stepped from the door and stopped, swaying unsteadily. Another man came from the house behind him, took Thieu by the arm, and carefully but firmly guided him down the three steps from the veranda toward the Renault. Like the first man, he lugged a heavy bag in one hand. When they reached the car, the man propped Thieu—Carwood could see now that the president was deeply drunk—against the fender while he groped for the door handle.

When Carwood tried to exit the car to help, the first man pushed him back, then held the door closed. "You stay!" he said. It was a command, not a request. "President not well. We help. Not you. Okay?"

"Whatever you say," Carwood replied. "Let's . . . keep calm. Okay?" A reflection from below caught his eye. A glint of gold. The heavy valise the man carried had tipped over on the ground, spilling some of its contents. Carwood heard a dull *clink* of metal on metal as the man bent to scoop up the loose objects. *Looks like Thieu isn't heading into exile a pauper*, Carwood thought. *The national treasury will never miss a bagful or two of gold and greenbacks*. There was an awkward moment as the man searched around at his feet with one hand while holding on to the president's leg— Thieu ever-so-slowly tilting away from his center of gravity—but before Thieu could fall, the first man let go of Carwood's door and grabbed him, pulled open the rear door, and manhandled the president onto the seat.

With Thieu safely stowed inside, the men loaded the bags into the trunk. The one with the M-16 climbed in beside his boss while the other went back into the house. He returned with two more bags, both of which appeared so heavy that he barely managed to keep them off the ground on his way to the car. The Renault sagged noticeably under the weight as the man squeezed into the car, sandwiching the president between himself and his partner.

"You go—airport! Now!" he commanded.

Carwood put the car in gear. As they approached the villa's gates he looked cautiously up and down the avenue. At this hour it was clear of traffic in both directions, with no parked cars in sight. Before he left the embassy to come here, he had gotten word from one of his informants that an assassination attempt would be made on President Thieu—tonight, the source told him. With that thought in mind, he stepped hard on the accelerator as soon as they cleared the gates and didn't turn on the headlights until they were well on their way to Tan Son Nhut.

* * *

Ambassador Martin was waiting for them on the tarmac beside a blacked-out Air America plane when Carwood pulled the Renault to a halt beside him. The big airplane's engines were already powered up, its props turning, but its navigation lights were off and the only illumination Carwood could see was a glow from the cockpit high above them.

In the backseat, Thieu stirred from his half-slumber and said something unintelligible to his men. Carwood looked back at the trio in his rearview mirror. Thieu's face was glazed with sweat, his expression blank. As his aides climbed out and busied themselves with the bags in the trunk, Thieu leaned forward and placed a hand on Carwood's shoulder. Carwood had felt only apprehension since the operation began and all the way out to the airfield, but now that feeling abruptly changed to pity, then sorrow. He had known Thieu for years. He wasn't a bad man, just a man caught in a bad situation. He had tried everything in his power to overcome increasingly unmanageable odds and, in the end, failed, but the failure wasn't entirely his fault. Now, there was nothing left to do—nothing that he or any of them could do.

"Thank you," Thieu said, his voice slurring slightly. "You have been my friend. I will not forget."

Carwood said nothing as Thieu slid across the seat and exited the car. His sorrow suddenly turned to anger as he realized that this really was the end. All that's left to do now is lower the curtain, strike the sets, and turn off the house lights on the way out. *Thank you? For what?* he thought. *How many had to suffer and die to get us here? South Vietnamese. North Vietnamese. American boys and others. Maybe a million or more, altogether. For what?*

He watched from the car as Thieu greeted Martin with a short bow and offered his hand. The ambassador hesitated long enough to make the message clear, then responded with a brief, perfunctory handshake. Neither man spoke. Finally, the former president of the Republic of South Vietnam—his head held low, a picture of defeat—turned and gazed up at the plane's open cargo door, slowly climbed the steps, and disappeared inside.

Martin angrily stalked away from the plane, shouting at the ground crew to send Thieu on his way.

Carwood pitied Martin. In their ultimate moments, both he and Thieu were joined together in defeat. History would judge them harshly—not because they had tried, but because they failed. He watched the ambassador stride briskly toward his waiting car. Martin couldn't give it up, even when they all knew, deep down, that the end had arrived.

After a moment, Carwood turned the Renault around and pointed it toward Saigon. *There's still a job to be done,* he thought. *Someone's got to turn out the lights.*

Wednesday, April 23

TWO DAYS AFTER THIEU'S RESIGNATION, HANOI rejected the South's chosen successor, Tran Van Huong. He was quickly replaced by Duong Van Minh, whose only mission was to negotiate a peaceful end to the war.

The South Vietnam government press office sent messengers around the city, dropping off yet another round of mimeographed news releases to every news bureau requesting press coverage of Minh's inauguration.

Lisette had had it with official announcements, news conferences, and government formality. She decided to pass up yet another news conference, and instead marched to the embassy where she confronted a hapless clerk. As Lisette went down her list of State Department sources, asking to speak to each one, the clerk would only repeat, "Unavailable."

"Christ, I've been after Ambassador Martin for days to give me something. Yesterday all I got was mush from Carwood. Carwood! God, is he the CIA's worst-kept secret of a secret agent? Oh, I mean analyst—yeah, right, *analyst!*"

She went on, "I can't believe this two-day power shift inside the Vietnam government is a surprise to Carwood, Martin, or the whole damn State Department. I bet you even knew about it. What are you . . . a GS-3?"

The aide looked up at her with a vacant stare—the kind of stare that says "no comment" without having to move his lips. By now there was no stopping her. "The CIA didn't know about this? How about this—where are the North Vietnamese tanks now? I mean, don't you know *anything*? Did you line up a ride out of the country for yourself? I bet you did!"

Hearing the commotion, Steve Carwood emerged from a nearby office. He told Lisette, "I'll give you a statement on the embassy and State's reaction to the Big Minh's inauguration." Then, as if to confide some deep-held secret, he told her, "Military defeat always carries with it terrible political repercussions. We can now only hope that the physical suffering of the vanquished can be reduced as much as humanly possible under the circumstances."

"What kind of bullshit is that?" Lisette snapped. "You've been talking government-speak for so long you don't even know when you're doing it. 'Suffering of the vanquished . . . under the circumstances.' Are you fucking nuts? Twenty years of fighting, how many lives? How much suffering and that's all you can say? Who talks like that? I don't even know what that fucking means, you asshole!"

Lisette turned on her heel, giving a now red-faced Carwood no chance to respond.

* * *

When she arrived back at the news bureau, Lisette began taking stock of her own situation—the North had surrounded the city, Americans were leaving every minute, "Big Minh" didn't have a chance of keeping South Vietnam intact, and the brass ring—a job as a network reporter—was still out of her grasp. So much for seeing the Rockettes at Christmas, she thought.

With her future uncertain, she absentmindedly gazed out the window, watching the street grow increasingly quiet. It was an hour before curfew, which was only enforced sporadically. The local police and soldiers had other concerns than keeping people off the streets at night—mainly saving their own skins.

When Tuan walked into her office, she told him, "Look outside. You can't even get a bowl of *pho* anymore. This is the endgame—Japan, France, and now the last of the Yanks are pulling out. Hell of a mess. I hope you have a plan."

"Miss Lisette?" Tuan addressed her with overly solicitous formality from time to time, which always made Lisette feel she was being played. "How is Miss Vo today?"

"Tuan, I'm okay. But you need to get out of the country. The communists will interrogate you. They will suspect you have secrets. They will question your loyalty because you worked for us, and especially for an American TV network. NBS has plenty of money and influence. We can help get you out."

"Thank you Miss Lisette. I will be okay. Vietnam is my country. I don't want to live in your Orange County. Vietnam is who I am. I will survive here. Here in my home."

"How long since the Operation Babylift crash?"

"Three weeks maybe," Tuan answered, wondering why Lisette had brought this up.

"I still cannot get that crash out of my head. I mean, I've seen corpses. But dead babies. For fifteen years GIs have been fucking Vietnamese women and leaving a trail of kids behind. What are they going to do with them? Give them to nice young couples in America and Australia like door prizes?"

Tuan kept encouraging her to continue. He was a good listener—a great listener, in fact. Like Lisette, Tuan had shown up at the bureau unannounced. He was a little younger than Lisette, strong, tall, and muscular—he always said it's because his mother made him drink milk every day until he was twelve. He was also fearless. Everybody simply assumed he had bought his way out of the army, just another one of the South Vietnam's "phantom soldiers." Tuan did nothing to disabuse his employers of that notion.

After staring silently out the window with Tuan at her side, Lisette finally suggested, "What the hell, let's take a drive, come on, what do you say?"

"Sure, let's do it," Tuan smiled.

They walked two blocks to fetch Lisette's car. Tuan opened the iron gates to the parking spot where she kept her Citroën protected and hidden away from prying eyes. Lisette hopped in and started the engine. She edged the Citroën forward as Tuan closed and locked the gate behind the car then jumped into the passenger seat.

They drove along the Saigon River. Just weeks ago, outdoor restaurants bustled there and lovers strolled along the river's edge, watching the lights from the channel markers and passing vessels. Now the restaurants were gone. No one was in sight. The few sampans, fishing boats, and barges that still plied the river didn't dare use their running lights. They slid by in darkness, carrying refugees hidden from view as they headed for open waters. Their only hope was to be picked up by one of the U.S. Navy vessels patrolling the South China Sea.

Lisette and Tuan drove along. A raindrop hit the windshield. Then another drop and another after that until a sheet of rain blocked their view. The first storm of the monsoon season had finally arrived. As the wipers slapped the rain away, the sound of artillery in the distance sounded like nothing more than the thunder that accompanies a warm April rain.

* * *

Riordan stood at the makeshift desk and watched heat waves blur the outline of a U.S. C-130 cargo plane on the nearby tarmac. A canvas fly had been strung over the tiny processing area to block the sun. It wasn't helping much. He felt like he was standing under a broiler. Behind him, fifteen of his SVN employees stood in a crowded knot, uncharacteristically quiet, as they waited for the official at the desk to call them up.

"You—next!" snapped the Vietnamese official, waving Riordan forward. As he stepped toward the desk, the entire mob of people behind him pressed against him.

"No—only you!" The official was not a happy man. The line of people wanting to board the aircraft was long and he had already turned away dozens, as evidenced by the overflowing trash bin at his side and the papers scattered underfoot. He looked warily at the crowd surrounding Riordan—an old grandmother, women with babies, teenagers, and children. Two of the men looked to be almost the same age as the tall American. "These people all with you?" he demanded.

"This is my family," Riordan answered. There was no irony in his voice—they were his family, as far as he was concerned.

The official looked skeptical but barely glanced at the documents. They carried the seal of the United States government and were signed by a State Department representative. He wasn't responsible. Slowly, he counted the number of pages—one page for each Vietnamese member of the group. He did not see a page for the American.

"You do not travel with your family?"

"I manage the Global Bank office on Tu Do Street," Riordan replied. "Do you know it? We're not planning to close the office, so I need to be here . . . for at least a little while longer."

The official fixed him with an unpleasant smile. "Yes, of course. But you will leave like all the Americans soon enough." He waved the people toward the gate and the waiting aircraft. "Go! All go! Leave your homeland like frightened cockroaches! Go before I change my mind!"

* * *

Carwood couldn't believe what he was hearing. Martin was uncharacteristically upbeat, now that Thieu had been managed out of the way. He was still insisting it was a game-changer. But

Thieu's absence didn't make a North Vietnamese invasion any less likely—in fact, Carwood believed, it was more likely every day. And from the looks of things, there weren't many days left.

They were seated outside on the veranda of the Hotel Continental, a favorite watering hole for Saigon's well-to-do, foreign correspondents, and the embassy crowd. The ambassador rambled on, almost to himself, while Carwood sat in silence.

"When Hanoi learns—hell, they probably already know—that Thieu is no longer in the picture," Martin said, "or in the country for that matter, they'll finally come to the table. I've got to get Kissinger off his ass and let him know the pot's on the boil and he's got to move quickly or we'll lose the advantage."

"Sir, it's not Thieu that Hanoi wants. It's Saigon. They finally have the South Vietnamese—and us—by the throat, and they're not about to let go."

"Nonsense! Forcing Thieu and his hardliners out is what Hanoi wanted all along. We'll get the National Assembly to appoint a president who'll be more conciliatory, someone who understands neutrality, like General Minh, and Hanoi will come to terms. They'll accept a power-sharing agreement because it will stop hostilities and make the North look good for a change. And it will mean they won't have to pacify the entire South, which they're in no position to do after spending all their resources on war for the past forty or fifty years."

Carwood shook his head. "That's not what our intel is telling us, Mister Ambassador. The scenario we're seeing and hearing from our sources is that the communists are more than ready, and able, to take over. The ARVN has been routed from every city and province north of Xuan Loc. That's only one hundred kilometers from here. The North Vietnamese Army is unopposed now. They've opened a corridor that runs straight south from the DMZ, and every division they can muster is moving at flank speed toward Saigon."

"We still have the Fleet sitting offshore. Hanoi won't dare invade the city. The bloodshed would be too great. If that happened they would be pariahs as far as the rest of the world is concerned—not that the world doesn't already see their intransigence."

"Sir, Hanoi doesn't care what the world sees. They never did. They have Saigon surrounded and they see us sitting here like a ripe pineapple, ready for picking. When Saigon falls, the country falls. South Vietnam will no longer exist. *That's* what they want. They've waited years for this moment, suffered for it—hell, they've sacrificed a million or more people on their side for it! They're not about to pass up this opportunity and share power with any South Vietnam government, no matter how conciliatory."

"Keep in mind, *Mister* Carwood, that the CIA doesn't run our foreign affairs and Director Colby doesn't give the State Department marching orders. As head of this mission I'm telling you to back off with your gloom-and-doom scenario! We play this my way. You and your spooks can cut and run if you like, but we're not abandoning this embassy, not on my watch. Kissinger has directed all nonessential personnel to leave and you can go with them for all I care. I'm not going anywhere. And I don't want to hear any more about evacuations."

"But sir . . ."

"Your objections have been noted. I'll take it under advisement."

Without giving Carwood another chance to speak, the ambassador rose, gathered up his dog's leash, and turned away. As they threaded their way between the seated diners, the little dog stopped, lifted his leg, and peed on the shoe of an unsuspecting Vietnamese woman seated at one of the tables.

Perfect, Carwood thought, watching the scene play out. *That's the American way. We just get up and leave—and piss on the people we're supposed to be helping!*

Washington, DC (Weds., 23 Apr.)—Today, President Gerald Ford announced the Vietnam War was "finished as far as America is concerned" but the U.S. still faced a crucial task: the safe evacuation of Americans who remained in Saigon, including the U.S. Ambassador, Graham Martin.

Thursday, April 24

"THU, COME IN HERE PLEASE!" AMBASSADOR Martin called as she rushed past his office door.

"Come in. Sit down. Sit down."

"Thank you, sir—Mr. Ambassador, I mean," Thu said as she stepped into his office and looked around for a place to sit. She selected the straight-backed mahogany Chippendale. She wasn't about to sink into one of the overstuffed, silk brocade chairs that were arranged in a semicircle in front of Martin's aircraft-carrier-size rosewood desk. Those seats were reserved for dignitaries. Martin especially liked to have admirals from Pacific Command headquarters in Honolulu sit in those chairs. It reduced their height and in doing so chipped away at their arrogance.

"Tea?" Martin offered, "I can have some sent in."

"No, thank you, sir. I'm fine."

"How long have you worked for the State Department, Miss Thu? And here at the embassy?"

"Five years, sir. Five years this May."

"You were granted a top-level secret clearance. That means we trust you, and depend on you, especially when we need someone to liaise with the Vietnamese nationals. I also want you to consider our meeting here classified. No need to stoke the rumor mill."

"Yes, of course," Thu replied as she wondered where the conversation was heading. She nervously smoothed the tunic of her *ao dai* and averted her eyes from Martin's, focusing instead on the miniature sword on his desk—a gift from the mayor of Saigon.

"I can count on you, right? Now, you do understand that our government loves to make contingency plans. I want to talk to you about this—the contingency plans," Martin said.

"Go on, sir. Please, go on." Thu was growing impatient. Martin was being hesitant and obtuse. She had work to do. All Thu could think about was the pile of envelopes Carwood had dropped on her desk. He wanted her to look up the names and addresses of every accredited correspondent, cross off the ones who had already left, and write the names of those still in town on the envelopes. He wanted it done right away. She thought to herself, *I've got a ton of work and everyone inside the embassy is running around like chickens trying to escape the soup pot. Where is this going?*

Martin poured himself some water from a silver pitcher and took a sip. He continued, "Thu, you do understand that when we create plans at the embassy, it doesn't mean we are actually going to implement those plans."

"Yes," Thu replied, "I understand."

"I want to assure you. Even though we have a plan, our personnel are not evacuating. Saigon is safe." Martin pulled a Gauloises Caporal cigarette from the pack on his desk and lit it with a smoldering cigarette from his ashtray. When he crushed out the old butt, ashes flew everywhere.

Growing impatient, Thu responded, "Would you not call Operation Babylift an evacuation, sir? You sent those Vietnamese people out. They were mostly the children of GIs. You are also sending Vietnamese out to refugee camps at Clarke Air Base in the Philippines and to Guam. We hear the talk." She shifted in her chair, trying to avoid having a loose cigarette ember burn a hole in her *ao dai*.

"Yes. Yes. But that is on a limited basis. Of course. We have fifteen hundred embassy employees here. They are *not* being evacuated. Let me be clear, there is no evacuation plan for our employees. And I hope I can count on you to support our mission as long as it takes."

"That number, sir. Fifteen hundred employees?"

'Yes, what about it."

"That is only the total number of *American* employees—1,486 to be exact. Why don't you mention Vietnamese employees?"

Ignoring her, Martin went on, "I need to know I can count on you. To be here. When I need you. No one is leaving. We are all together—Americans, Vietnamese. It is a contingency plan."

"Yes, sir," she responded. Still puzzled by the whole exchange, she started to get up.

Martin continued, "Although . . . you might hear the phrase Frequent Wind, and something about using the roof of the embassy or the CIA station to escape by helicopter. Well, Frequent Wind is the contingency. It's not going to happen."

"Yes, Frequent Wind. It is only a plan. Are Vinh and I included in your Frequent Wind?"

"There is no need. What good would that do? If it comes to an evacuation, you and Vinh will be included. Is that clear?"

"Perfectly. Thank you, sir. May I go now?"

"Yes. You may go now."

Thu left the ambassador's office and, as she walked down the hallway shaking her head in disbelief, she saw Carwood heading toward her.

Carwood and Thu had worked on the same floor for as long as he had been in Vietnam. Whenever he wanted to keep projects out of his own section—to avoid office rumors—he gave the work to Thu. Like addressing the pile of envelopes on her desk. Carwood admitted to a couple of his friends that he also had an office crush on her. He liked her naïveté and earnestness, to say nothing of her stunning good looks.

Once, when she was attending English classes for Vietnamese employees, she came into Carwood's office and showed him an assignment she had completed and asked him to read it. The class had been assigned to write an essay titled, "Traditional Dishes of Vietnam." Thu produced a beautifully written, perfectly punctuated essay. She described in elaborate detail the ceramics factory near her hamlet where they produced the traditional hand-painted "dishes of Vietnam."

Carwood praised the piece and then started to laugh, suggesting the teacher might have been expecting a report on "dishes" such as spring rolls and *pho*—not dinnerware. Thu turned red from embarrassment. Her eyes filled with tears. She ran to the ladies' room and would not come out even at the urging of another female worker Carwood sent in to talk to her. She couldn't face him, at least not that day.

For weeks, Carwood tried to apologize. Over time her embarrassment subsided, and the episode became their private joke, creating a permanent bond between them.

"I'll get those envelopes done for you right away," Thu told him, hoping she could avoid questions about her meeting with Martin.

"I heard you had a meeting with Old Man?" Carwood said. He paused, waiting for her to offer details.

"Heard? You saw me leave his office a minute ago."

"What did he tell you?"

"I can't go into it. He told me not to talk about it."

"Look, he's been meeting with every Vietnamese employee here," Carwood said, interrupting her before she could finish. "Don't believe the rumors you hear about not evacuating. Does that sound like what he called you in for? It is what he's been telling everyone. Is that what he told you?"

"I suppose . . . that could be what he talked to me about."

"Did he mention 'Frequent Wind'?"

"Come on Carwood, stop asking. You are my special friend but I cannot tell you."

"Never mind. You don't have to answer. What's your husband's name?"

"Vinh."

"Vinh what?"

"Vinh Anh Nguyen."

"Age?" Carwood asked, taking a notebook from his pocket.

"Twenty-seven."

"How old are you?"

"Twenty-six. Carwood, what is this all about?"

"Do you have any relatives in Saigon?"

"No. They are all dead."

"Thu, let me say it this way. Martin is delusional."

"What do you mean, 'delusional'?"

"He's not well, physically or mentally. He is fooling himself. He doesn't see what is happening."

"He said many times that when the time came, we would be rewarded for our loyalty. We would have instructions on where to go, if there is an evacuation."

"And do you have these instructions?"

"I do not. But they have been promised."

"Don't be so damn stupid!" Carwood blurted out before he could catch himself.

"You are scaring me now! And you are being a little bit rude!"

"You can't count on Martin to make good on his promises. Listen to me. When it is time, I will send for you to come to Le P'tit Bistrot. There you will get instructions and the paperwork you need to get out of Saigon. Do you know the place?"

"Yes. Yes. I know it."

"Just be there when I tell you. I'll get you out."

* * *

Nuoc Thi Quanh sat alone in her bedroom, trying to decide what to do next. Incredibly, her mother and father—her entire family— had chosen to go to America with Pham's husband, Matt. *Let them* go, she thought. *As soon as the war ends they will return, despite what they say.*

She thought about her fiancé, who was off somewhere with his helicopter unit. Nuoc had not heard from him in almost a week, but he was an experienced Air Force officer and a pilot. She was sure he was all right. But what would she do, all alone, if the Northern soldiers managed to invade the city?

What she wasn't going to do was wait around until that happened. Her music teacher, Truc Vu, would be in his office at the Opera House now. If anyone could advise her, it would be him. After all, she was always his favorite student.

As she was about to leave, a tall American entered the courtyard.

"Nuoc?" he said. "Are you Nuoc Thi Quanh—Pham's sister?"

Hearing her sister's name surprised her. She had not seen Pham in over a year—not since Pham's last visit to Vietnam, after she had married and moved to California.

"Who are you?" she said.

"I'm Pham's husband, Matt. A couple of hours ago I helped your family onto a plane for the Philippines."

"They were foolish to leave! They are giving up their home, their country! For what?"

"Everyone knows the North Vietnamese have the city surrounded. What happens next is anyone's guess. Your father is worried. He asked me to find you and help get you out."

"My place is here, with my husband—my fiancé. We will be married as soon as this stupid war ends. It won't be as bad as everyone thinks. The communists will be no worse than the miserable government we already have."

"Your father told me your fiancé and his unit are somewhere out there right now, probably up in Phan Rang, trying to hold back the North Vietnamese. If he isn't killed in the fighting, he will be captured when the NVA overruns the rest of this country, including Saigon. It's happened before—are you old enough to remember the Tet Offensive in '68? There will be reprisals. Anyone who is allied with the South or with its soldiers will be punished."

"I don't believe you and I'm not going anywhere until I see my fiancé again!"

Matt stood silently, trying to think of a way to move her forward. He liked that she was willing to stand her ground, though. She reminded him of her big sister Pham.

"Tell you what," he said, finally. "Take two days, no more, to locate your guy and decide what you'll do. I've got a Marine buddy at the embassy—I'll see if he can get us a couple of exit visas. I'll even get one for your fiancé and find a way to get us out of the country. Civilian evacuations of South Vietnamese nationals have stopped, but there may still be some flights out, or maybe a ship that will take us. But you have to promise me—we meet back here no later than Thursday, okay?"

Nuoc looked doubtful. "I'll meet you here, but I'm still not going anywhere without my fiancé."

"Then let's leave it there for now," he said. "Meanwhile, be careful. Everything I've seen tells me this city could fall quickly. We don't want to be here when that happens."

Friday, April 25

RIORDAN SAT IN THE BACK OF a sweltering cyclo and watched the same official process—and turn away—people at the gate. Four SVN employees sat with him and another six waited in a second cyclo. After an hour, the official got up from his seat and left the tent and was replaced by another man. When Riordan was sure the first official was gone, he and the group headed for the tent.

The line was even longer today, with dozens of anxious, obviously frightened nationals already in the queue and more arriving every minute. Riordan and his group took their places in line and inched forward with the rest. They had passed scrutiny once. Was it possible they could do it twice, or more than twice? And what about the others at the bank waiting to take their turn—the odds were even greater against their going. It simply wasn't possible. They would be caught, and then what?

Once again the official eyed Riordan and the group's papers warily. Then, without a word, he waved the group past the desk with a resigned shrug.

"Go!" he said.

"To the plane?" Riordan replied, momentarily stunned.

"You not want to go?" said the official, now equally confused.

"No! No! We're going! I mean, they're going—to the plane!"

Before the official could speak again, Riordan began hustling his group toward the gate, urging them on. He didn't have to hurry. As soon as they stepped away from the desk, the crush of people behind them surged forward, shouting all at once in Vietnamese. The official disappeared behind the crowd.

Riordan couldn't believe their luck. But would it last? Twenty-five gone, he thought as he headed back toward the city. Only seventy-three left to go.

* * *

The ride from Nuoc's home to central Saigon was only a few kilometers, and she covered the distance on her bicycle in good time. The streets were strangely empty. When she arrived at the Opera House she was disappointed to find no one there. The grounds were vacant and the building was locked. Truc Vu was nowhere to be found.

An old woman passing by told her that everyone had gone away because they were frightened of the North Vietnamese. *They're all afraid!* thought Nuoc—her mother and aunts were so afraid, they let the Americans talk them into leaving their own homes. Who cares! The North Vietnamese are still Vietnamese, after all. Let them come! What did it have to do with her? She had no interest in politics. She cared only about what her life would be like after she and her husband were married.

But she still needed to find Truc Vu. She went to the rear entry of the Opera House and pounded on the door. At first there was no response. Then, as she was about to give up, the door opened a crack and a small, elderly man peered out.

"Truc Vu!" she cried. "I was hoping to find you. I need to talk."

"Why are you even here, Nuoc?" he said, hurrying her inside, then closing and locking the door behind them. "Everyone who can go has already left Saigon. You should be gone, too! It is no longer safe here in the city."

Truc Vu's tiny office looked like a typhoon had blown through it. Sheet music was scattered everywhere, piled on his desk and strewn across the floor. His leather satchel was brimming with papers. The old teacher seemed distracted, as though he had forgotten something and wanted to find it, but Nuoc had interrupted him.

"It looks like you are leaving, too," she said.

"Yes, tonight! My son knows a way we can travel west to Can Tho, where our cousins live, without encountering the Northern soldiers. We have to go right away, my son says. Tomorrow could be too late." Truc Vu hesitated, seeing the crestfallen look on Nuoc's face. "But what about you? Where will you go?"

"I am staying. I need to be here when my fiancé returns."

"And where is he?"

"He's a helicopter pilot. I'm not sure where, but they're not far from the city."

Truc Vu inhaled sharply. "Oh no, no, no," he said. "That is not good. Surely you know that many soldiers have died already trying to hold back the North, and many more will perish as the fighting continues. You must think of yourself! Save yourself!"

"How can I leave if he knows I am here waiting for him?"

"He would not want you to stay here if it cost your life! If your soldier survives he will come and find you, I am sure of it. I would offer to take you with us but our little Deux Chevaux cannot carry any more—there is barely room for our family! Do you have anyone who can help you?"

Nuoc looked away, lost in thought. "There might be a way. I need to think about this . . ."

"Dear Nuoc, you were always my brightest pupil. Think carefully, but please do not wait any longer than necessary." The old teacher looked infinitely sad. "We are seeing the end of Saigon, and Vietnam, as we have always known it. Better to leave now. I believe my son is correct when he says tomorrow may be too late."

No Exit Visas
Không có thị thực xuất cảnh
Sans Visa de Sortie

* * *

Jean Paul nailed it to the front door of Le P'tit. He knew it would do little to discourage desperate evacuees. But he had to try anyway. The steady stream of humanity looking for a way out of Saigon was building on the boulevard and too many of them were wandering into his bar, going table-to-table looking for someone, anyone who could give them hope of obtaining an exit visa.

Le P'tit was jammed. Lately, most of the customers were strangers, people Jean Paul had never seen before. The crowd inside was nothing compared to the South Vietnamese who were gathering on the sidewalk asking anyone who walked in: "You sell me exit visa? *Xin vu ra y lam on.* Please?"

The scene was pretty much the same in front of Givral's, the coffee shop and patisserie on the corner of Tu Do and Le Loi that had been run by the same Vietnamese woman since 1960. Givral's usually reliable rumor mill was spinning out of control. The latest talk on the street had a CIA analyst spurning his former lover when she pleaded for help getting out of the country. She then shot herself and died in a pool of blood on the street, but not without first taking the life of their eighteen-month-old baby.

The bookshop and newsstand, across the street from the Continental Palace was jam-packed. Where the city's intellectuals once stood in line on Fridays, waiting for the bundle of *Paris Match* magazines to arrive by post, they now huddled inside, beseeching the owner for help. "You must know someone, anyone who can get me an exit visa!" cried one Saigon University professor, adding, "Look at these hands, they were not made for the labor camps."

Outside, an Algerian holding a sheaf of genuine exit visa blanks was negotiating with a woman who needed five for her family. He demanded a thousand U.S. dollars—each. She haggled until he agreed to two thousand, four hundred fifty dollars for all five. It was all the money she had. As soon as she handed over the money, he thrust the papers into her hands and disappeared around the corner. She didn't discover his sleight-of-hand until too late. The top sheet was indeed an exit visa; the rest of the pages were blank.

In front of the national post office—the only place in Saigon where anyone could still make an international phone call—a woman clutching a U.S. phone number on a scrap of paper and fifty thousand piasters stood in a queue that wrapped halfway around the building. She had worked for the Air Force Information Office until 1973, the year her American employers departed.

When her turn to use one of the three available public phones arrived, her call wouldn't go through. Confused, she asked the clerk for help.

"My colonel, Colonel Biederman, promised to get me to the States when he left Vietnam," she explained. "If I can talk to him, I know he will help me."

The clerk looked perplexed. "This number is old. It is probably out of service."

"Please, sir," the woman pleaded, but her requests went unanswered. The clerk gently moved her aside and called to the next person in line.

Nearby at the Rex Hotel, workers had barricaded the doors to keep out people seeking shelter. Barricades had appeared at City Hall and other public buildings as well. Across from the Rex, the broad steps of the Opera House where teenagers gathered on Friday evenings to chat with their friends and flirt with one another were now clogged with families that had given up hope of escaping the city. No one could help them now. All they could do was sit there with their belongings. Waiting.

Throughout the city, Vietnamese continued to badger anyone who looked American or European. They stood on every corner, pleading:

"You sell visa? Exit visa? *Xin vu ra y lam on?*"

"Please, sir? Exit visas for my family?"

Those without political influence or connections quickly realized that their fate—their lives—would be in the hands of their decades-long Communist enemies. For those who had worked for American companies, the military, or the U.S. government, a favorable outcome was by no means certain. Global Bank and Pan Am were seeking ways to get Vietnamese employees evacuated, moving mountains of paperwork and piles of money and chartering aircraft to get them out of the country. For most of the other Vietnamese, their former U.S. employers had ignored their pleas or disappeared.

Vietnamese brave enough to step inside Le P'tit stood out against the backdrop of expats and foreign journalists. They sat alone and ordered the cheapest drink on the menu, a local 33 Beer—*Ba Muoi Ba*—with ice. After twirling the glass a bit and taking a few sips, they'd ask, "Perhaps you know someone who can get an exit visa? It is for my family. It is not for me. Money is no problem."

Jean Paul's answer was always the same: "I know of no one, but stay close. Luck may find you."

Standing at his post behind the bar, Jean Paul turned to a new customer who had sat down on a stool. "Isn't it funny, where people come when times are desperate, Padre, my bar and your church, and now even the church has arrived here," Jean Paul mused, filling the priest's glass from a bottle of Hennessey that he had stashed on the shelves behind the bar. Tossing the empty into the trash, he added, "A perfect union, booze and God. Shall we drink or shall we pray, Padre?"

"Maybe a little bit of both," Father André Dessault answered. As archbishop of Saigon, he had been baptizing, marrying, and burying his parishioners at the Cathedral de Notre Dame for two decades. It was a job he held since the country was partitioned in the 1950s. His salt and pepper hair was jet-black then. He was lean and strong. Women often fanned themselves and giggled after he passed, as if his dimpled chin, liquid gray eyes, and porcelain white teeth where too much to take. There was always plenty of gossip about how he had an open heart for widows and bar girls seeking salvation.

"It's happening all over again," Father Dessault told Jean Paul, "I know the signs. At first, the high officials charter planes to send the rest of their money to Geneva. Then their families suddenly need a vacation in Paris and off they go. The foreign governments and companies are getting their employees out on charter flights, their Vietnamese wives and children will go with them. Girlfriends, especially those whose boyfriends have wives in the States, will weep. But this time it will be worse. This time it is *total* defeat. South Vietnam is wounded, bleeding, and crawling in the gutter. The communists will finish her. There will be no mercy."

Jean Paul simply shrugged and nodded in response as he mopped the bar with a rag, saying in a low voice, "It is a pity nothing can be done."

"Jean Paul," Father Dessault, said harshly and a little too loud. "What!"

He had Jean Paul's attention. The priest lowered his voice and whispered, "I know you can help me, Jean Paul. I know you can! You have your ways and your secrets. You know you do." He leaned in, and was hardly audible, "There are more than a hundred of my parishioners hiding in the Cathedral. It's the first place they'll look. I've got another maybe five hundred in orphanages and convents around the city. Centre Caritas can't take any more, we've already got three hundred hidden there. I checked. The American C-130s are still flying, and the U.S. Air Force sergeants who are booking people onboard are not looking too closely at anyone's papers. Fake or not, if you've got an exit visa and a halfway believable story, they will let you through."

"Padre, you are breaking my heart." Then, making sure no one was within earshot, Jean Paul added, "Bring in a dozen, no, make it ten at a time. I mean it, small groups. Have some of the women come with foreigners—find some fake boyfriends for them, the more they look like lovers or married the better. That way no one will suspect."

* * *

As soon as Father Dessault arrived with the first batch, Jean Paul motioned to them to follow and walked the group to the rear of the bar, unlocked the back door, then led them down a long alleyway with trash underfoot and laundry waving above. Two more turns and then, between the narrow canyons of Saigon's slums, they had arrived at the front door of a low, yellow ochre building. Jean Paul knocked.

"Let them in. Quickly," came a voice from inside.

The group nearly filled the space. In one corner, a sweat-soaked, shirtless American—whom she called Carwood—was sorting papers on a table. A Vietnamese woman who appeared to be in her forties was wearing a shirtwaist dress and had a camera slung from her neck. Incense burned in the Buddhist shrine along the far wall. A Christmas tree bulb made the shrine glow from behind.

"Stand here. No there, in front of the sheet on the wall." The Vietnamese woman aimed her Polaroid camera. She photographed each of the newcomers and handed them the picture. The windows were covered so that no one in the neighborhood could see the camera flash.

"Wait till it dries, then give it back to me." She then dunked the photo into a pot of tea, swirled it around a couple of times, and held it over the stove to dry it again. The American pulled a blank exit visa from a stack, swiped the back of the photo with a brush full of mucilage from a pot and glued it to the visa along with tax stamps. He hung it on a string to continue drying.

In turn, each of the refugees was handed their new counterfeit exit visa. As the refugees admired their new documents, Jean Paul instructed Dessault, "Now as soon as we get ten, put them on the army truck. It's right around the corner. You will see it.

Go quickly. Close the back. The driver will take you to Tan Son Nhut. Good luck."

Before the group departed, the Vietnamese woman sized up the evacuees. Pointing to a fiftyish man and to a woman of about the same age, she said, "You are the father. You are the mother. These are your children and those are their husbands and wives. The little ones are your grandchildren. You are a now a cook. You have a job at a restaurant in Orange County, California." She handed them a card. "Now say, *Orange County*."

"*Arange ca thi.*"

"No, *Orange County*."

"*Arange cow thi!*"

"All right, don't talk. Just nod yes, no. Go."

For hours, Father Dessault brought a steady stream of refugees to Le P'tit. As quickly as each group arrived, Jean Paul funneled them through the alleys to the apartment where they got their counterfeit exit visas. Then another ten or so would arrive. When they couldn't fit one more soul into the truck, the driver drove for the air base and shuffled them onto C-130 refugee flights. Meanwhile, another truck would return empty, ready to take the next group on the first leg of their journey to freedom.

Saturday, April 26

THEY WORKED THROUGH THE NIGHT AND by sunrise Jean Paul and Father Dessault had smuggled more than 260 people through their counterfeit visa operation and onto the departing C-130s. As quickly as the planes landed at Clark Air Base in the Philippines, they taxied to the terminal and unceremoniously disgorged the refugees from their rear cargo ramps. The moment the last stragglers exited, the crew chiefs raised the ramps and the planes returned to the runway and took off. On the way back to Saigon, they refueled in midair to cut their time on the ground at TSN, where they risked being struck by artillery. Midair refueling also shaved time off the return flight. Back at Tan Son Nhut, they picked up more refugees and a fresh flight crew and made another about-face to Clark.

On and on it went. Finally, Jean Paul began to worry.

"Okay, Padre," he said. "We've got to close down. We can't risk our operation or the people running it. The White Mice are bound to discover our little scheme. Round up everyone who's left and keep them out of sight until tonight, then bring them here. Only this time, we're heading for the Saigon River."

* * *

Right on schedule, twenty-eight refugees showed up as soon as it was dark. Jean Paul loaded them into two trucks, one driven by him and Dessault, the other by Carwood and the Aussie pilot, Cameron Fletcher. He shoved a few thousand U.S. dollars into his pockets and a chrome-plated .45-caliber pistol into his waistband. *"Plus les choses changent plus elles restent les memes." The more things change the more they stay the same,* Jean Paul uttered, recalling his own escape from Hanoi two decades ago. This time though, Jean Paul was alone. His parents were dead. His brothers and sisters had all gone off to Paris. His wife had divorced him. He was alone save for the Vietnamese cargo in the back of the army truck, Father Dessault sitting shotgun. Carwood and the Aussie pilot followed in the second truck.

"Over there. We're taking the embassy yacht," Jean Paul told the priest. The vintage yacht, with its flawlessly maintained white-painted hull, varnished mahogany, and polished brass fittings, was a sharp contrast to the sampans and barges and patrol boats that plied the river. The yacht had seen glorious days as a party boat for dignitaries, generals, journalists. "We are going to steal it right out from under the nose of the U.S. government. Too bad you are a priest. This *would* be a story to tell the grandchildren."

While Father Dessault and the Aussie waited, Jean Paul made his way across the dock and sneaked up the gangway. He pulled out his pistol and held it behind his back. He wanted to make sure the Padre saw the gun. He crept along the upper deck, inching his way toward the wheelhouse, all within view of Father Dessault. When he reached the door, he slowly turned the knob, and eased the door open enough to slip inside and shut it behind him.

The captain, who was seated at the wheel, whirled to face the intruder.

"It's about fucking time you got here."

"I had to make it look good for the Padre. Christ, I thought you were going to leave!"

"You think I would leave without putting on our little charade? Can't have the ambassador telling everyone all is well and then

have it look like he ordered the embassy yacht—one of the U.S.
Navy's prized possessions—to leave because he thinks it is too dangerous here. I hope your Padre friend has a big mouth and tells
everyone how we were hijacked and forced to leave."

"I *weel* make sure of it," Jean Paul replied with an exaggerated
French accent. "Okay, let's get our passengers onboard. I'll tell the
Padre that you thought taking a bribe was better than being tied
up in the engine room. He'll never suspect."

Jean Paul signaled for the two trucks to pull up to the ramp. His
human cargo scrambled aboard and were hidden below decks. A
U.S. Navy ship had become another overloaded vessel on its way to
the open ocean—the shiny yacht squeezed in among the freighters,
fishing boats, sampans, and makeshift rafts built from scavenged
lumber and truck tires that clogged the Saigon River that night.

Before they got under way, Jean Paul summoned one of the refugees who spoke a fair amount of English and told him, "You are
in charge, now. The captain has been well paid to get you all out
of here. No need to use force. Here is some cash. You may need it
to bribe the harbormaster, or who knows who out there. Take it.
Take the pistol."

The captain smiled and nodded in agreement as he fired up the
diesel engine.

As Jean Paul turned to leave the bridge, the captain called out
to him, "Hey, maybe I'll see you in the States. Maybe you'll get a
house in Falls Church out of it, maybe a liquor store too."

As they tossed the lines onto the dock, Jean Paul walked down
the gangway with Father Dessault and got in the truck. They drove
back to Le P'tit, this time following Carwood and Fletcher in the
other vehicle.

The rumble of artillery from Ton Son Nhut picked up, died
down for a minute or two, then picked up again.

"It's going to be fine."

"Yes, it will be fine."

"I wonder, Jean Paul, have you got any of your Hennessy left?"

"I think I may have a bottle or two stashed."

"Look, Padre. The prostitutes have all gone."

"Yes. Now I start to worry."

Sunday, April 27

L ISE! NBS NEWS . . . Is LISETTE Vo here?" Carwood called out, as he stood on a wooden beer crate in front of Le P'tit's long cypress bar. He held a sheaf of manila envelopes and looked for familiar faces among the crowd of journalists packed into the café this afternoon.

"Collins, Emile . . . okay, there you are." As Collins emerged from the WC, Carwood thrust the official-looking envelope into his hands. Collins puzzled over it, wondering what all the commotion was about. The envelope was sealed with a label that read *U.S. Embassy Standard Instructions and Advice to Civilians in an Emergency*.

"Hey, pay attention, people!" Carwood said loudly, trying to restore order as conversations regarding the mysterious envelopes broke out around the room.

"Esposito . . . *Legend?* Jack Star . . . *Tribune?*"

"Whoa, I'm here! Give me my packet," Lisette called out from a table by the piano. "I'll take Sam's, too. Go ahead, cross him off," she said as she took the envelopes labeled *Lisette Vo, NBS News* and *Sam Esposito, Washington Legend*.

"Jack Star? You here?"

"Yeah, I'm here," the *Tribune* reporter answered from his perch on the piano bench.

161

Carwood asked the people in front to pass his envelope to him, adding, "Hey Jack, didn't you cover World War II? Time you went home, sir."

"Yeah, I was at the Big One, smart aleck. I covered Korea, too!" Star testily replied. "And I wrote my copy with a quill pen."

"Okay, moving on. Esper?"

"Present."

Carwood handed the packet back to the table where George Esper was seated with a group from his office. "Here, take this one to Peter. Make sure Arnett gets his personal copy.

"Mike Ebara . . . *Asahi Shimbun?* Here you go." Carwood tossed the packet to him.

After fifteen minutes, Carwood had distributed all the envelopes but one. Turning to Jean Paul he added quietly, "I've got envelope for you as well, Jean Paul. Here you go. Looks like you are now a correspondent for *Agence France-Presse*. You'll need a cover if your other plans don't work out."

"Thank you, my friend, that is most thoughtful," Jean Paul replied. "But I will not be going with you. I have other things to do before I leave. Don't worry, I can take care of myself."

"Okay, then. All right, listen up folks!" Carwood called out. He again asked Jean Paul if the door was locked.

"I've been through every newspaper, wire service, and broadcast office in the Caravelle and across the street at the Rex. Not too many of you guys are left. Most of the offices look like no one has been in them for weeks. I guess if you want to find journalists at this point, you look for them in a bar," which got a halfhearted laugh.

Carwood went on, "These are your instructions and exit packages for leaving Vietnam. Each packet contains your helicopter landing and embarkation point. These pickup points are not the same for everyone and none of them are at the embassy—so please, when you hear the signal, do not all head for the embassy. Your ride won't be there."

"Care to share the signal with the class?" Esper chimed in.

"Okay. This is for your ears only. When the evacuation is ordered, the secret code will be broadcast on Armed Forces Radio and you will immediately proceed to your pickup point. Have your bag packed. If you have a wife, if you have a girlfriend, if you have children, bring them with you to the embarkation point. Do not expect to come back for your dependents. This is not a dress rehearsal."

Carwood again looked around the café to be sure he was speaking only to journalists.

"Please stay tuned to Armed Forces Radio 90.1 FM," he said. "You will hear a code phrase: 'The temperature in Saigon is 105 degrees and rising.' This 'weather report' will be followed immediately by the song 'White Christmas.' When you hear 'White Christmas,' go! And, let me be clear, share this information with *no one*! I repeat, *no one*!"

Mike Ebara raised his hand.

"Yeah, Mike. What's up?"

"Mr. Carwood, how does 'White Christmas' go? Can you tell me please? I've never heard that song."

Before Carwood could respond, Jack Star turned around on the bench, put down his beer, and began playing "White Christmas" on the piano. A few people in the crowd started singing along. Then a few more and then everyone joined in.

"I'm dreaming of a white Christmas, just like the ones I used to know. Where the treetops glisten, and children listen to hear sleigh bells in the snow . . ."

"Okay, a children's song. For Christmas." Mike nodded, indicating he got it.

"No, Mike, not a children's song. It is a song about two soldiers—friends—who must put war behind them. It is a song about coming home."

* * *

Carwood waited at the bar after the others left. It wasn't long before he heard a quiet knock on the door. It was Thu, as they had planned.

"Come inside, quickly," he said. "I've been waiting for you."

He handed her the last envelope and repeated what he had told the journalists.

"This is your way out. Remember—you won't be leaving from the embassy. That will be the central evacuation point, but we've arranged other sites scattered around the city. You, and your husband Vinh, will be extracted from a different location. It's all in there. I'll see you before then, but we can't talk about this. Not to anyone. Meanwhile, listen to the radio for the signal. When you hear it, don't hesitate. Just go."

* * *

Jean Paul had not seen much of Lei Hoa since the couple divorced five years ago.

When she walked in this time, she was as beautiful as he had remembered. *How did I blow it with one of the best-looking women in Saigon?* he thought as he leaned forward over the bar to see two pairs of eyes looking up at him. Twin girls, Solange and Sandrine, four years old with long, straight black hair tied back and the most stunningly liquid blue eyes. Jean Paul had seen such eyes in only one other person—his mother.

"It's about time you got here, I was ready to send someone to kidnap you and the girls. We need to leave. Right now. Girls, Lei Hoa—meet my friend from Melbourne, Cameron Fletcher. He's giving us a ride."

Lei Hoa looked incredulous. "What? We're driving to Thailand?"

"No, ma'am," Fletcher countered, "We are going for a ride in my little silver airplane. Would you like to go up in my airplane, girls?" he asked, directing his question to the twins, who nodded enthusiastically.

"Oh, right, we'll casually drive over to Tan Son Nhut. I will fly away with my girls and we'll go shopping in Bangkok tomorrow."

"Partially right," Fletcher agreed, "Except we will not be departing from Tan Son Nhut."

Lei Hoa was becoming worried, bordering on fearful. As she drew her daughters closer she said, "The only other airport is at Bien Hoa. There is no way we can get there either. The North has cut off the highway. What are you talking about?"

"The North Vietnamese are invading from the east and north, blocking us from reaching Bien Hoa. But Vo Van Kiet highway to the west is still open. They've taken Vung Tau to the south but it will be weeks before their forces can interrupt travel west of Saigon. The highway is clear, at least for now. That is where we are headed."

Lei Hoa interjected, "Okay, then what? There is no airport there. What are you talking about?"

"You know the cement plant? It's about twenty kilometers out of town. It's huge. I know you have seen it. That is where we are heading. That is where the plane is. You, the girls, Jean Paul, and me—we are going to fly out from there right under, or should I say over, the noses of the North Vietnamese Army."

Jean Paul hesitated and then added, "Fletcher, I'm sorry to tell you but I have added a few more passengers to our manifest—two Vietnamese women who worked at NBS and three Vietnamese guys from the *Legend*. They have to come with us, too. I made a promise."

"That'll be swell, mate, the more the merrier!" Fletcher answered as he looked over the group. "Weight could be a bit tricky. Five adult Vietnamese, I'd say about 250 kilos. The twins about thirty, tops. Then you and me at around eighty kilos each. Should make for an interesting ride."

Fletcher explained that they would fly out in an Air America plane, a Helio Courier that the company kept hidden at the cement plant—presuming the fuel had not been siphoned off.

No one, especially Lei Hoa, looked assured. Even though the Helio was built for short takeoff and landing, it would take some doing to get off the ground with eight adults and two children aboard.

* * *

Air America operated a hodgepodge fleet of airplanes—as small as Cessna 150s and as large as C-130s. Among them were a dozen or more Helio Couriers secreted in locations all over South Vietnam. They typically flew into Laos, where the pilots would buy opium from local tribesmen in exchange for small arms and cash, which the indigenous tribes then used to fight the North Vietnamese. It was a secret guerilla war, being run by the United States a kilometer or two beyond the border.

After picking up the opium using airstrips hacked into the jungle, Air America would then fly at night to undercover locations—among them the cement plant. There, they would destroy the opium by burning it. A quantity always seemed to slip through the cracks. This was instead processed into the purest heroin in the world, so pure and so powerful that it didn't have to be injected, it only had to be smoked to get high.

Since the Helio needed only four hundred feet to take off—less in a strong headwind—they could fly into and out of clearings in tribal villages deep inside heavily canopied jungles that were barely visible from the air. When the pilots returned at night, they landed with their engine at barely above idle and without navigation or landing lights. No one ever suspected that the pasture right in front of the plant was a runway, or that the factory—a few kilometers outside the city center—was its hiding place.

* * *

As Jean Paul reached up to shut off the light over the bar, a satchel bomb landed in front of Le P'tit. The explosion that followed knocked everyone to the floor, showering them with broken glass and filling the room with smoke.

"Stay down!" Jean Paul ordered as he saw two figures advancing toward them. As they stepped to the curb, one of the men raised a weapon and sprayed a short burst of machine gun fire over their heads.

"Come out with your hands showing!" the other man yelled. "No harm will come to you if you obey. You have ten seconds. Come out now!"

Jean Paul crept toward the bar on his belly. Fumbling with his keys, he felt underneath the bar until he found the keyhole that unlocked a front panel, giving him access to a secret compartment. Still hugging the floor, he reached in and grabbed an AK-47 and slid it across the floor to Fletcher. He then grabbed a pistol—an American .45.

"Lei Hoa, take this," Jean Paul whispered as he racked the slide on the pistol to chamber a round. He reached into the compartment again, and pulled out another AK-47 and a dozen loaded magazines in a canvas bag.

Fletcher and Jean Paul nodded to each other, then rose up simultaneously, partially obscured by the smoke, weapons in hand. Jean Paul shouted, "The bar is closed for the night! No service."

One of the attackers shouted back, "Come out now or you will be killed."

Another added, "Come out! *Now!*"

Jean Paul got the response he wanted. From the direction of their voices, he and Fletcher now knew approximately where to aim. In the shadows cast by the dim streetlights, they could see the distinctive silhouettes of North Vietnamese Army helmets. Without a word they both took aim and fired. The soldiers dropped to the ground, dead.

"I knew you should have put out the 'Closed' sign," said Fletcher.

Jean Paul ordered everyone to stay low and follow him to Lisette's Citroën, and shepherded them inside. He retrieved the keys from under the mat, started the car, and pulled away from the curb, heading for the highway.

"I think we can leave for holiday now," Jean Paul said to his passengers. "Our airplane is waiting."

* * *

Matt Moran lay in the darkness listening to the artillery pound the airfield miles away. Sleep wasn't happening. His week had come and gone in a rush—first the landing at TSN, then rounding up Pham's family, the Quanhs, then the contentious wrangling with the bureaucrats at the airfield until he finally saw them all safe aboard the plane. All except Nuoc, Pham's sister, who was somewhere out there in a Saigon gone haywire.

Suddenly a whistling sound followed by a loud *pop* came from high above. A bright white mortar flare lit the sky. As the flare swung like a pendulum beneath its parachute, shadows on the ground around Matt's makeshift bed on the Quanhs' lanai leaped and swerved like crazed Halloween lantern effects. A moment ago, Saigon was empty, devoid of life. Now it seemed alive, crawling with dark figures in the surrounding undergrowth. The sounds, the smells, the eerie, menacing night shadows. It all seemed so familiar.

His heart nearly stopped as he looked around and realized where he was. The DMZ. On patrol, night location, deep in the boonies.

Is this a dream? he thought. The thatch roof overhead gave no clue. *Is this real?*

He couldn't tell. In the dark, alone, he was on his own, hunkered down in a listening post outside the perimeter.

Outside the wire. Waiting for Charlie. First line of defense.

Instinctively, he felt around his sleeping poncho for his M-16. Gone!

What the hell is going on here?!

A noise in the bushes caught his attention. Heart pounding, muscles tight as a coiled spring, he made no move, his long-forgotten jungle training reasserting itself. Only his eyeballs rotated toward the sound—slowly, no faster than the second hand on a watch. The bush rustled again. Still moving in slow motion, he felt his pockets for the folding knife he had absentmindedly bought on his way into town. Without a sound, he slipped the knife out of his back pocket and worked it open, his hands slippery with sweat. At least he had a weapon!

Come on out, motherfucker! he whispered silently. *I'm ready now! Come and get me!*

It took every ounce of strength to hold his position as the bush moved again. If he waited too long and was discovered, he was a dead man. If he acted too quickly he could find himself staring into a muzzle flash—the last thing he'd ever see. He tensed, ready to leap.

A rat appeared, scurrying out from under the bush. Then a second rat joined it in the open and the two ran off into the darkness.

For the first time in what seemed like minutes—*hours?*—Matt let out a long breath, and then inhaled slowly, still maintaining his frozen position in total silence. He willed himself to relax. After a few moments and a few more breaths he felt calm enough to look around. The house behind him, the lanai overhead, the courtyard bordered with shrubbery—it all took on a more familiar aspect, changed form before his eyes. He was no longer in the jungle. He was back in Saigon. Suddenly, he was overtaken by uncontrollable shaking.

He lay back on the cot, his mind racing. He'd heard about guys who came back haunted from combat, but it had never happened to him. When he left the war he thought it was all behind him. With Pham he was okay. Now, here in Saigon, it all came back again, it was all too real.

I'm okay, he said to himself. *I'm okay.*

His calm restored, Matt ran through the events of the past week in his mind. So far it had been one hell of a roller-coaster ride, now capped off with a flashback that he never saw coming. Wondering what could happen next, he remembered that Nuoc had agreed to rendezvous with him here tomorrow. He worried that she might not show. He was still thinking about how he—they—would ever get out of Saigon when sleep finally came over him.

* * *

Jean Paul drove as fast as he dared with the headlights off—praying there were no obstacles or artillery craters in the road. When they pulled up to the factory, Fletcher led the group inside through a side entrance.

Two sliding, floor-to-ceiling garage doors took up the entire end of the building. When the two men tried to open them, they found them jammed shut.

"It looks like they're rusted solid, mate," said Fletcher. "They've been left too long like this, we'll never pull them apart. We'll have to find something to make them open."

He turned and disappeared into the recesses of the abandoned factory and returned with five bricks of American military C-4 plastic explosives and a spool of detonation cord.

"Here, I think you know how to use these," he told Jean Paul as he handed him the explosives. Jean Paul set to work, depositing a small amount of the pliable C-4 along the base of the massive doors. He pressed his thumb into each wad of explosives, knowing that would focus the blast outward, taking out the doors, without harming the people inside. All that remained was to link them together with the detonation cord, light it, and take cover.

As Jean Paul set up the charges, Fletcher pushed away the pile of cartons that obscured the Helio from the view of anyone who might peer into the windows. He found a ladder, climbed up, opened the filler cap on top of each wing and peered inside.

"Fueled and ready to go. Marvelous."

He then opened the side doors of the plane, unlatched the back seats, pulled them from their runners, and tossed them out onto the floor. Along with the seats he tossed out the life raft, life preservers, and fire extinguisher to lighten the plane as much as possible.

"Okay mates, saddle up," Fletcher ordered. "The adult men first, then the women and then the kids. Everyone find a place as close to the front seat as you can. I want you all to keep as much weight forward as possible." As soon as the men boarded, he said, "Okay, Lei Hoa—your turn. I'll help the girls up."

Fletcher kicked the chocks away and climbed into the left seat. He pulled out the choke, set the mixture to full rich, and hit the starter. The engine turned over and caught for a second before it coughed, expelled a cloud of oily blue smoke, sputtered, and died. "We need to clean out its lungs!" Fletcher shouted as he hit the starter again. This time the engine shuddered and sprang to life.

Jean Paul lit the fuse to the C-4 then ran to the plane. As soon as he climbed into the right seat, the charges ignited, blowing out the entire west end of the building and revealing the grass runway.

As Fletcher taxied out onto the open field he added full flaps. Once under the starlit sky, he pressed both brakes and held tight while he ran up the engine to the redline on the tachometer. As soon as he released the brakes, the turbo-charged engine gave the Helio the boost it needed. The tail wheel lifted off the ground and the plane lurched into the air, quickly gaining the altitude it needed to clear the trees and power lines at the far end of the field.

"Okay, now what?" Jean Paul shouted as they climbed.

"We are going to land on the *Midway*. It's out there. All we have to do is find it."

"You can land this on an aircraft carrier?"

"I'll let you know. I've never tried."

* * *

With its engine at cruising speed, Fletcher guided the Helio out over the South China Sea, hoping to find the American fleet before he ran out of fuel. Meanwhile, he told Jean Paul to try several frequencies on the radio that he thought would reach the carrier fleet. No luck. Jean Paul then switched to the standard emergency frequency. No help there. The channel was so cluttered with English and Vietnamese pilots looking for navigation assistance that communication was hopeless.

As Fletcher pressed on, the sky began to brighten in the east. They could see an approaching line of clouds that reduced their ceiling to five hundred feet. It started to rain. Fletcher eased back on the throttle and trimmed the nose down before settling in at three hundred feet above the sea.

Another thirty minutes passed. Finally, Jean Paul called out, "There's a chopper heading in that direction, southeast!"

"I guess we'll follow. I hope he knows where he's going."

"There, look! I saw a flash!" Through the light rain, the carrier appeared straight ahead, no more than five kilometers out.

"How could something that big look so small from the air?" Fletcher said. "Jean Paul—let's send them a message. There's paper and pencil in the glove box. Write this down: 'No radio, Req VFR Landing Immed. Low fuel. Ten souls on board.' That should do it. Do you still have the .45?" Fletcher asked. Lei Hoa immediately handed the gun to Jean Paul. "Now stick the note in the barrel— make sure it is unloaded, please—then we are going to make a low pass and deliver our little message."

As Fletcher flew over the ship, he pulled full flaps and waggled his wings—a universal sign of surrender that let the deck crew know they were not a threat. Jean Paul shoved the pistol out of the window and let go. It hit the deck and bounced a couple of times as the sailors scrambled to retrieve it. Fletcher banked right. Jean Paul looked back and saw a crewmember reading the paper and giving a thumbs-up sign.

"Look!" Jean Paul shouted. "They're pushing a helicopter overboard! They're clearing the runway for us."

Using the ship's signal lamp a sailor flashed a message: "Cleared to land. VFR. Winds 5 Kts E." With that Fletcher set up about one hundred yards alongside the carrier for the downwind leg of his landing, mentally calculating how rapidly the ship pitched. He wanted the deck to be at a slight uphill angle when he touched down.

Fletcher turned to his final approach. His timing was perfect. The crew lined up along both sides of the runway, watching in anticipation and ready to help.

Fletcher kept descending, flying close to stall speed, bleeding off airspeed—eighty, seventy, sixty, forty knots. With the stall warning horn blasting in their ears, Fletcher cut power and pushed the nose down slightly.

"Just a few more feet and we'll be over the runway, my friends," he said under his breath. "That's it, a little more—and . . . yes!"

Less than three feet above the deck, Fletcher pulled back hard on the yoke. The Helio dropped instantly and rolled no more than a dozen feet forward before it stopped, then began rolling back.

"I don't think we want to go back, do you?" Fletcher said, as he tapped the brakes. He cut the engine and exclaimed, "Damn!"

"Damn what?" Jean Paul asked.

"This is a U.S. Navy ship. No booze allowed, mate! Unless one of you jokers back there brought something to drink, I'm refueling and heading for Melbourne straightaway!"

Monday, April 28

To Riordan's continuing disbelief, his ruse had worked every time—nine times—with groups ranging from six to eleven. Incredibly, all were waved through onto waiting U.S. aircraft and whisked off to sanctuaries in Hong Kong, Guam, or the Philippines. He wasn't concerned about where they went, only that they had escaped Saigon—and the North Vietnamese, their bitter enemies of more than twenty years at war.

Mrs. Em Bah had insisted on staying with him to the end, helping him clear the way with not only the South Vietnamese authorities but also with the concerns and complaints that inevitably arose as each group took their turn confronting exile.

"Only nine remain," she said to Riordan as they prepared for their next, and hopefully last, trip to the airfield. "I think we all go now."

"With a group this size, we'll need to take a bus to Tan Son Nhut. Have everyone ready here at 0900 hours."

"We all go—you too."

Riordan managed a smile. "This time I will. It looks like my work here is done. We'll go together."

DEPARTMENT OF THE ARMY
HEADQUARTERS
3RD BATTALION, 10TH SPECIAL FORCES GROUP (AIRBORNE)
FORT CARSON, COLORADO 80913

O 28 9181Z APR 28

FM AMEMBASSY SAIGON

TO SECRETARY OF STATE

SENSITIVE EXCLUSIVELY EYES ONLY

DELIVER AT OPENING OF BUSINESS VIA KISSINGER CHANNELS
WH8644

APRIL 29, 1975

HK:

DESPITE REPTS TO CONTRARY, CITY CALM, EMB IN CONTROL.

AS EXPECTED, NV HOLDING BACK. SUGGEST WAITING ON
FURTHER TALKS.

I PREDICT WILL BE HERE STATUS QUO NEXT YR THIS TIME.

ALL BEST,

GMARTIN

* * *

By midmorning, Riordan grew concerned that the bus wouldn't show at all. The chaos and fear in Saigon had increased with each day. Services like electricity and water were sporadic. Homes were shuttered and vehicles abandoned as people tried to find a way out of the city and through the ring of heavily armed NVA reported to be swarming the surrounding countryside. Sandbagged revetments now guarded the entrances to most public buildings. Police and military checkpoints were everywhere. Bus service seemed impossible, but somehow it continued with haphazard schedules while people queued on street corners to flag down anything that looked like it would stop to pick them up.

When a vehicle finally appeared, it wasn't the local bus he had anticipated. It was a U.S. Embassy bus, empty except for the driver, with a sign above the windshield that read Tan Son Nhut. Riordan ran into the road to force it to stop. If anyone questioned why he was escorting a group of SVN nationals to the airport, he wasn't sure what he would say.

"I can't pick you up, mister," said the driver, an American Marine who looked to be about fifteen. "You're not from the embassy, and I'm not authorized to pick up anyone else—and besides, I've still got to make a run to the airport for the embassy people."

"I'm an official with Global Bank and I'm escorting these people who are manifested to fly out today on a MAC flight. If we don't get there in time, they may not make it."

"Like I said . . ."

"Tell you what—I'm leaving with them and you can have my moped when you get back here." Riordan dug into his pocket. "Here are the keys. It's a real nice bike—a red Yamaha. A new one. It's yours."

* * *

Riordan and his people rode in silence, clustered into a tight group at the back of the bus. The U.S. Embassy logo painted on the side and front enabled them to cruise past one checkpoint after another until they reached the main gates to the airport. An armored personnel carrier with a platoon of helmeted, white-spat wearing *Quan Canh*—the Vietnamese military police—blocked their way.

A tough-looking QC sergeant entered the bus first. He took one look at Riordan and the civilians huddled together and warily backed off again, only to be replaced by the ranking officer, a captain.

When Riordan stood to speak, the officer reached for his sidearm.

"*Chao ong, chao ong, Dai uy!*" Riordan quickly said in as calm a voice as he could muster as he sat back down. "As you can see, this is the U.S. Embassy bus. We need to go to the departure tent for the MAC flight leaving today. I'm with the American Global Bank and these people are all in my charge."

"Who are these people?" the officer demanded. "Vietnamese not leaving Saigon! Americans only!"

"This is my wife," said Riordan, indicating Mrs. Em Bah, "and these are my sons and daughters."

"Why they not look like you? Where are passports?"

"I have adoption papers for each of them . . . and embassy and State Department documents showing they are my legal dependents and are allowed to leave with me."

The officer looked unconvinced. "Give me papers. I will call embassy!"

Riordan had no choice but to hand over the documents, hoping that no one—or no one of any consequence—was manning the security desk at the embassy. The officer motioned for him to remain seated and barked a similar order in Vietnamese to the people around him; then, like the sergeant, backed off the bus with his eyes on the group.

They watched through the bus windows as the officer and the other soldiers looked through the papers, arguing loudly about how to proceed. Riordan began to sweat, but it wasn't from the heat in the bus. Suddenly, Mrs. Em Bah stood and calmly walked toward the open side door. She stepped down and addressed the senior officer in Vietnamese, who stepped aside to speak with her. Riordan couldn't hear what they said, but he noticed the woman was holding a small paper bag. With a smile, she handed it to the officer, who opened it and glanced at the contents. After a moment, he gave a curt bow and waved her back onto the bus, handing her their documents. Then he shouted an order to the driver of the personnel carrier. The armored vehicle roared to life and began backing away from the gate.

The Marine in the bus driver's seat didn't wait for the signal to go. He put the bus in gear and as soon as the PC cleared the gate he drove straight through toward the departure tent and the airfield beyond. To Riordan's relief, the cargo plane was still parked out there in the heat, waiting for the order to take off.

"What did you say to that officer?" Riordan asked Mrs. Em Bah. "And what was in the bag?"

"I have worked in a bank in Saigon for three years," she replied. "We have resources, and I have learned a few things while I was there. Let me say this. A little sweetness makes even difficult situations better."

* * *

As Riordan's group boarded the plane, a commotion at the departure gate made him stop and turn. A well-dressed Vietnamese woman and three children were wailing loudly as they clutched at an ARVN soldier in full battle dress, who was tearfully saying what appeared to be his final good-byes to his family. Meanwhile, the Vietnamese guards were pulling the distraught officer back from the gate. They managed to separate the group and roughly pushed the woman and children out toward the waiting plane.

At that moment, an American colonel that Riordan recognized from the embassy ran up and tore the guards away from the soldier, then hustled the officer through the gate, blocking the guards from the man.

"Get on the plane!" he shouted over his shoulder to the soldier.

The officer tried to protest. "My country still needs me! How can I turn my back on it now?" he yelled back, anguish in his voice.

"Don't be a damn fool," said the colonel. "You can see that it's over. We're all leaving! Get on the plane and take care of your family!"

The soldier hesitated then bolted toward the woman, scooping up the two smallest children as they ran together to the plane. The C-130's big Allison engines were thundering and its props spinning as the family ran onto the tailgate ramp, which the crew chief quickly raised to block any further interference from the Vietnamese on the tarmac. The engine roar swelled as the plane rolled forward onto the airstrip.

Riordan strapped himself into a sling seat and for a moment felt a confusing mix of relief and regret. As the plane soared into the sky and out toward the Pacific, he looked through a porthole window at the receding coastline. He wondered what would happen to Saigon and to the people on the ground when the NVA invaded. And he wondered whether he—or any of his fellow refugees— would ever return.

Saigon, South Vietnam. Monday, April 28—In a desperate attempt to save Saigon from being destroyed by advancing North Vietnamese troops, South Vietnamese officials have announced this morning that Gen. Dung Van Minh will be installed as pres- ident in ceremonies to be held later today. Minh will replace President Tran Van Houng, who earlier this month replaced the ousted Nguyen Van Thieu.

Minh, or "Big Minh" as he is known here, is an influential mili- tary and political leader. He is regarded as a neutralist who will act in accordance with Hanoi's wishes. According to sources on both sides of the conflict, he is in the best position to negotiate a quick end to the war.

With Saigon in chaos and the South Vietnamese government desperate to end the fighting, there is little hope of preserving any remaining vestiges of South Vietnam and the life the people have known here since the nation was partitioned in 1954.

The situation is perilous. Communist forces are less than a mile from the city center, travel between Saigon and Bien Hoa has been cut off by the North, and the Viet Cong openly hold their own news conferences in Saigon. Saigon residents are scrambling to get on mercy flights out of Tan Son Nhut Air Base, where transport planes take off within no more than five seconds of one another.

Though the Northern army artillery batteries are poised to obliterate the runways of TSN air base, they continue to hold off, fearing a reentry of American air and ground forces massing offshore in a flotilla of warships. Although the North's forces are poised to obliterate Saigon's remaining defenses, including Tan Son Nhut Air Base, its only lifeline to the outside world, they continue to hold off . . .

Esposito/04/28/1975/Saigon/URGENT

-30-

Sam finished typing his story into the Telex and waited in silence for a full minute. Another minute passed, then the green Telex machine chimed *bing, bing, bing* loudly and began printing a reply:

Received Legend/04/28/1975/DC/ Understood URGENT.

The message confirmed that his copy had reached the *Legend*'s wire room half a world away. His one-page "take" would be ripped from the Telex, rolled up, and placed inside a plastic cylinder, then shoved into a metal tube to be delivered pneumatically to the International Desk. When the cylinder landed in the editor's in-basket, its red band marked *URGENT* ensured it would get immediate attention.

Sam gave his copy one last look before tossing it into the waste-basket. The Telex machine again came to life with an insistent *bing bing bing* and began typing another note:

04/28/1975 Esposito: Come Home/Need you home/ Int. Ed.

Sam read it without bothering to rip the paper from the machine. He then toggled off the power switch, shut off the light and ceiling fan, and walked out of the now dark and vacant *Legend* news bureau where he had worked for a dozen years. As he locked the door behind him, he thought about tossing the key through the mail slot, but changed his mind. He might yet have another story to file before he went home, he thought, shoving the key into his pocket.

As he headed back to his apartment at the Caravelle Hotel, he noticed that the mobs of people begging for exit visas had diminished, but there were still people hanging about desperately seeking an escape.

"You—American! You help get me exit visa? I pay you."

"I know you, mister. You *bao chi*, you smart man. You remember I help you one time? You help me now?"

Now there were waves of people walking, biking, pushing carts—all heading for one of two destinations, south to the Saigon River or west to Tan Son Nhut. Today's rumor for those who heard it: *Forget the paperwork, forget IDs, forget visas, just show up. Show up, tell a good story, and you'll get out.*

At the Caravelle, Sam rode the elevator to the eleventh floor and walked down the exterior hallway to his apartment. As he opened the door, a sleepy female voice came from within.

"Sam? You're back, I must have fallen asleep, what time is it?"

"It's nearly ten o'clock," he answered as he removed his clothes, dropped his glasses on the nightstand, and slid between the cool sheets. Her jet-black hair cascading on the pillow and the warmth of her full breasts were ample reason for Sam to return.

"You feel so good Lise," Sam whispered, as they made love and then fell back onto the sheets, idly watching the ceiling fan slowly twirl above them, feeling the coolness of the breeze on their naked bodies.

"Wow, this beats 'emergency sex,'" Lisette sighed, recalling how they became lovers. "Emergency sex," was their running joke and repeating it over and over again was their way of maintaining a distance between them.

But this time Lisette felt it was different. Sam felt it, too. "Sam, we've done it. We did our job. It's over. We can go home. You and me. Today. We can put on our clothes, walk out the front door and catch a ride to Tan Son Nhut. We'd be on a flight within the hour. It's that simple. What do you say, Sam? Let's go home."

Sam smiled broadly over the thought of leaving without a moment's hesitation, skipping the heartfelt goodbyes and vows to keep in touch. He wanted to be with Lisette. But then a thousand thoughts raced through his mind. He hadn't been back to the world in ten years. Where would he, they live? Would the Legend still want him? But mostly he thought, would covering Washington politics or writing ponderous editorials bore him to death.

Caressing Lisette, his eyes met meet hers, and it brought him back to the present. He now wondered, am I ready for another go. But just then the phone rang. He fumbled for his glasses and put them on as he clumsily reached for the receiver.

"Hello?"

"Ha, ha, Ong Esposito! You and lady friend have good time?" came the voice on the line. "This your friend from the North."

"Christ! Don't you guys have anything better to do than follow reporters around? Who the hell is this?"

"You remember me? This is your friend from the cyclo-drome."

That got Sam's attention. "Lise, give me something to write with, quick!" She fumbled around until she located a ballpoint pen and a hotel stationery pad and handed them to him.

"Yes, I remember you now. What—no more secret messages and meetings? Now you call me? Brave North Vietnamese fellow talking to a decadent American?"

"Your friend Captain Trung, he wants to say good-bye to you. He gives me instructions. Be at Tan Son Nhut before dusk. Hide outside the fence west of the runway. Take your TV friend with you and tell her to bring her camera. Trung promises to have a present for her, a special show for her American Uncle, Uncle Walter!"

Sam covered the mouthpiece and turned toward Lisette.

"Hey, Lise!" he whispered. "He's got a news tip for you that he says will get you on the *NBS Evening News*, maybe then Walter Cronkite will know who you are! How is it that these fuckers know so much about us and what we watch on TV, and we don't know shit about them?"

To prove his point, Sam asked the caller, "Hey, asshole—who's a better pitcher, Catfish Hunter or Bill 'Spaceman' Lee?"

"What?"

"Catfish Hunter or Bill Lee. Who is the better pitcher?"

"Of course, Catfish Hunter, he win Cy Young last year. But I still root for Red Sox!"

"How do you know this shit?"

"I listen to your American baseball on Armed Forces Radio. Learned English, too, from your guy who says 'Goood Morning Vietnam,' and DJ Chris Noel—she is one hot babe!" The caller hung up.

"Holy crap, Lise, we get our asses handed to us twelve thousand miles from home, and meanwhile *they* know that Americans are pulling out their TV tables, popping their Swanson chicken dinners in the oven, and sitting down to Walter Cronkite. Mom says to Dad, 'Hey, let's watch the news. Let's watch some villages burn.

Let's watch our boys getting slaughtered on Hamburger Hill. Too much to take, Dad? Twist the dial, no problem. Hey, let's watch M.A.S.H. instead—same shit, only the blood's fake and the jokes are real!'"

Lisette pulled the sheets over her head—her way of letting Sam know she was ignoring him.

"Lise, put on your clothes, we've got things to do." He handed her bra to her and, as she reached for it, he snatched it away, adding, "Well, maybe we do have some time . . ."

* * *

WBYX-TV
Washington, DC

Ms. Lisette Vo
Correspondent, NBS NEWS
Saigon, South Vietnam

Dear Ms. Vo,

I have admired your work on NBS-TV news for many years. You have certainly done a superlative job of bringing the Vietnam War home to millions of Americans who have come to trust your judgment and honesty. Your Peabody Awards are but a small testament to what you have achieved.

But now, the Vietnam War has nearly ended. That chapter in American life is quickly coming to a close, along with your involvement in it as a journalist. I am sure you must thinking about your future.

I hope you will think about including us when you consider your options for future employment. I would like to invite you to visit with me and our news people here at WBYX. We are working on something very new and very exiting—totally unprecedented when it comes to bringing the news to TV viewers. It's *cable*. We'll deliver news twenty-hours-a-day, seven-days-a-week, nonstop. This is the future. Broadcast is over.

I would like you to consider being a part of it.

Please let me know when you return to the States. If you do decide to come and see us, give me a call and we'll arrange for your travel to Washington.

I am very much looking forward to visiting with you here in Washington.

With warmest regards,
Edward Foster III
Chief Executive Officer
WBYX-TV

* * *

Hidden among the tall weeds surrounding Tan Son Nhut, Sam, Lisette and Tuan waited as dusk approached. Trung had promised Lisette a story worthy of *NBS Evening News*, and Lisette had nothing to lose by taking him at his word.

The three had picked a spot close enough to the runway to watch the departing mercy flights pass overhead barely three-hundred feet above them. As quickly as one plane got airborne, another was already rumbling down the runway. Between the cargo and passenger planes, a lone A-119 gunship lumbered down the runway and took off.

The twin-tail A-119, originally a cargo hauler, was retrofitted for use as a defense and attack plane. Its squared-off shape and capacious fuselage had earned it the nickname "Flying Boxcar." In this version, its side cargo doors had been removed to accommodate four six-barrel Gatling guns, each capable of firing six thousand rounds of ammunition per minute. The guns ejected so many spent cartridges and at such a rapid clip that flight crews brought snow shovels on board to gather up the brass and throw it overboard. Every fifth bullet on the ammunition belt was a tracer that glowed bright red to illuminate the firing trajectory. In attack mode, the A-119 looked like it was spewing fire.

For the past month these gunships patrolled the skies above Tan Son Nhut. If the enemy dared to fire at the airfield, the A-119 would answer with so much firepower that the gun emplacement, along with the soldiers manning it, would be vaporized. The A-119s dealt a similar hand to the increasing number of snipers hidden in the weeds around the base—half of them Viet Cong hoping to knock an enemy plane out of the sky, and the other half South Vietnamese who were angered at being abandoned and fired at their own people as they flew away. Sometimes the snipers fired at each other.

As they watched one aircraft after another fly out, Sam, Lisette, and Tuan sat, mystified as to what Trung had in store for them.

* * *

The air traffic controllers had their hands full. There were so many outbound flights that there was almost no separation between take-offs, a normal procedure to avoid turbulence. The tower focused on a single objective: launch as many planes as possible as fast as possible. It was the Berlin Airlift in reverse; instead of bringing supplies into a beleaguered city, the mission was to get people out. The evacuees included American contract workers and their families, American sympathizers, Vietnamese who had worked for the Americans, and the hundreds of orphaned children of Americans and ethnic Vietnamese.

A C-130 loaded with refugees and fuel was first in line on the taxiway. Before he reached the runway, the tower ordered, "VN5673, cleared for takeoff runway Zero-Seven right."

The pilot inched his plane forward. As he started to turn onto the active runway, he simultaneously pushed the throttles to the firewall. He quickly glanced to the left, making a final check for any aircraft that might be approaching. What he saw made him hit his brakes. A tight cluster of dots appeared on the horizon, a smudge in the sky that grew larger and more distinct with each second. The objects were heading toward the runway without landing lights or red and green navigation lights.

"TSN Control, we have traffic approaching, do you want me to hold short?"

The controller also spotted the unidentified craft. So had Saigon's air defenses. An F-5 fighter squadron out of Bien Hoa Air Base a few miles away had been scrambled. The A-119 gunship patrolling above TSN began to climb so that it could launch a counterattack against the intruders from above.

The air traffic controller's voice was calm. "VN5673, you are cleared for immediate takeoff. Can't promise runway Zero-Seven will still exist if you hold for incoming traffic."

The pilot glanced left again. Reality sunk in. An enemy fighter squadron was closing fast. He repeated, "Cleared for takeoff," to let the controller know he got the message, then he turned his craft onto runway Zero-Seven, applied full throttles, and pulled gently back on the yoke. The C-130 rapidly gained speed, became airborne, and climbed away from the field.

With the taxiway jammed and enemy aircraft closing in, the tower controllers looked over the field. Despite the pressure and peril, this was their domain. They were like the guys who play speed chess in New York's Washington Square, who can instantly form a mental picture of where every piece is on the board and where it needs to move. And, like the chess players, the tower controllers were thinking six moves ahead.

The next plane moving up the taxiway was another C-130. With the first craft barely airborne, the controller ordered: "Cleared for takeoff, runway Zero-Seven right." The pilot obliged immediately.

"That's two. Three to go," the controller told his counterpart in the tower. As the enemy squadron continued its approach he added, "Maybe the A-119 will get them. If they can intercept in time, we'll be good for at least another day of flying."

The next aircraft lined up on the taxiway was an Air America DC-3, followed by a VNAF C-47. The air traffic controller directed the

Air America flight to taxiway Whiskey Three, which intersected the active runway. The order meant the DC-3 pilot had to cross the runway between planes taking off. The pilot obliged and made the turn. With his feet hard on the brakes, he used the seconds he had to rev up the twin Pratt & Whitney turbine engines so that he could slingshot his plane across the active runway. It worked. Before he traveled fifty feet the DC-3 rose off the ground and began to climb.

Air Traffic Control had swept every plane into the air except for the C-47, which remained at the end of the taxiway, farthest from the approaching enemy.

"VN6553, hold your position," the tower ordered.

"VN6553, holding position."

"Taxiway Whiskey Eleven is now the active runway," the controller announced. "You are cleared for takeoff."

"VN6573 cleared for takeoff," the pilot replied as he picked up speed on the narrow taxiway. Not only was he taking off toward the enemy fighters, he was taking off with wind at his back. The C-47 would need faster groundspeed and much more runway to get airborne. With a full load of passengers and fuel, his takeoff roll would be longer. Just as the first of the attacking aircraft—Trung's Dragonfly squadron—crossed the outer marker, the planes dropped two bombs on the adjacent runway. The C-47 was heading straight for the attackers.

Then the second wave of Dragonflies flew past, releasing their bombs for a direct hit on the runway. The C-47 pilot pulled back hard on the yoke and forced his plane into the sky.

As the A-119 jockeyed into position to attack the enemy aircraft, two of the fighters split off, gaining altitude and an advantage over the lumbering gunship. Prey had now become predator as the Dragonflies turned their twin guns against the A-119. The bullets pulverized the gunship's aluminum tail boom. Mortally wounded, the A-119 spun in lazy corkscrew loops toward the earth. One parachute, another, then another, blossomed in the sky as the plane smashed into the airfield below, killing the pilot.

Shocked at what was happening in front of them, Tuan captured it all on film from his vantage point at the far end of the runway. By now the runway had been shredded as if by the claws of a giant eagle. As the attackers passed low overhead, Sam and Lisette were astounded to recognize Trung's insignia on the lead Dragonfly and that he had waved to them. The Dragonflies that followed him climbed as they turned to rejoin his formation, putting them in position to fly over the airfield for a second bombing run. But instead of turning back to the air base, Trung shot skyward. He made a climbing turn and then, diving toward earth, leveled out no more than fifty feet off the ground. He bore down on Sam, Lisette, and Tuan crouching in the field.

Sam, Lisette, and Tuan were at first mystified and then horrified as Trung fired a long burst from his guns in their direction. But he was not aiming at his friends. A sniper, hiding 500 yards from Sam, Lisette, and Tuan, had made a fatal mistake by leaving the cover off his scope a little too long. Long enough for Trung to catch a glint of the setting sun reflecting off the lens.

When Lisette turned to see what Trung was aiming at, she saw a single muzzle-flash from the sniper's rifle. Before anyone even heard the report of that one shot, Trung's cannon fire ripped through the weeds, tearing the sniper into a thousand shards of flesh, bone, and blood. Trung then turned toward the setting sun and disappeared below the horizon.

"I guess we got our story," Sam said matter-of-factly, staring down at his jacket as he held the fabric away from his chest to keep the bloodstain from growing larger.

Lisette looked at Sam, looked at the bloody jacket, then back at Sam as he looked up and into her eyes, a quizzical expression on his face.

Tuan rushed to his side, "Sam, Sam you're hit!" he cried. He gently eased Sam to the ground and pulled away the shirt to get a better look. Lisette leaned over and pressed her hands hard against the pulsing wound, hoping to stop it from oozing more blood.

Sam lifted his hand and touched her hair, saying, "Lise, look, you've got some blood on you. Let's wash that off when we get home." Then, with Lisette silhouetted by the sun, he dropped his arm, smiled, and closed his eyes.

"Sam . . . Sam! Oh my God, Sam. You can't do this. Do *not* do this! Please don't Sam. Sam! You can't leave me. I need you, Sam!"

After a moment, Tuan said softly, "We have to go," Lisette barely felt his hand tugging on her shoulder as he pulled her to her feet.

"I will bring Sam home," he said, as he led her away. "I promise you. I will bring him home."

Tuesday, April 29

SOMETIME BEFORE DAWN, CARWOOD WOKE TO a thunderous incoming artillery barrage. It was directed at the air base, four miles from where he was sleeping, but the opening salvo was so powerful it shook the building. In the darkness he was momentarily disoriented. He was still fully clothed and for a moment he didn't know where he was. Then he recalled that he had opted to sleep on the couch in his office at the embassy.

A strange orange glow at the window got him to his feet. In the distance, Tan Son Nhut was ablaze. The oily black smoke that rose above the flames meant the fuel dump must have been hit, he thought, just as another salvo landed, adding to the fire.

He ran into the hall. All of the lights were on and people were rushing around. Most of his staff and other embassy workers hurriedly carted boxes of files out of their offices. Everything was in disarray. Papers littered the floor, boxes were piled one atop another. Carwood could see that the files were mostly documents and folders marked TOP SECRET. He stopped one of the younger staffers—the kid was new to the embassy, Carwood didn't know his name—and looked into the box he was carrying. It was filled with film canisters and contact sheets, sensitive photos the CIA had collected over the years.

"Where are you going with that?" Carwood demanded.

"We were told to destroy everything," the kid replied, a worried expression on his face.

"Who gave the order?"

"Mr. McWhorter, sir. He said we can't take any of it with us when the choppers come to get us out."

Carwood turned away and stopped another of his men, Timson, as he backed a hand truck stacked with file boxes toward the elevator.

"Did Ambassador Martin okay this?" Carwood asked.

"I don't know if he even knows about it," Timson replied. "The ambassador learned about the evac airlift we've been running for our South Vietnamese workers and their families and canceled it about an hour ago—pissed as hell—but McWhorter told us to pack up and be ready to move. Mac also told the Navy guys to keep the choppers coming."

"Coming for who?"

"We've got two thousand South Vietnamese personnel to evacuate or they'll die here, for sure. North Vietnam's not waiting any longer. They started shelling the air base overnight—destroyed both runways, we heard, and shut down all fixed-wing operations. No more flights in or out of Tan Son Nhut. We were busing embassy workers out there and evacuating them from the military compound until midnight, but it looks like we'll have to airlift them from here now—if the ambassador ever changes his mind. We'll be going too, we don't know when, but soon."

Carwood did a quick mental calculation. Helicopters to airlift a couple of thousand evacuees? Plus the six or eight hundred Americans still left in Saigon? Maybe if they had a week. He remembered what Huan Dinh had said about Hanoi wanting to take Saigon before the first of May. That would make the deadline tomorrow, the last day of April. Time's up. Ready or not.

"I've got to talk to Martin . . . and McWhorter, see what's really going on," Carwood said. "You're in charge up here, Timson. Most of these files have already been copied back to Washington, so destroy it all—papers, photos, everything."

"Sure, boss. But there's a shitload to get rid of. We're shredding and burning as fast as we can, but not sure how much time we've got left."

"You know the drill. Start with the classified docs and crypto gear. Leave the Sat-Comm equipment in place until we're ready to fly out of here—we might need it. Take the rest up to the roof and torch it. We've got a dozen fifty-five-gallon drums up there and a stockpile of sodium nitrate that'll turn it all into slag in no time. Whatever can't burn or be dismantled, have your men smash in place. I'm sure one of the engineers has an ax or a sledgehammer you can use."

"You got it. My guys will make sure nothing's left behind."

"Go to it," Carwood said. "I'll be back as soon as I find out what I can."

* * *

The chaos upstairs was nothing compared to what Carwood found when he got down to street level. Overnight, the grounds around the embassy building had filled with South Vietnamese men, women, and children, and hundreds, maybe a thousand or more, were clamoring outside the fences, trying to gain entry. He made his way through the crowd to a space the Marine guards had cleared near the swimming pool. They were checking papers and frisking the men lined up behind them. In Saigon, everyone was armed, but the Marines weren't about to let armed civilians onto their aircraft. As each man handed over his weapon, the Marines tossed it into the swimming pool. Carwood could see the bottom of the pool was already piled deep with handguns and automatic weapons of every sort.

"Gunny, what's going on here?" he asked a Marine sergeant he recognized.

"Trying to process these people for extraction, Mr. Carwood. We were told the choppers would be coming here now because no one's getting out through Tan Son Nhut. We're moving everyone who's cleared next door to the recreation center until the birds arrive."

They were interrupted by a deafening roar from above as a Navy CH-46 Sea Knight helicopter, a smaller version of the big twin-blade Chinooks flown by the Army, appeared overhead and rapidly descended onto the embassy roof.

"Right on time, sir!"

Carwood left the Marines to their work and fought his way back through the crowd to the embassy's main entrance. In the lobby he nearly collided with McWhorter, who was hurrying toward the elevators.

"Steve! I'm glad to see you!" McWhorter said, keeping his stride. As Carwood fell in beside him he lowered his voice. "Don't know if you heard, but Kissinger has ordered all U.S. and allied personnel out. Now."

"What do you mean, out?"

"Out of Saigon. Out of the country. They're sending choppers to take us all offshore. We'll regroup on the *Okinawa*. You've got to round up your people and get them to the roof for extraction."

"And the ambassador? Is he going with us?"

"He'll have to. SecState says go, we go."

"When I spoke to Martin yesterday, he was still insisting we could pull this out of the fire. Now I hear he's called off the flights taking our SVN people out to Subic! We can't leave them behind—they'll be slaughtered, their families will be slaughtered, and the Navy doesn't have enough choppers to get everyone out in whatever time we have left."

"We're working on it. Kissinger's orders said evacuate all embassy personnel, Vietnamese, and third-country nationals who worked for us. That includes American civilians and accredited correspondents—anyone the North might want to round up as potential hostages. Or spies. CINCPAC is already sending CH-46s on a constant rotation out to the ships and back, and they've promised us CH-53s if we can clear a landing zone here in the compound big enough for them to drop into. They're too heavy to set down on the roof helipad."

Carwood looked dismayed. "I've flown in those CH-46s—they seat only a couple dozen passengers! They might be able to stuff in two or even three times that number of Vietnamese, but those people will have to leave behind everything they own, and any flight coming here and then straight back to the carriers will burn lots of fuel if they've got too much weight on the return trip. Hell, they might not even be able to make a round trip!"

McWhorter stopped short of the elevator. "Our job is to get everyone onboard those helicopters as they come in, not count noses or worry about fuel!" he said, impatience in his voice. As he stepped into the elevator he turned back and held the door, fixing Carwood with a level gaze. "You take care of your section. We'll take care of the SVNs. Just be sure you've got every one of your people accounted for and on those birds and out of here when your time comes. Now, like you, I've got things to take care of. The ambassador's convening a meeting of all the department chiefs in one hour. I'll see you there."

* * *

At exactly 10:51 a.m., Chip Nolan, a contract employee for Armed Forces Radio Network and the last American disc jockey in Vietnam, shook out an envelope containing a prerecorded cartridge and popped it into the Gates Automatic Programmer at the AFRN studio at 9 Hong Thap Tu street, a few blocks from the embassy. When he pressed the play button the message, recorded as a continuous loop, began broadcasting on the station's frequency at 90.1 FM.

The message said, "The temperature in Saigon is 105 degrees and rising," followed by the song "White Christmas." It played over and over and over again.

Chip took one last look around what had been his home and office for the past two years, walked to the studio exit, flipped off the light switch, and closed the door behind him. Out of habit, he hung a dog-eared cardboard GONE FOR COFFEE sign on the doorknob—the sign that he used whenever he took a break, whether it was to take a quick piss or quit for the day.

As he started to walk away, a thought occurred to him. He turned back and took a ballpoint pen from his shirt pocket, then wrote on the sign: BACK IN 10 MINUTES. He smiled as he looked at his handiwork.

"I guess we get the last laugh after all," he said to no one.

The sun was high and the tropical heat had already begun to build when he made his way out to the courtyard. He ripped open his evacuation package and glanced at the instructions, then began to whistle "White Christmas" as he headed off to his embarkation point—the football pitch near the university.

* * *

The sun was well up when Matt awoke. He was still bedded down on the cot outside on the Quanhs' lanai. He remembered the night before and tried to recall details about what had happened, but it was already fading, like a bad dream. He got up and shrugged it off. Time to saddle up and move out.

He felt relieved when Nuoc rode into the courtyard on her bicycle. She explained that she had spent the past two nights with family friends in Cholon, the ethnic-Chinese district at the western edge of Saigon. As immigrant shop keepers—neutrals in the conflict—they didn't fear reprisals if the North Vietnamese were to take over.

Nuoc looked at the cot where Matt had slept. "Why did you stay out here?" she said. "There are beds inside and there's no one else here now."

"I figured I'd wait out here on the porch in case you showed up during the night."

"Ride around at night? No way, man!" she said, pointing beyond the courtyard. "It's crazy out there! The streets are empty, like there's nothing but ghosts walking around. Even the food vendors have disappeared. But I can make a meal for us here, there's plenty of food in the house."

"I'll go for that. Besides, I think we'd better wait until later before we try to move around the city. I heard a lot of small-arms fire in the middle of the night. The NVA are probing the city's defenses, looking for weak points, and I was told the VC are everywhere in Saigon, acting like everyday citizens while they wait for their signal."

"What signal?"

"Rock and roll, Nuoc. Rock and roll."

* * *

McWhorter had to raise his voice to be heard over the clamor in the room.

"Okay, keep it down! Keep it down back there! Can we get a little quiet, please?"

The embassy's conference room was jammed with people, all talking at once. Each section head was there, along with Marine officers and noncoms in civilian clothes from the Grounds Security Force and a group of Air Force officers who had come in from the recently shut-down TSN Operations Center. Carwood stood near the front with Timson, the CIA's chief of Comms.

There was no panic in the room, but the air was tense with concern. When everyone settled down, Ambassador Martin slowly rose from his chair at the end of the long table. Those who had not seen him in the previous days were shocked by his appearance. He looked like a very ill old man. His complexion was pallid and he repeatedly coughed into his handkerchief.

"I want you all to know this is not—I repeat, *not*—the beginning of the end of our involvement in South Vietnam," he said, his voice barely audible to those in the back of the room. "The North has not invaded the city and we at the State Department do not believe they will invade. As such, I have ordered these airlift evacuations to stop."

A tremor of disbelief ran through the room. One of the Marine security officers stepped forward from the crowd.

"Mr. Ambassador . . . Sir . . . Two of my men were killed in this morning's rocket attack. The shelling has closed Tan Son Nhut and NVA tanks and troops have already penetrated the city. They waited this long but they're coming in now. If we don't get these people out there's going to be a bloodbath, and we won't be able to stop it!"

"Stand down, Colonel!" Martin said, calmly but firmly. "State is still running this show, not Defense. Your orders are to secure the embassy. *Not* to mount an unauthorized and uncalled-for humanitarian mission."

Carwood didn't let the ambassador continue. "We now have a thousand or more people inside the embassy grounds," he said. "They came here for asylum. The colonel is right—we won't be able to protect them! And even if the North Vietnamese don't set foot in the embassy—a big *if*, given the way they've ignored the peace agreement they signed with us—those people can't hole up here forever. They were *our* people, our allies. We still have time to get them out—"

"Mr. Carwood! You don't give the orders in my embassy! The CIA, like the military, serves a support function—I suggest you remember that. The Vietnamese who are in the compound now can stay while this sorts itself out, but until you and I receive orders to abandon this mission, civilian evacuations will cease. Meanwhile, we have been instructed to move all nonessential staff out to the Fleet. Continue to use the roof helipad so the people in the courtyard won't see what you're doing. We don't want a panic on our hands!"

* * *

Outside the conference room, after the ambassador had returned to his office, Carwood huddled with the Marine officers. All agreed that they needed to continue the civilian airlift, despite what the ambassador said.

"We *will* have a panic if those people in the courtyard think we're not going to help them," the colonel said. "I've got one hundred and thirty Marines, including those we've already detailed to the other evac points around the city, and we're spread pretty thin here at the embassy. And there's hundreds more people outside still trying to get in—those we have an obligation to, and those who are just scared shitless and hoping to hitch a ride out with the rest."

"Who are you letting in now?" asked Carwood.

"Anyone with an ID issued by the embassy, along with their immediate family members."

"Okay, at least that will limit the flow somewhat. But we still need to increase the number of people we can fly out at a time. Those Phrogs, the CH-46s, can't carry enough."

"We have Navy CH-53s on standby out at the fleet, and I got word before the meeting that the *Midway* will soon be on-station with a detachment of Air Force H-53s. Those big boys can take about a hundred Vietnamese at a load. Only problem is, they're too heavy to touch down on the roof. We'd need to clear an LZ in the courtyard for them."

"So what's preventing that?"

The Marine colonel gave Carwood an exasperated look. "That damn tamarind tree is smack in the middle of the yard, it covers half the parking area, and the ambassador told me point-blank that if we cut it down he'd court-martial me and any man who put an ax to it. He said it's been there since the embassy was built and it's 'a symbol of our presence here in Vietnam,' as he put it."

"Jesus!" Carwood thought for a moment. "Screw it. The tree has to come down. I'll deal with the ambassador—and, if necessary, defend you, or maybe both of us, at any trial. But it's not going to get any easier when those big choppers start coming in. Your men will have their hands full keeping the people out there from mob-bing them as soon as they touch down."

"We know what happened when Da Nang was overrun," said the colonel. "Don't you worry, the Marines have some experience when it comes to organizing a fallback—and this won't be our first rodeo. I was a young buck private in China when the Kuomintang fell to Mao's communists and we had to evacuate Chiang Kai-shek's entire army to Taiwan. We did a good job then and we can do it now!"

* * *

Ever since Carwood told her about the evacuation plan, Thu kept her transistor radio tuned to Armed Forces Radio. She was in her office at the embassy when at last she heard the song, "White Christmas." She immediately set her own plan in motion.

Her bag was packed and waiting behind the door. Thu avoided the elevator and took the stairs to the first floor, exited by a side door, and walked as casually as possible to the parking area. She pulled her Honda out from the row of motorbikes and slowly walked it toward a rear gate. Just as she reached the gate, Ambassador Martin entered the compound followed by his cook and two body-guards, one carrying a pair of suitcases and the other leading his Yorkshire terrier on a leash.

"Taking a trip, Mr. Ambassador?" Thu said, as Martin brushed past her, avoiding eye contact.

Thu was not about to let it go. She wheeled her bike around and blocked his way.

"You have room for your dog but not Vietnamese people. Is that your 'contingency' plan?" she said.

As Martin stammered unintelligibly, Thu turned her back and moved past. The Marine guard opened the gate. Martin didn't see him give her a thumbs-up as she passed.

Getting through the crowds massing at the wall was her next obstacle. She gunned the engine and blasted the horn. The crowd parted enough to let her through.

Thu sped to the Cholon district, less than three kilometers away, hoping Vinh had heard the signal as well. As she steered down the alley behind their apartment, she could see Vinh already standing outside, holding a suitcase. He hopped on behind her and Thu turned toward their assigned rendezvous point, the University of Saigon's football pitch.

People mobbed the streets, many of them on foot, all heading for Tan Son Nhut. As quickly as the refugees abandoned their homes and shops, looters followed, smashing windows and breaking down security grates to grab anything of value.

"The university is only a kilometer away," Thu shouted. "As soon as we cross the canal we'll be there. The helicopter will be waiting."

As they rounded the corner, Thu and Vinh could see a big Marine helicopter, a Jolly Green Giant, settling to the ground in the distance. The chopper was huge—it could seat fifty passengers and pack in twice that number in a pinch. Fortunately, the plan to keep the pickup locations secret worked. The chopper would be able to move in and out so quickly there wouldn't be time for panicked crowds to gather and rush the scene.

"There's the bridge!" Thu yelled. "Almost there!"

As they neared the overpass, two North Vietnamese soldiers ran up the embankment and began waving everyone back. Several people in the street, realizing they were enemy soldiers, panicked and started to run toward the bridge. To stop them, one of the soldiers fired a burst over their heads with his AK-47. The crowd turned as one, ducking away from the bullets, just as the bridge exploded, sending wood and debris flying everywhere. The shockwave knocked Thu and Vinh off the bike and sent it skidding across the road, where it slammed against a utility pole.

Everyone scattered, screaming. With a ferocious roar, the Jolly Green Giant rose in the distance, turned, and hurtled away from the area. Within seconds the streets around Vinh and Thu were empty. In the confusion, the North Vietnamese soldiers had also vanished.

Vinh didn't hesitate. He got to his feet and, hobbling on his withered leg, retrieved the motorbike and wheeled it over to Thu, who was kneeling by the curb, rummaging through her broken suitcase.

"Do not bother with that now!" Vinh said. "Our lives are more important than clothes and perfumes. Now we need to leave!"

"I'm not looking for our things," Thu replied, pulling out a wallet—stuffed with U.S. dollars—that she had hidden in the lining. "It's this that we will need when we leave."

As Thu jumped on the backseat, she glanced around to see the helicopter flying toward the sea where the U.S. Navy ships would be waiting.

She yelled to Vinh, "We have to get to the CIA station on Gia Long Street! We'll never get near the embassy, not anymore. The CIA evacuation point is our last chance!"

* * *

"Kowalski! Get in there and spell that man! I want this tree gone—*today!*"

The gunnery sergeant was furious. The tamarind tree was proving to be made of ironwood. With two axes swinging at once, even his biggest Marines barely dented it. He knew that if they didn't get the embassy courtyard clear in a hurry, the inbound choppers would have no place to set down. He couldn't let that happen.

"Where's that chain saw! We called for it an hour ago! Tell those engineers I want to see it up here on the double, and that means now!"

Two building maintenance engineers—the only two remaining at the compound—ran up from the equipment shed. One of them held a chain saw, and the look on his face told the sergeant there was something wrong.

"We had to dig this out of the tool locker," the man said, breathless. "No telling when the last time it was used. The carb's all gummed up and—"

"Are you telling me your equipment has a *problem?*" the sergeant bellowed. "I don't want to hear it! You get that friggin' saw running—*now!*—or I will personally tear you a new asshole!"

Crouched down on the grass, the engineers worked anxiously, dousing the saw with solvent while scraping away at the crud caking the engine. Finally, one of them sprayed ether into the carburetor while the other repeatedly yanked the machine's starter cord. The saw sputtered, then coughed into life.

"Outstanding!" the sergeant yelled over the engine roar. "Now cut 'er down!"

It took less than five minutes to fell the tamarind and cut the limbs into pieces small enough to be carried away. The courtyard was clear.

"Let's get some paint on that asphalt! We need a bull's-eye big enough for the choppers to see—and some lights, once it gets dark. They'll be coming in quick and then getting the hell out quick, so we gotta clear their path."

The Marines went to work setting up the LZ, detailing men for crowd control, organizing the outgoing Vietnamese into separate lifts the helicopters could rapidly load. When the first H-53, a USAF chopper from the carrier *Midway*, roared down out of the sky, they were ready for it. The big chopper barely touched the asphalt, loaded up, then turned 360 degrees and flew out the way it came in—between the trees and buildings surrounding the embassy.

While the Marines worked in the courtyard, the smaller Sea Knight helicopters continued to take American evacuees off the rooftop and fly them out to the Fleet. The tension inside and outside the embassy spiked when both LZs began operating at the same time, until Timson, the CIA Comms chief, took over as air traffic controller, coordinating the landings and takeoffs for both LZs.

All went well for a while until the incoming helicopters abruptly disappeared when the chopper pilots reported heavy smoke coming from the embassy roof. Thinking the building had been attacked, the Fleet ordered them to back off.

Carwood, too, saw the smoke pouring off the roof. He ran up the stairs, exiting the rooftop door in time to see three of his men furiously attempting to douse the flames in their burn barrels.

"It's the sodium nitrate!" one of them yelled. "Once it gets going—man, you can't stop it!"

The fifty-five-gallon drums they were using to destroy their equipment had melted inches-deep into the roof's built-up asphalt surface. Carwood and his men could only watch and wait until the fiery substance burned itself out. After a few minutes the flames died down, the smoke dissipated, and the air cleared. Carwood went to the roof edge and whistled loudly to the men below, signaling the all-clear.

The airlift was back on.

* * *

Like a massive prehistoric beast, the scarred, battle-worn North Vietnamese T-59 tank clanked and growled to a halt a few meters short of the Ong Lanh Bridge. Below, the Saigon River moved listlessly, absent of traffic, its piers and moorings—normally crowded with river commerce—now empty. Across the span was the heart of the city, the central district, where most of the important buildings and offices were located. Directly ahead were the reconnaissance targets for this scouting mission—the embassies of the despised Americans and the equally despised French, as well as the soon-to-be-defeated nationalist government's command center, the Presidential Palace.

Colonel Binh Anh Le squinted through the tank's periscope at the empty, trash-strewn streets. Darkness was coming early, a result of the heavy monsoon clouds that hung low overhead, a thick, damp blanket that blocked the sunlight and cast a gray pall across the scene.

The colonel's mood was equally gray. He should have been elated. Seven years to get here, he thought. More like an eternity since he left his mother and father in Hanoi and followed his brothers down the Ho Chi Minh trail through Laos. Then, he was a lowly assistant gunner in his first tank—*Shining Star* they called it when they set out, *Rusting Star* as the weeks wore on—a snarling, foul-smelling, mechanically troubled antique leftover from the French war that somehow carried them all the way down into the southern Kontum wilderness. It took months, traversing terrifyingly steep mountain passes, then descending into jungle swamps that swallowed vehicles whole, fording one unnamed forest stream after another, grinding over teeth-rattling corduroy roads laboriously fashioned from logs. Through it all they endured countless nightmare days and nights when huge, thundering explosions— bombs dropped from invisible bombers high overhead—laid entire mountainsides to waste. Many comrades disappeared in those raids, vaporized or buried under the torn earth. The colonel recalled how he barely escaped with his own life in the first battle he took part in, their attack on a Montagnard and American military encampment at Polei Kleng, a victory that left his tank a smoking ruin but presaged the beginning of the long war's end.

"Do we cross, comrade colonel?" his driver asked from the dark innards of the tank, beneath and to the left of the colonel's turret seat. Squeezed in among the racks of high-explosive cannon shells, the driver, a beardless youth named Kang, looked to be about fifteen or sixteen at the most. Looked very much like himself, Le thought, when he drove the *Rusting Star*.

The colonel released the turret latch and raised the hatch cover. He wanted a better look at the Saigon he had heard so much about but had only seen in grainy photos and newsreels. Slowly lifting his head above the turret, he cautiously scanned the empty streets for enemy soldiers. Nothing moved. Perhaps the snipers were already asleep at this hour, he thought. He looked up the broad avenue that stretched away from the bridge—Nguyen Thai Hoc, according to his map. The city within view was impressive, much bigger than the Hanoi he remembered, with taller buildings. He hoped they would not have to destroy it when the invasion began.

He ordered the driver to move forward, slowly. As the tank crossed the bridge and neared an intersection, a high-pitched whine signaled a vehicle rapidly approaching, then suddenly a motorbike with two people astride burst into the intersection. Its driver was already swerving onto Nguyen Thai Hoc when he spotted the tank. Too late to turn away, the man slammed on the brakes and swerved to a stop in the middle of the street, nearly throwing his passenger, a young woman, onto the pavement.

Han, the tank gunner, reacted immediately, swiveling the turret around while simultaneously lowering the big 100-mm cannon to bear directly on the target. Kang also quickly sighted in on the motorbike with the tank's forward-mounted machine gun.

Before they could fire, the colonel commanded them to wait—he could see the pair was unarmed. They appeared to be two teenagers, civilians, probably trying to find a way to escape the inevitable invasion. For long moments, he watched the pair while the young couple stared back at him in silence. He imagined they were terrified—he would be, if he were staring down the barrel of a tank.

If the young man was afraid he didn't show it. He slowly edged forward to stand in front of the woman, who looked thoroughly surprised at encountering a tank—an enemy tank, no less—in the middle of Saigon, but who also showed no fear. When the tank didn't fire the man said something to the woman that the colonel couldn't hear, then he calmly righted the motorbike. Tentatively, the two began walking the bike out of the intersection, their gaze never leaving the tank, until they reached the corner of a building. The man nodded once at the soldier in the turret and without a word they disappeared around the corner.

The colonel let out a sigh of relief. After all the killing and bloodshed he had seen in the years and months leading up to this moment, an encounter that did not result in lives lost was an unexpectedly welcome event. He suddenly felt lighter in spirit, the monsoon clouds notwithstanding.

"You did well by not firing," he said to the crew over the tank's intercom. "Remember, we did not come here to kill civilians. We came to liberate them. The southern forces that have been our enemies all these years will be defeated, and later they will be reeducated and perhaps punished to truly understand their error. But we are still one people. We are all Vietnamese. And when we are victorious we must balance justice with mercy.

"Now forward, comrade Kang—follow the river south to the next crossing, then let us return to our camp until we are called to fight again, if that is necessary. I think we have seen what we needed to see tonight. But be alert! Unlike those young people, there may be others about who are armed and eager to engage us. The South has not yet surrendered. There is still much to do before we claim Saigon as our prize!"

* * *

Nuoc sat quietly as she waited for Matt to return. He had gone in search of a motorbike, saying he knew where several had been abandoned after their owners disappeared. Pham always told her how resourceful he was. And dependable. It looked like Big Sister was right, as always.

Before Matt arrived Nuoc hadn't been afraid, but now that he had come all this way to help the family flee Saigon, now that she knew how much her sister Pham worried for their safety, she began to realize how dangerous their situation was, if the world beyond Saigon was afraid for them. On top of that, she still had not heard from her fiancé and no one she had spoken to knew the outcome of the battles at Phan Rang and Xuan Loc—other than that the

South's forces had been badly defeated. Fear was beginning to creep into her consciousness.

The sound of an approaching motorbike startled her away from her thoughts. She stayed hidden in the alley, not recognizing the driver in his black helmet and sunglasses until he stopped in front of her hiding place.

"Matt! Why are you scaring me like that?" she said, emerging from the shadows. "I thought you were some cyclo boy coming to get me!"

"Only me, Nuoc. Just in case there are any NVA around—I don't want to be picked out as an American, so this is the best disguise I could come up with on short notice."

"Nice bike. You buy it or steal it?"

"Hey, us ex-military types don't steal—we appropriate. People are leaving stuff all over the place. I found this Yamaha parked next to one of the embassy buses, both with keys in the ignition. I figured someone wanted to pass it along."

"Well, the White Mice are all gone, along with everyone else, so I guess it's ours now." She straddled the seat and gripped him around the waist. "Where to, cyclo boy?"

"I'm thinking the U.S. Embassy is our only way out of Saigon now." He looked up the empty street, not a car moving and no one in sight. "Hang on, Nuoc—if we hurry, I'll bet we can beat the traffic."

* * *

As day turned to dusk, Matt and Nuoc cruised the now-deserted boulevards, heading for the central downtown district. It was beyond strange to see Saigon so empty—a city normally so crowded that pedestrians crossing the streets often did so with a prayer on their lips and their eyes closed, hoping the drivers would simply choose to avoid an accident. Neither of them spoke, hushed by the eerie silence beyond the whine of their motorbike. Occasionally, another motorbike or car appeared, but each time the vehicles veered away like fighter jets taking evasive action. Fear ruled the city.

They crossed the Saigon River and headed northeast. Matt kept to the side streets, parallel to Vo Van Kiet, the graceful, palm-lined drive along the waterfront, hoping to avoid any sort of confrontation. He recognized enough landmarks to know where he was and how to get to the embassy. It wasn't far now.

When they entered the intersection at Nguyen Thai Hoc, a major boulevard that ran west from the river toward the Presidential Palace and its surrounding park, Saigon's sprawling central greenspace, a sudden movement on his right caught Matt's attention. What he saw when he turned startled him so much he almost let go of the handlebars.

A tank—*a fucking North Vietnamese tank!*—sat guarding the intersection, no more than fifty yards from them, its cannon and machine guns pointed in their direction.

His first thought was to get away, hit the gas and try to get past the intersection or behind one of the buildings before the tank's guns ripped them apart. At the same moment he realized they would never make it. He slammed on the brakes and threw the bike into a spin. They were too exposed, too far from the nearest wall of protection. He let the bike stop and fall, and he and Nuoc stood there facing the guns, both of them hoping the tank crew might take them prisoner—or end it quickly. Either way, they were done for.

The tank trained its guns directly at them but didn't fire. Matt knew the tankers could see them—he could see a man's head peeking from the turret, his eyes intent, watching silently. Long, breathless seconds passed.

"Nuoc," he said quietly. "I don't know what's going on here but we may be catching a break. Maybe they're out of ammo. Maybe they don't want to fire—draw attention to themselves. Whatever. I think it's our move."

He bent slowly, never taking his eyes off the man in the turret, and reached for the bike's handlebar. When there was no reaction, he lifted the bike upright, waited a few seconds, then began to roll it toward the nearest corner. Nuoc followed in silence, like Matt keeping her eyes focused on the tank, while the turret with its big gun rotated to remain aimed directly at them, keeping pace as they walked. They expected the tank to fire with every step.

It seemed an eternity passed before they reached the corner. Finally, they neared the wall of an imposing stone building— safety, if their luck held out a few seconds longer. Matt wanted to say something, yell something, ask the tankers why they were letting them live. He restrained himself, then momentarily thought about throwing a salute before discarding the idea. The NVA was still the enemy. They would have killed them if they wanted to.

When Nuoc reached the edge of the building, Matt hesitated long enough to nod toward the man in the tank, then he too stepped out of sight behind the wall.

Then they ran, pushing the motorbike ahead of them as fast as they could. When they reached an alley, Matt stopped and kick-started the engine to life. They jumped on and raced away, the rear tire smoking.

"Someday when this is over, remind me to ask you what *that* was all about!" he yelled as he banged through the gears.

"When this is over, I don't want to be reminded about *any* of it!" she yelled back over the engine's whine.

* * *

With Tuan urging her onward, Lisette ran until her burning lungs demanded a halt. The embassy was a few blocks north—they could see the compound's lights against the night sky and hear the helicopters roaring in and out on short intervals.

As they rested in a doorway alcove, three South Vietnamese soldiers rounded the corner across from them, heading in the same direction. The soldiers didn't see them in the shadows. At the same moment a half-dozen uniformed North Vietnamese PAVN soldiers, wearing pith helmets and backpacks, materialized less than ten yards from their doorway. Without hesitation the People's Army soldiers aimed and fired on full automatic at the South Vietnamese trio, who fell where they stood. Two of the PAVN soldiers ran up to the now-prostrate figures and shot each man again at point-blank range.

Lisette's breath stopped and her legs nearly gave way beneath her. She had seen the aftermath of many firefights and was no stranger to death and corpses. But she had never seen men gunned down at close range. As she watched the PAVN soldiers deliver the death blows, the savagery of the moment made her cry out despite herself.

The soldiers reacted as one, spinning around in a defensive crouch, their gun sights suddenly trained on Lisette and Tuan.

Before they could fire, Tuan raised his hands and cried, *"Quyết thắng! Quyết thắng!"*

One of the PAVN soldiers—their leader, apparently—ordered the others to hold their fire. Cautiously, he motioned Tuan forward and the two spoke briefly while Lisette stood transfixed, her gaze locked on the other soldiers, their gun muzzles locked on her.

The leader nodded and turned away from Tuan. He ordered the others to move on, but as he began to follow he hesitated, then turned and took three steps back toward Lisette. He raised his weapon and pointed it directly at her. Lisette froze in terror.

"Saigon is ours now," he said calmly in a cold, flat voice. "Do not be here tomorrow. Your good fortune has saved you this time, but it may not continue."

Then he spun on his heel and ran to catch up with the others, who were already disappearing into the darkness in the direction of the Presidential Palace.

"We must go, quickly!" Tuan urged, taking Lisette by the elbow. "If we can reach the embassy we'll be all right, the helicopters are still evacuating people from the compound. This way!"

Lisette tried to catch her breath. "Tuan! What . . . what was that? They let us go! They killed those soldiers without a word or . . . or a warning, or anything . . . but they let us go!"

"Yes, and they told us not to be here if they should come back! We must be very careful now!"

"But . . ." Lisette's mind was racing. She found it difficult to breathe. To walk. To think.

"Don't stop," Tuan urged, pulling her onward. "We need to find a way to get you out. *Now!*"

* * *

The streets surrounding the U.S. Embassy were absolute chaos. Thousands of city residents crowded the compound environs, all vying to reach its sanctuary and secure a chance to be among those being evacuated by the big helicopters shuttling in and lifting off from the embassy courtyard and roof. Though dawn was still hours away, big floodlights had been turned on inside the compound and atop the embassy walls, transforming the darkness into day. People ran in every direction, mothers hustling small children ahead of them, men with babies in their arms, old *mamasans* and *papasans* with anxious, bewildered looks on their faces. On the side street behind the French Embassy they encountered a group of SVN soldiers tearing off their uniforms and hurriedly donning civilian clothes. A man raced up on a bicycle only to be thrown down onto the sidewalk by another man who pushed a cart overflowing with house furnishings.

As Lisette and Tuan came around to the front of the embassy, the noise of the crowd swelled—a thousand voices shouting as one, pleading, demanding, screaming in fear. Several people had climbed onto the compound fence and were attempting to scale it. Behind the fence, U.S. Marine guards held their rifles ready as they warned the climbers to drop back or be shot. Somewhere beyond their field of vision a shot rang out, causing several of the would-be fence scalers to leap back into the crowd.

"We have to get to the main gate," Tuan shouted to Lisette. "We don't know how many helicopters will come or for how long. Do you think they will recognize you?"

"I have my press credentials and passport—the Marine guards will let us in!" she replied, her voice almost lost in the din. "We'll tell them you're my husband! They'll have to get us out!"

They pushed into the crowd but the crush was impossible. Hundreds of bodies stood between them and the gate, no one willing to give way. Tuan shouldered the camera and kept his arm locked in Lisette's. As they struggled to move forward, a man in front of Lisette turned half-around and screamed at her to keep back. Tuan, tall and athletic, shoved the man away and stepped in front of Lisette to block any further threat. As she recoiled from the man, she felt her shoulder bag being pulled from her arm. She tried to turn but it was too late—the bag and whoever had grabbed it had disappeared into the mass of people behind her.

"My bag!" she shouted. "Someone took my bag! Tuan, all my IDs—they're gone!"

Tuan tried to turn and push past her to find the thief. It was no use. A hundred angry, agitated, fearful faces stared back at him. The bag was gone.

They had no choice but to continue toward the embassy. It seemed to take forever, but they finally neared the main gate, which was padlocked with a heavy chain. As an added precaution, one of the embassy's military vehicles was parked hard against the inside of the gate.

It took a full minute for Lisette to get one of the Marine guard's attention. "I'm an American!" she shouted at the top of her lungs. "I'm here with my husband—we need to get in!"

At first the young Marine ignored her. A hundred Vietnamese faces much like hers looked back at him, all screaming for him to notice. Finally, he heard the word "American" and looked toward her.

"ID!" he yelled without stepping forward or moving from his position. "If you're American, show me your ID!"

"Someone stole my bag!" she yelled back, "It had my passport and press pass—if you let us in, I can prove who I am! I'm a NBS reporter. I'm accredited. And I am an American. The ambassador's people know me!"

"No ID, no entry!" the Marine said, turning away. A fence-climber leaped onto the gate and the Marine shouldered his weapon, pointing it straight at the man from three feet away. The man thought better and dropped back.

"Sir! I need to get in!" Lisette shouted. "The embassy will vouch for me! Please!"

"Not happening!" the Marine said curtly. "No ID, no entry. Now step back! Step away from the gate!" He raised his rifle to his shoulder, his threat clear.

Lisette slumped back against Tuan. As she did, more bodies quickly surged between them and the fence. Within seconds, they were again yards from the gate, as though pulled by a strong riptide away from shore. She knew it was futile to try again.

"If we can find someone from the embassy staff, somewhere around the grounds," she cried to Tuan. "There must be someone out here that I'll know and will let us in!"

Tuan looked over the heads of the crowd to the grounds beyond the fence. "I think it is hopeless," he said. "I see no embassy personnel, only Marines. The embassy people are already being evacuated—they all may be gone by now. We have to find another way."

* * *

At the other end of the crowd, Matt Moran and Nuoc were finding entry to the embassy and their hoped-for ticket out to be just as impossible. They had come this far but now it seemed their luck had turned against them. As they pushed away from the edge of the melee, Matt thought he spotted a familiar face. He hurriedly pulled Nuoc along as he threaded through the sea of bodies until they were within shouting distance of Lisette and Tuan.

"Miss Vo! Lisette Vo!"

Lisette heard her name called and scanned the crowd. An upraised arm waved frantically, then Matt Moran emerged from the crush of bodies with a young woman in tow.

"Do I know you?" she said.

"We met last week in Saigon. I told you that I came back to Vietnam to find my wife's sister—this is her, Nuoc."

"I remember now. Matt, right? What are you doing here?"

"Trying to get the hell out!" he yelled, pushing through the bodies toward them. "I thought you'd be on one of those choppers by now!"

"Not without my ID—someone in the crowd took my bag. Now the Marines won't let us onto the embassy grounds."

"We can't get in either," he said. "Saigon's no longer in the government's control. The NVA are everywhere—we were almost run down by one of their tanks, and we heard there are sapper squads running around targeting all the main buildings. None of us are safe here!"

"We know. We had a close encounter of our own—something I don't ever want to repeat. The question is, what do we do now? Where can we go?"

"Hello, I'm Nuoc, Matt's sister-in-law," Nuoc said, inserting herself between them. "I think there may be another way. My boyfriend—I mean, my fiancé—is a helicopter pilot with the air force. We heard his unit pulled back to Saigon, or somewhere near Saigon, after the communists took Phan Rang. I haven't been able to contact him and I'm sure he's trying to get in touch with me somehow, but there's no way we can communicate with the telephones down."

"He could be anywhere—" Matt began, but Lisette cut him off.

"No! We were told yesterday that all of the intact airborne units were relocated to Tan Son Nhut," she said. "If Nuoc's fiancé is out there he might not be able to get into the city—"

"Yeah, and us getting out there would be just as much of a long shot," Matt interjected.

"Everyone is trying to get out of Saigon at this point," said Tuan. "I don't think the communists care right now where people go—there's nowhere to run. The soldiers will be concentrating on eliminating any opposition and securing the city's important buildings and resources. Listen—do you hear any more helicopters landing at the embassy? I think the evacuation from here is already over. Tan Son Nhut may be the only place—the last place—you can get out."

They looked to each other. What Tuan said made sense.

"Then we have to go now, right now!" Lisette said.

* * *

"No one's leaving Saigon, not anymore," Matt said. "Those people trying to get into the embassy? They left their cars and mopeds all over the place. I found a Yamaha with the keys in it and rode it here with Nuoc. I'll go back around the embassy to see if it's still there—if not, I'm sure I can find something else that can take us all out to Tan Son Nhut."

"All right. Take Nuoc and see what you can find," said Lisette, snapping the lens cover off her camera. "I need to get some of this on film. Tuan and I will wait for you here. Be careful!"

As Matt and Nuoc headed off, Lisette turned to face Tuan.

"Before we do this, Tuan, I need to know what went on back there, when the North Vietnamese soldiers shot those three South Vietnamese troops. What you said—'Quyết thắng'—that's the North Vietnamese Army's slogan: 'Determined to win.' Was that your passcode? Are you with them, with the North? Tell me! Who are you?"

"I am your friend."

"Bullshit! Why did they back off—for *you*?"

"Please . . . I am from the South, Lisette. I love the Saigon people. But I have always followed Ho Chi Minh. You could not know. My father was a student in Paris with Uncle Ho before our war with the French. They marched together against the occupation of our country! When they returned to Vietnam, my father introduced me to him. Ho Chi Minh was a great man, a patriot! His vision will unify the country. You'll see!"

"All this time—when you would disappear and go off on your own—taking care of family, you said! I never suspected."

"Listen to me, I beg you."

"No! You lied to me. Now Sam is dead, and you're on the side of the people who killed him. *You* killed him. You may as well have pulled the trigger! Damn you! No—*fuck you*! Fuck you, you bastard!"

Tuan shook his head. "No. No. No Lise . . . Miss . . . Lisette. Please. I would not let that happen! If I knew, I would have stopped it. I would have stopped you and Sam from going."

"Get away from me, you son of a bitch!" Lisette screamed, pushing Tuan away, her tears mingling with the sweat and dirt on her face.

"I'm sorry you had to find out this way now. I had to keep the secret from you. It was not easy! But I never let harm come to you."

"Harm? What do you call lying to me for ten years?"

Tuan looked at her with a mixture of pity and regret. "Now you must go, and I stay. Perhaps one day you can forgive me. If not forgive, at least understand."

He took a brightly colored cloth from his pocket and unfolded it so she could see. It was an armband made from a small flag—a red and blue flag with a bright yellow star in the center, the banner of the Viet Cong National Liberation Front. Lisette had seen those flags many times before, scattered across battlefields and hidden in tunnels from the Mekong Delta to the DMZ.

Tuan pulled on the armband and pinned it to his sleeve. "Good-bye, Lisette. We have waited and suffered many years for this day. Now I must go and join my comrades."

"*Viet Nam cong hoa!*" he shouted as he ran off into the dark.

* * *

Lisette wordlessly watched Tuan go. She wanted him to leave, but now she felt abandoned and alone. First Sam . . . now Tuan. She couldn't think. How could she have been so blind?

Matt and Nuoc roared up on a motorcycle, breaking her spell.

"I couldn't find a car," he said, "but there are lots of motorbikes lying around. This is the bike that Nuoc and I rode over here. I'll find another for you and Tuan. Where's your buddy?"

"He's not coming with us," was all Lisette could say. There was an awkward moment and Matt could see she didn't want to discuss it further, so he let it go.

"Look, we can take time to find another ride," he said, "or we can all go now on Nuoc's bike. It's fast and there's plenty of room for the three of us, and it's still got gas in the tank. I say we *dee-dee* the heck outta here before we find any more trouble—or it finds us!"

Shouldering her camera, Lisette squeezed onto the motorbike behind Nuoc.

What's done is done, she thought. *Who knows what's next?*

"I need to get to the airport in a hurry, driver!" she called out, gripping Nuoc by the belt.

"Okay, then. Hang on, ladies!" he shouted back as he dropped it into gear, and together they sped off toward Tan Son Nhut.

* * *

Official White House text of President Ford's April 29 statement on the U.S. evacuation from Vietnam:

(From the White House, 29 Apr. 1975)

During the past week, I had ordered the reduction of American personnel in the United States mission in Saigon to levels that could be quickly evacuated during emergency, while enabling that mission to continue to fulfill its duties.

During the day on Monday, Washington time, the airport at Saigon came under persistent rocket as well as artillery fire and was effectively closed. The military situation in the area deteriorated rapidly.

I therefore ordered the evacuation of all American personnel remaining in South Vietnam.

The evacuation has been completed. I commend the personnel of the armed forces who accomplished it, as well as Ambassador Graham Martin and the staff of his mission who served so well under difficult conditions.

This action closes a chapter in the American experience. I ask all Americans to close ranks, to avoid recrimination about the past, to look ahead to the many goals we share and to work together on the great tasks that remain to be accomplished.

* * *

The helicopter evacuations at the embassy continued into the night. By midnight, nearly two thousand Vietnamese, American, and allied civilians—including most of the Saigon press corps—and almost all of the embassy personnel had been ferried out to the ships offshore.

Hundreds of Vietnamese were still massed in the courtyard, nervously waiting their turn, while others outside the embassy gates threw themselves at the fences and clambered over the compound walls wherever they could find an entry point. With the Marines preoccupied with the airlift, there was no one to stop them.

The crowd inside the compound again swelled to more than a thousand. Unlike the waiting evacuees, the newer arrivals knew they were not assured of a place on the departing choppers, and a murmur of discontent rippled throughout the compound.

Carwood went in search of the Marine colonel and found him with Timson, who looked exhausted but was still manning the radio.

"Colonel, has the ambassador been evac'ed yet? I don't like what I'm hearing and seeing out there."

"No, I don't like it either. If we don't wrap this up we're going to have a real situation on our hands. And, no, the ambassador is still holed up in his office, refusing to get on a chopper."

"Well, going down with this ship isn't an option." Carwood thought for a moment. "I'll go see the ambassador. Maybe I can talk some sense into him. One way or another we've got to get him—and ourselves—out of here!"

* * *

As Carwood made his way to the ambassador's office, one of the Marine guards ran in from the compound.

"Mr. Carwood! Mr. Timson sent me to find you. He said the civilian airlift has been terminated—orders from the White House! He told me to give you this."

He handed Carwood a note scrawled in Timson's handwriting. It read:

The following message is from the President of the U.S. and should be passed on by the first helicopter in contact with Amb. Martin. Americans only will be transported. Ambassador Martin will board the first available helicopter and that helicopter will broadcast "Tiger, Tiger, Tiger," once airborne and en route.

* * *

"Jesus!" Carwood exclaimed, crumpling the note into his pocket. "Go back and tell Timson, and your colonel—don't let this get out! We'll have a riot on our hands if those people out there hear about it!"

He hurried toward Martin's office. McWhorter was standing outside the door, blocking anyone from entering.

"No time to chat," Carwood said, shoving McWhorter aside.

Inside the office, the ambassador sat at his desk. His complexion was gray, and his lip quivered. He looked like he was on the verge of collapse "Yes, yes, we saw the president's message, Mr. Carwood," he said. "But I'm not going anywhere. This is still my mission and I feel there's still time—"

Carwood cut him off. "Still time! Time is what we had yesterday! Mr. Ambassador, you have to go *now*, sir!"

He ran to the window and pushed open the sash. "Have you looked out there? Do you see all those people? If you're still here when the North takes this embassy, you will be fine. You will not be harmed. You will be treated as a diplomat and eventually sent home. Not those people. They will be treated quite differently. They will be considered traitors."

"Don't be insubordinate, Carwood. You are on thin—" Outside, a baby began to wail, interrupting him.

"Do you hear that, Mr. Ambassador?" Carwood didn't let up. "Do you know *why* you hear it? It's quiet out there now—the helicopters have stopped coming for those people. But as long as they know you're in here they will stay there and hope the airlift will continue. When you leave, they will leave, because they'll know there's no one here to protect them. You've got to go. It's all you can do for them now."

* * *

Matt twisted the Yamaha's throttle to its limit and held it there. The little two-stroke engine screamed in protest and he prayed it would hold long enough for them to reach the airport. TSN was somewhere up ahead in the darkness—not far now, he hoped.

Though the horizon was still pitch-black, the sky was beginning to lighten in the east, and Matt, Nuoc, and Lisette—the three of them clutched together straddling the motorbike—could see enough to know that the road was littered with burned-out vehicles, broken furniture, overturned straw baskets half-filled with articles of clothing, framed photographs, cookpots, blankets, books, papers, and all the other detritus left behind by what must have been a panicked mob. Few of those people were visible now, but here and there stragglers and a few goats wandered about, aimless and dazed.

A light in the distance marked the military entrance to Tan Son Nhut. Matt tensed. No telling what kind of reception they would get when they got there. He hoped it wouldn't be a "shoot first, ask questions later" scenario.

They reached the gate and found it wide open, hanging crookedly on broken hinges, its sentries nowhere in sight. Dozens of large, shallow craters in and around the roadway, along with a telltale odor of burned gunpowder, gave stark evidence that the area had been the target of a recent shelling. Just inside the gate they could make out the dark, boxy shape of an armored personnel carrier, twisted and broken almost beyond recognition. Grass still smoldered in a wide circle around it.

Matt didn't slow as they passed through the gate and sped toward the helicopter flight line. Ahead of them, fire and explosions lit the night.

As they approached a row of low corrugated-steel buildings, they could see dozens of helicopters—Hueys, big twin-blade Chinooks, Cobra gunships, diminutive light observation choppers, or "loaches"—all parked haphazardly across the tarmac.

"Looks like somebody beat a hasty retreat!" he shouted over his shoulder to Lisette and Nuoc.

Neither answered. Nuoc was focused on looking for anything she recognized. Suddenly she spotted a Huey with a gaping, blood-red shark's mouth and jagged teeth painted across the nose.

"There!" she cried. "Sharks and Dolphins—that's Phuong's air cav troop! He must be somewhere near here!"

Matt turned the motorbike toward the nearest building and pulled up outside. As he neared the door, he yelled, "Hello! Anyone in there? Can someone help us? *Chúng ta cần giúp đỡ!*"

The door opened a crack and a chrome .45 pistol barrel poked out, followed slowly by a heavyset Vietnamese man dressed in SVN uniform fatigue pants and boots and a brightly patterned Hawaiian shirt.

"Who are you?" the man shouted. "This is a military barracks— no civilians here! Go away!"

Nuoc stepped forward, unafraid. "We are looking for Captain Minh Van Phuong. He's a pilot with the One-Seven-Four Air Cav—I am hoping to find him here! Do you know him? Can you help us?"

"Go away!" the man repeated. "No pilots here! Maybe in BOQ hooch—over there!" He waved the pistol toward the next building, then retreated back inside and slammed the door shut.

Just then a huge explosion ripped through one of the buildings on the far side of the field, followed within a heartbeat by a second blast, then a violent salvo of rounds. Two buildings disintegrated, the others erupting in flames.

"Mortars!" Matt said. "They'll be coming here soon—these choppers will be prime targets as soon as it gets lighter and the gunners spot them. Let's spread out and see if we can find anyone else. We don't even know if Phuong is here."

"He's here, I'm sure of it!" Nuoc replied, the conviction in her voice tinged with fear. She ran toward the next building. "We have to find him!"

The first two buildings they tried were empty and locked. The third opened when Nuoc banged on the door. She spoke to the man who answered, then called to Lisette and Matt.

"He's here! They're going to get him!"

Moments later a uniformed SVN officer appeared. When he saw Nuoc he looked stunned, then the two rushed to embrace.

Matt waited a few seconds, then interrupted. "We're happy you found your guy, Nuoc, but we need to get the hell out of here, and quick! Those mortars will be falling on us next! Can the captain fly us out in one of these choppers?"

Nuoc's fiancé answered for her. "Yes! Most of our squadron has already gone—heading offshore to find the American fleet. We have more helicopters than pilots now. My men are dividing up the people here to try to take everyone out, if possible. I can fly one of the Hueys but not the bigger Chinooks, so I can only take us and a few more—ten or twelve, maybe, if some are children."

More artillery exploded across the airfield, much closer this time. Phuong said, "The women and children are inside. Their husbands were in my unit—many of them killed defending Phan Rang—so we brought their families here, hoping to get them out. We can't leave them behind."

He ducked back inside and emerged moments later with six women. One carried an infant, the others guided a group of children ahead of them. He waved Lisette, Matt, and Nuoc forward and together they hurried out toward the flight line.

"This is all the weight a Huey can carry, I think," he said, surveying the group. "Now we need to find a ship with enough fuel—not all of them were refueled after we arrived." As they approached the nearest chopper he motioned to Matt and pointed toward another of the Hueys. Each had a blue dolphin painted across its nose.

"We have to take one of these empty slicks—the gunships can't carry the weight and won't have room for us. Check the fuel levels in those two—I'll show you how."

The first Huey they checked was low on fuel. So was the second and third. Desperately, they raced from one empty chopper to another. Suddenly a new noise split the air—a deafening, terrifying screech like a Greyhound bus being dragged sideways over concrete. It was a sound Matt recognized instantly from his tour on the DMZ: the distinctive roar of 122-millimeter rockets flying directly overhead.

Six years of civilian life on the California coast vanished in a flash. Instinct kicked in.

"INCOMING!" he yelled, diving for cover and dragging Lisette and Nuoc with him. The other women and children ducked back against the outer wall of the building, screaming in terror. Matt watched as one, then another, then several fiery explosions bloomed on the tarmac a few meters beyond the flight line.

"They're walking them this way! As soon as their spotters get our range they'll fire for effect. Phuong, we've got to get one of these ships into the air right now!"

"Over here!" Phuong yelled from a Huey in the next row. The first ships they had tried were newer and in better condition than the rest. This was one of the older ones, a veteran of a thousand sorties into battlefield landing zones. It was still stripped for action—the side doors had been discarded and the interior was fitted with sling seats fore and aft that ran the width of the bird. A bare diamond-plate steel floor stretched across the passenger and cargo area from the engine firewall to the back of the pilots' seats.

The ship's age and worn condition didn't matter now. It had fuel.

As Matt and Phuong prepped the chopper, Lisette tried to ignore the artillery raining down across the field and had Nuoc film her while she did a brief report on the events swirling around them. She didn't know how, or whether, she would ever get the footage into the hands of her network, but she had to try—even if it turned out to be her epitaph.

Phuong had the blades spinning by the time Lisette and Nuoc finished. They helped the other women aboard and climbed into the chopper. Matt handed the children up to them then released the ground tethers and strapped himself into the co-pilot's seat. Phuong motioned for him to put on his headset.

"It's not fully refueled but it will have to do!" Phuong shouted over the turbine whine. "I don't know how far we can fly on this—

we have to reach the ships offshore, but we don't know where off-shore!"

"Just go—we'll worry about that once we're outta here!" Matt replied.

Suddenly, an artillery round slammed into the roof of the building that Phuong had left moments ago. Within seconds, the other pilots from Phuong's unit and dozens of civilians sheltered in the building rushed outside and ran toward the remaining choppers. Several people made straight for the Huey that Phuong and Matt were struggling to get airborne.

"If they rush us, we'll never get off the ground!" Phuong yelled.

As he spoke, two men and a woman reached the door and threw themselves onto the deck. A dozen panicked, screaming people followed on their heels, all desperate to escape the explosions coming closer with every second. Ahead of the group was a young woman carrying a baby and pulling a small child behind her. She reached the Huey as it began to lift off and threw the baby at Nuoc, who caught the infant in her arms while the mother struggled to push the child up onto the deck. One of the men grabbed the child by his shirt and hauled him aboard as the chopper began to pull away with the woman running alongside. "Go!" she screamed. "Go!" Her face was a mask of anguish as she watched the chopper rise, her children aboard but herself unable to catch up. At the last possible second another man on the deck stepped down onto the skid and grabbed the woman's arm, lifting her up and into the chopper.

Phuong pulled back on the cyclic and the ship lifted slowly, laboring to get into the air. He tried to tip the nose forward but the controls were sluggish. Too much weight! He looked around and saw there were more than a dozen passengers now crammed in the back, with others still trying to climb aboard. One man standing on the chopper's skid waved a silver pistol as he screamed something unintelligible over the rotor noise.

"Somebody push him off!" Phuong screamed. "We're at our limit now—we won't get airborne with him or anyone else, it's too much!"

Matt turned to follow Phuong's panicked gaze and found himself staring at the man with the Hawaiian shirt. Without thinking he threw off his seat harness and launched himself at the man. The two grappled as Phuong put the barely airborne chopper into a spin, hoping to throw the man off-balance. The ship pitched wildly as they struggled. Cursing hysterically, the man tried to aim the gun at Matt, who was quicker and grabbed at it, gripping it tightly around the hammer to prevent it from firing. Finally, Matt managed to free his other hand and punched the man as hard as he could, hitting him square between the eyes, knocking him back out the door. The man disappeared from view.

Exhausted, Matt fell back onto the deck, when suddenly a pistol shot exploded right outside the door. The shot was wild, the bullet ricocheting off the door frame.

He rolled toward the doorway and saw the man clinging to the starboard skid, eyes bulging with fear. With his legs wrapped around the skid, his weight was enough to keep them from lifting more than a few feet off the ground. Matt didn't know if the gunshot was deliberate or accidental, but he knew that another round in the wrong place would spell disaster.

Beyond the door, the mortar and rocket fire leaped closer with each explosion. As they watched, one of the big Chinooks at the back of the line took a direct hit, erupting in flames.

Before Matt could move, Lisette reached across him toward the doorway and grabbed the camera by its long telephone lens. Wielding it like a baseball bat, she swung with all her strength. The camera smashed hard against the man's head and burst open, spilling out a four-hundred-foot-long streamer of exposed movie film. Stunned, the man on the skid dropped the gun, then lost his grip and fell to the tarmac.

The chopper lifted like a balloon that had been held under water. Phuong powered up and the ship careened across the tarmac, at first low to the ground, struggling to rise, then swiftly gaining altitude as the big rotor blades clawed at the air. Fiery explosions surrounded them on all sides as Phuong pointed the nose toward the rising sun beyond the coast.

When they cleared the airfield, with the sounds of war receding behind them, the people packed into the crowded Huey breathed a collective sigh of relief. They had escaped. With little more than each other to cling to in the open cargo area, those who had managed to make it aboard at the last moment looked silently at Lisette and Nuoc with smiles of gratitude.

"That was nice work—nailing that man with the gun," Nuoc said to Lisette over the noise of the wind and rotors. "You saved us!"

"Yeah, but I wish I could have saved the film," Lise replied. "I had some good footage on that reel."

As the chopper raced toward the sea, cool air swept the open cockpit. The infant in the woman's arms, who had somehow managed to sleep through the last hour's chaos, woke up and began to cry.

Everyone cheered.

* * *

At 0430 hours, under a still-black sky, Carwood stood on the embassy rooftop awaiting the ambassador. With him was McWhorter, who fussed with the luggage and the numerous boxes his aides had carried up during the past hour.

"You know, we made the Vietnamese abandon their luggage in the courtyard," Carwood said, "so we could put more people on the helicopters. They had to leave their country of birth with nothing. Nothing! You could probably take a dozen of them with you if you leave all that behind."

McWhorter avoided Carwood's gaze. "This is all diplomatic stuff. High priority. We can't leave it behind."

"Yeah, I'm sure. Especially this ceramic elephant." Carwood toed one of the boxes with his shoe. "Leaving that here could be a real security risk."

"Look, Carwood, the ambassador is exiting a wartime post—under duress—that he has fought to maintain under the most difficult circumstances imaginable. Do you want to tell him he can't take any personal items?"

"There are still four or five hundred embassy-credentialed Vietnamese down there in the courtyard, by my count. Do you want to tell them that we're not evacuating them, too?"

"I told you—the choppers are coming back for them. We spoke to CINCPAC and they're waiting for the ships to refuel. They'll be here."

"Sure they will. But you won't. *Vaya con Dios*, McWhorter. I'll be sure to look you up when we all get back to The World."

The rooftop door opened and Ambassador Graham Martin slowly stepped out onto the helipad. He didn't have long to wait. Within minutes a Navy Sea Knight helicopter appeared out of the dark sky and quickly set down on the roof. Carwood offered his hand and Martin took it and held it briefly, then without a word he turned away and climbed aboard the chopper with McWhorter and the last of his personal staff.

Just the end of another era, thought Carwood as he watched them go. Leaving the roof, he wondered how the Romans felt when the Visigoths chased them out.

As the ambassador's helicopter headed toward the sea, its pilot set a course for their waiting carrier, the USS *Okinawa*. When they cleared the coast he spoke the three prearranged code words into his helmet mic:

"Tiger! Tiger! Tiger!"

Wednesday, April 30

YOU LOOK LIKE YOU COULD USE some java, Mr. Carwood." The Marine held a thermos filled with coffee from the commissary, a welcome sight. He handed Carwood a mug. "Long night, sir."

Carwood looked up and saw that the darkness had become dawn. Like the Marines and the last of the embassy staff, he had worked through the night to keep the operation moving, making sure the mobs outside the compound didn't get in and the thousands of Vietnamese still inside were protected while the evacuations continued. Meanwhile, the choppers roared in every few minutes, flying out of the darkness from every direction, landing both on the embassy roof and in the courtyard, touching down only long enough to load up another few dozen evacuees and then blasting away in a fury of rotor wash and noise. Now that the evacuations had ceased, Carwood felt drained and empty, like he had been through a battle.

"Thanks, buddy," he said, inhaling the hot brew. "Reminds me of a night I spent at a Special Forces camp on the Song Ve River in '67. I was just passing through, but we got probed around midnight and it was all-hands for the rest of the night. We never knew where they were coming from or when. The gunships were on constant rotation around the perimeter, chewing up the scenery nonstop while dust-offs shuttled out the casualties."

"Yes, sir. I was at Khe Sanh around that time. Incoming mortars and rockets day and night. Wasn't no picnic. Last night was a bitch but at least no one's shooting at us here."

No sooner were the words out of the Marine's mouth when a burst of incoming automatic rifle fire sent them and everyone else in the compound running and ducking for cover. More shots followed, which gave away the shooter's position on a nearby rooftop.

"Is anyone hit?" the gunnery sergeant yelled from behind them. After several replies assured him that there were no casualties—as of yet—he bellowed, "Uncle Sam gave you Marines rifles for a reason! Someone get a bead on that sonofabitch and put him down!"

The shooter opened up again and bullets spattered off the patio and embassy walls. A woman screamed somewhere beyond the swimming pool. Two Marines immediately returned fire from opposite ends of the courtyard. Carwood looked to where they were aiming—at the top of a building less than a block away. The Marines' rounds found their mark. The shooter's head snapped back and his rifle, easily recognizable as a black M-16, toppled over the roof ledge and fell to the ground several stories below.

"Do you think that was VC or NVA?" asked the Marine with the coffee. "Are they here in the city already?"

"Based on that M-16 he was firing, I'd say he was on our side— or used to be," the sergeant replied. "There are plenty of ARVN troops and South Vietnamese civilians really pissed off that these people in here might be getting out of the country without them."

"We got reports last night that the evac choppers were taking fire from positions along the river between here and the ships," Carwood added. "Turned out the only military off in that direction were South Vietnamese. There's a lot of hard feelings right now."

With the sun up the day was quickly growing hotter. Before the shooting, Carwood had been thinking about shedding the flak jacket he'd worn through the night. He decided to keep it on, at least for now.

He went back into the embassy and climbed the stairs to the fourth floor, where he found Timson and three other CIA staffers smashing the remaining communications equipment. They were taking turns bashing the gear with a sledgehammer so heavy that the men could barely swing it, and each time the sledge struck the Sat-Comm console the machine's powerful magnets held it fast, requiring two or more men to pull it free. The men were soaked with sweat, but they laughed like schoolboys as they gleefully destroyed what had been their most important career work until two days ago.

"Listen up," said Carwood. "Now that the ambassador's off-shore we don't know when the airlift will resume or even if it will resume. There are still a lot of people in the courtyard that have to be evac'ed. I can't believe CINCPAC or the ambassador, who's probably debriefing the admiral right now, will simply abandon them. But whatever happens from this point forward, you've got to be ready to grab the next chopper that comes in—you may not get another chance."

"Yeah, with the embassy staff out of here, things are breaking down pretty quickly," Timson said, panting with effort as he lowered the sledge. "People are already looting the lower floor offices. They'll be up here as soon as they know we're gone."

"So finish up here as quick as you can and get to the roof. I'll send some of the Marines up with you. Barricade yourselves up there and wait for a chopper—there's not much more you can do here."

"What are you going to do, boss?"

"I have to get over to Gia Long. We're still taking our people out of there, no matter what CINCPAC says or does. I don't know if I'll be able to get back here, so you'll be on your own. Just be sure you're up on the roof when your chopper comes in. And be on it! That's an order!"

* * *

It didn't take long for Thu and Vinh to reach the street where the CIA kept its offices and apartments for the station chief and senior officials. The building, an otherwise featureless multistory cube with balconied apartments and a rooftop penthouse, was nevertheless one of Saigon's more desirable addresses. The fact that the American Central Intelligence Agency used it for their headquarters was an open secret in Saigon.

Now, as Thu and Vinh abandoned their motorbike and ran to what they knew could be their last chance to escape Saigon, it was clear that far too many of Saigon's residents knew what they knew. The building was surrounded by hundreds of people hoping to leave on one of the helicopters landing and taking off from the roof. Unfortunately for those still out on the street, the gates were locked and Marine guards held their ground inside, keeping the crowds at bay.

Vinh and Thu looked for a way around the mob and into the building. After ten frantic minutes of searching, encountering one locked door after another, they couldn't find an unsecured point of entry.

"What can we do now?" Vinh said. His limp was worse after the fall from the motorcycle. He tried not to let it show, but Thu had noticed.

"Thu!" The voice seemed to come out of nowhere. "Thu! Up here!"

They looked up and saw the face of a Marine guard above them at the top of the courtyard wall. Miraculously, the guard—who was usually assigned to the embassy's security staff—had recognized Thu in the swarm of people milling around the building. He waved them toward a small service door in the wall, then met them there and, before anyone else could notice or react, let the pair through and into the yard.

"Take the stairs to the roof," said the guard. "Elevator's no longer working. When you get up there, you'll have to queue up with everyone else, but we've got choppers coming as fast as they can to take people out. We don't know how long we can keep it up—or keep everyone out—so you'd better get moving."

"Thank you, corporal! Thank you!" Thu said, taking his hand.

"Don't thank me now," he replied. "Thank me when we're all out on the ship. Now move out!"

They made their way up to the eighth floor, ascending slowly through the darkened stairwell, surrounded by people they couldn't see. Whether from anxiousness, or resignation, or emotional exhaustion, no one spoke. Vinh struggled with each step.

When they finally emerged onto the broad, flat roof of the building, they found a long line of people ahead of them, all waiting their turn to climb a ladder leading to the top of a small cooling tower that served as a makeshift helipad. Air America Hueys were coming in at ten-minute intervals, taking a dozen or more people at a time off the roof.

Three of the helicopters swooped in, quickly loaded the evacuees, then flew off again before Thu and Vinh reached the bottom rungs of the ladder. They inched upward, hoping to be among the next group out. As another chopper was about to land, word spread through the crowd below that NVA tanks and troops were nearing Gia Long Street. When this news reached the rooftop, people began to panic. The crowd behind Thu and Vinh surged forward the instant the Huey touched down above them.

Thu looked up and saw Carwood in the helicopter. The people on the ladder began pushing past one another, fighting and clawing to get into the Huey, threatening to overwhelm it. The chopper wobbled precariously as it hovered above the cooling tower roof, unable to overcome the weight that increased with each person that grabbed on to it. Carwood tried shoving them back, then he reached out and punched a man away from the door, sending him tumbling backward.

Thu's eyes locked on Carwood's. He recognized her and called out, but his words were lost in the commotion of the helicopter and the yelling mob. He waved her toward him.

She turned around, expecting to see Vinh close behind her, but he was far below, struggling to climb. "Go without me!" he screamed. Thu hesitated. She looked up at Carwood, then turned back toward Vinh and loosened her grip on the ladder.

As she slid down the ladder into Vinh's arms, she whispered, "I slipped." Clinging to one another, they watched the Huey lift off and speed away. Carwood was gone.

The helicopters stopped coming after the melee on the rooftop. Reluctantly, Thu and Vinh made their way back down to the courtyard. As they stepped out onto Gia Long Street, a North Vietnamese tank rumbled into view at the far corner, followed by a squad of rifle-carrying, pith-helmeted soldiers.

The couple could only stand and silently watch as the soldiers approached, realizing they now had no chance to escape Saigon.

"Perhaps it won't be too bad," Vinh said at last, holding Thu close. "We are together. That is what matters."

* * *

The thunder of artillery faded as the Huey swiftly covered the distance between Tan Son Nhut and the South China Sea. When it crossed the coast, Matt Moran looked down at the white sand beaches of Vung Tau, the picturesque peninsula resort early French colonials called Cap Saint Jacques, the "Pearl of the Orient."

Sitting in the co-pilot's seat, Matt felt a pang of homesickness as he recalled the idyllic days he'd spent there with Pham on in-country R&R, and it suddenly reminded him that he hadn't spoken to or sent a message to her in the week since he'd landed in Saigon. She knew the country was imploding and would be crazy with worry by now. He had to get a message out as soon as they landed, he thought—whenever and wherever that might be.

As the coastline receded behind them they could see nothing but a vast, empty ocean ahead. Somewhere out there, they all prayed, was the American Seventh Fleet. That thought gave them little comfort at the moment. It was a stomach-churning ride as Phuong struggled to maintain a steady altitude. Battered by powerful air currents off the alternately night-cooled, sun-warmed water, the overweight chopper rose and fell in dizzying leaps, sometimes sinking hundreds of feet in seconds toward the foaming waves, then rising again like an express elevator as a warm thermal propelled it back up into the sky. Matt and Phuong were strapped into their seats in the cockpit, but behind them on the cargo deck the wind tore at their passengers through the gaping open doors. They could only cling tightly to the children and one another, crying out each time the helicopter pitched wildly.

Matt and Phuong anxiously scanned the cloudless sky. The sun, at first blinding as it rose out of the sea directly ahead of them, was now high enough over the water to let them see without their dark helmet visors. Suddenly, Matt stiffened and yelled.

"Chopper at ten o'clock! There's another behind him!"

"It's one of our Chinooks!" Phuong replied. "And I've got a couple of Hueys coming up on our port-side rear!"

"Phuong, I see ships on the horizon, south-southeast! Looks like a friggin' city out there!" Matt squirmed around against his seat harness. "Everyone! U.S. Navy, straight ahead!" They looked at him blankly and he realized there was no way they could hear what he was shouting. He gave a two-thumbs-up gesture, grinning madly. "Almost home!"

Phuong raised a finger to signal Matt, then he tapped a gauge on the instrument panel.

"We'd better be," he said into his mic. "We're pretty close to *bingo*, as the jet boys say. Out of fuel!"

Within minutes the sky around them was swarming with helicopters, all converging on the steel-gray ships ahead. With no control tower to guide them, each pilot had to set his own course and somehow ensure that his airspace didn't encroach on other choppers flying above, below, and beside him at airspeeds of a hundred knots or more. Adding to the confusion, dozens of pilots were now in contact with different ships below, many of them talking on different radio frequencies, in English and in Vietnamese—an airborne Tower of Babel, thought Matt.

"We've got to find a carrier!" he said to Phuong. "We can't put this thing down on a ship unless it's got a helipad, and I'm not seeing any from here."

Phuong shook his head. "I'm not seeing any carriers either! There should be three or four."

"They may be running behind this group."

"Yeah, way behind." Matt was worried before. Now he was *really* worried. "Phuong—how long can we stay airborne?"

"Not long! We have to set down somewhere very soon! If we can't find a ship big enough to land on, I can hover on one until we get everyone off!"

"Everyone but you! What'll you do?"

"I'll ditch in the water and hope they pick me up before the sharks get me!"

They flew in silence, each man searching for an open deck somewhere among the ships below. The ocean that had seemed so empty minutes ago was now crowded with vessels of every size and description. Some were South Vietnamese Navy ships, some civilian cargo steamers, even some tiny fishing skiffs. All were jam-packed with refugees standing or sitting on their decks. They passed what looked like a large commercial trawler that had so many people that it was hard to tell which way the boat was facing.

Well, any port in a storm, thought Matt. He eyeballed the fuel gauge. It was either broken or stuck—as far below the empty mark as it could go. Despite the cool air blowing through the Huey, he was soaked with sweat.

"There!" Phuong yelled. "That ship's got a big afterdeck. We have to go for it—no more time on the clock!"

Looking left and right to avoid the choppers that seemed to be everywhere around them, Phuong pitched the nose steeply and dove for the ship. The briskly snapping ensigns on the ship's radar mast told him the winds at deck level were strong, causing the monstrous bulk of the destroyer to pitch and roll on the ocean swells. He decided to take it straight in, drop the tail at the last moment, and flare down quickly, hoping the air cushion generated by the Huey's rotors—the "doughnut"—would give them a soft enough landing even on a heaving ship. After hundreds of hours on the cyclic, much of it in combat under fire, he trusted his nerve and his flying skills. Still, he whispered a silent prayer to his ancestors—just to be sure.

"Watch out!" Matt yelled as a dark shadow three times their size—a twin-blade helicopter as big as a locomotive—careened into view off their starboard side. Phuong veered left and down as the Chinook passed within yards, its prop-wash driving them toward the water. The Huey dropped like a stone and suddenly they were looking up at the ship's deck railings. Phuong went to maximum power, fighting the controls. The Huey's turbine screamed and the chopper shuddered and shook like a wet dog, but their rapid descent slowed, then stopped, and gradually they began to rise.

"Whoooee!" Matt cried. "Phuong, you are *numbah one* chopper pilot! But let's not try that again!"

Phuong let out a long breath. "Roger that! We need to put this bird down, and now!"

They lifted toward the destroyer's deck and Phuong zeroed in on the helipad, a tiny circle painted on the afterdeck. They never saw the Huey coming at them from out of the sun, above and behind them, until both choppers' shadows converged on the ship's deck, just as they touched down.

The second Huey was wildly out of control, its panicked pilot attempting to find room on the crowded stern only to discover that he had badly miscalculated. Before he could lift away, his skids contacted Phuong's spinning rotor blades, shattering them into a thousand pieces, throwing shrapnel in all directions. As the ship's crew dove for cover, the still-airborne Huey spun crazily, careened off the roof of Phuong's now-rotorless chopper, and slammed into a steel cargo locker, then bounced hard, rolled twice, and pitched over the side of the ship.

As they watched in horror, helpless to react, Phuong, Matt, and the others in their Huey clung to anything they could hang on to as their bird slid sickeningly across the ship's deck, following the other helicopter's debris-strewn path.

Just as it reached the edge of the deck, the Huey's skids hooked the mangled railing, preventing the Huey from falling into the ocean. It hung there, threatening to break loose, as sailors rushed in to pull the occupants to safety.

Matt was the last one to scramble out. He looked at the wreckage, then back at Phuong.

"You're one hell of a pilot, Captain," he said with a wink, "but I think your landings need a little work!"

* * *

The lead tank of the People's Army Fifth Tank Brigade, its number 843 carefully painted on its turret, sped unimpeded along the wide boulevard toward the Presidential Palace. Sitting in the open turret hatch, enjoying the morning breeze that fluttered the red pennant above him, Colonel Binh Ang Le marveled at the fact that they had met so little resistance entering the city. He supposed he shouldn't be surprised. The streets were littered with South Vietnamese Army uniforms, and on nearly every corner the young men who presumably discarded them wandered aimlessly, dressed only in their underwear.

A vanquished army, the colonel thought. *Did we ever really believe we would see this day?*

Behind him, tank number 390 raced to keep up, followed by a convoy of military trucks and vehicles trailing behind. Like the deck of the colonel's tank, all of the vehicles were crowded with infantrymen laughing and shouting to one another. Ever since this morning, when they were ordered into the city in force—only to find it empty and quiet—a mixture of relief and giddy excitement had permeated their ranks.

The boulevard they traveled ran through a grassy park flanked on both sides by tall, leafy shade trees. Directly ahead were the imposing wrought-iron gates fronting the palace. As the tanks pulled up to the entrance, the colonel could see that the gates were closed tight, with a heavy, padlocked chain double-wrapped around the center columns.

He hesitated only a moment. "Break through!" he ordered.

The driver, Kang, stuck his head out of the hatch below and looked up at the colonel. "Crash into them?" he asked, wanting to be sure he heard correctly.

"The Southern forces have kept us from this victory for too long," answered the colonel. "I think it is only fitting that we strike down the last barrier, and not knock on their door as though we are asking to be admitted. Go ahead, smash them down!"

Without another word Kang shifted the tank into gear. Smoke belched from the exhaust stack as the diesel engine revved to a menacing growl. The tank churned forward, knocking one gate aside and tearing the other from its hinges. Troops from the tanks and trucks behind them swarmed onto the palace grounds and up the building's broad marble steps. Moments later, a cheer went up as the yellow, red-striped South Vietnamese flag atop the palace fluttered down the flagpole. It was quickly replaced by a red banner with a gold star, the flag of North Vietnam.

The colonel checked his wristwatch. The time was 1100 hours. He smiled, amazed as always that the cheap, military-issue watch was the one thing he owned that had survived with him until now.

* * *

From his vantage point atop the tank, now parked in the shade at the edge of the palace grounds, Colonel Binh Ang Le watched the troops relaxing out on the grass as his thoughts wandered to his home in Hanoi. He tried to imagine what it looked like now, after so many years of war. He looked forward to returning there to see his family again.

His gaze shifted to the stark white palace, and beyond it to the tall city buildings of central Saigon.

This is ours now, he said to himself. *We have won!*

* * *

Aboard the USS Anchorage, *South China Sea*

"C'mon, Gunny—I've got to make this call."

Matt hated to plead, but the Marine sergeant blocked his way.

"After what I've been through, my wife needs to know I made it out!"

The old Marine's face was impassive as he scrutinized the dirty, disheveled longhair standing in front of him in the ship's passageway. So this college boy claims he's a former grunt?

"If you was up on the 'Z like you say, what outfit?"

"Kilo Company, Second Battalion, First Marine Regiment," Matt instantly replied. "Quang Tri, Con Thien, and the Rockpile."

"Who was your CO?"

"Captain Barcena in '67, Henderson in '68. Barcena got the Navy Cross while I was there. Henderson caught a frag after I left and I heard he didn't make it."

"Yeah, he didn't—I knew him too, served with him in the Crotch before he went in-country. Good man."

The sergeant paused; then, "Okay. Once a Marine, always a Marine—even with that stateside haircut. You get one call! And keep it short! If the Old Man ever hears I let you use our comm, he'll make a tobacco pouch outta my ball sack!"

Five minutes later Matt was in the ship's radio room, a radio handset jammed against his ear, waiting—hoping—to hear Pham pick up. He almost dropped the handset when he heard her voice.

"Hello? This is Pham. Who's calling?"

"Pham! It's me, baby!"

"Matt! Oh my God, it's you! Where are you? Are you okay?"

"I'm on a ship and I've got Nuoc and her guy with me. We made it out! We're coming home!"

* * *

Standing on the afterdeck, feeling the cool breeze blowing off the sea, Lisette held the mic to her lips while she collected her thoughts. Next to her, Nuoc and Phuong held each other close. They watched as a squad of ship's Marines shoved the remnants of their mangled Huey across the last few feet of the destroyer's deck and, shouting encouragement to one other, with a final heave pushed the metal carcass overboard. It plummeted seventy feet to the sea below, made a mighty splash, then quickly disappeared, leaving no trace on the ocean's surface.

Finally, she nodded to the ensign who had volunteered to hold her battered camera.

"Let's do this," she said. As the camera whirred, she began her monologue.

"Today, April 30, 1975, I'm reporting to you from the rescue ship USS *Anchorage*, off the coast of Vietnam in the South China Sea. Within the past twenty-four hours Saigon and the South Vietnamese government have fallen to the communist forces of the North. After years of struggle and millions of lives lost, their decades-long war is over . . ."

Behind her, far out in the distance, the fighting had ceased but the coastline was a tableau of smoke and fire. It wasn't the faraway smoke that was making her eyes water.

Better end this now, she thought, *before I start bawling like a baby.*

"The American presence here—limited to diplomatic and financial assistance since U.S. troops pulled out in 1973, after nearly a dozen years of bloody and ultimately pointless warfare— also ended hours before the communists took control. Ironically, it is American sailors and Marines here on these ships that are once again helping the beleaguered citizens of South Vietnam. When

they are finally aboard this and other ships waiting out here, we—
meaning myself along with the United States of America—will
leave this scarred and tortured land, perhaps forever . . .

"This is Lisette Vo, *NBS News*, reporting from the deck of the
USS *Anchorage*—off the coast of what was once the Republic of
South Vietnam."

April 30, 1976

O NE YEAR LATER TO THE DAY, a U.S. Air Force C-141 lifted off the runway at Tan Son Nhut Airport outside Ho Chi Minh City and set a course for Washington, D.C., more than eighteen hours' flying time and half the world away. After rendezvousing with a USAF KC-135 tanker over the Bering Sea, the transport continued on to Andrews Air Force Base, where a reception party of military and civilians waited in the warm Maryland sun.

After landing and taxiing to a stop in front of the somber group, the transport's tail ramp lowered, a sergeant gave a soft-spoken command, and all of the military men, including an Air Force chaplain and eight U.S. Marines in formal dress blues, snapped to attention.

The civilians in the group included Lisette Vo, Estelle Waverly—publisher of the *Washington Legend*—and Sam Esposito's mother and father.

A large van with U.S. government plates and a black Cadillac hearse from the Marino & Messina Funeral Home were parked nearby. Their drivers stood next to the vehicles, hands folded, watching as the plane's air crew walked down the incline, took up positions on either side of the ramp, and, like the military members, came to attention.

The Marines ascended the ramp in formation and re-emerged moments later with the first of six flag-draped coffins. Each of the coffins was carried in mute ceremony to the van. The bodies in the coffins were, until recently, among the 2,646 Americans listed as Missing in Action after the U.S. military ceased combat operations and left Vietnam in 1973.

As the van drove away, the Marines returned to the plane, marched up the ramp, and carried out the last flag-draped coffin. In it was Sam Esposito.

Tuan kept his promise. Sam was home.

* * *

"Lisette, you covered the Vietnam War for over a decade and barely escaped from Saigon last April when the North Vietnamese captured the city and ended the war. A year has passed since then. What are your thoughts on this anniversary of your return to the States?"

Barry Chase leaned forward in his chair, eager to hear his guest's response. Lisette Vo was a newsmaker in more ways than one—a courageous wartime journalist and, since her return to the U.S., a celebrated figure for her outspoken commentary on the war. He knew this interview would be a terrific lead for his weekend show, the *Sunday News Hour*.

Lisette paused for a moment, collecting her thoughts, then replied, "I've got a lot of emotions to sort out, Barry. As you know, this week we welcomed home the remains of Sam Esposito, who was killed during the time you just described, the fall of Saigon. I lost a friend and we all lost a great journalist. In fact, sixty-four reporters died covering the war. I made it out. I still haven't come to grips with that."

"Do you think you made a difference, reporting from Vietnam for ten years? Was it worth it?"

"Yes. I think what I did—what we journalists did—was important and valuable. The world certainly changed during that time. France fought a war there, then we fought our own war for another decade, then the South Vietnamese struggled to hold on until the

North finally overwhelmed them. Someone needed to be there to describe the events as they happened, otherwise who would ever know? Colonialism as an institution in Indochina ended with Vietnam. The war changed America, too. It was the longest war in our history and, whether you fought in it, avoided it, or openly protested against it, the Vietnam War defined our entire generation."

"What about the Vietnam you left—the country, the people?"

"Reprisals by Hanoi against the people they defeated are just wrong. The communists have put tens of thousands of former South Vietnamese military and civilians into forced-labor camps under brutal conditions. In the name of 'progress' they make highly educated lawyers, scholars, and writers work at menial jobs. What a waste. Meanwhile, their economy is failing and the U.S. embargo hurts all of them—not only our former enemies but also the people who were once our allies. I hope this will change."

"And the deaths?"

"During our war alone, more than fifty-thousand American servicemen and women died, and it's estimated that a million North and South Vietnamese soldiers and perhaps two million Vietnamese civilians were killed. Fortunately, the killing has stopped. There have been no mass executions as there were in Cambodia at the hands of the Khmer Rouge.

"Refugees—the 'boat people'—keep fleeing Vietnam. I've heard that over one million Vietnamese have left the country as of this year, and they're still leaving by any means possible. Many of them die trying—drowned at sea, taken by pirates. It's another legacy of a terrible war, one that goes on and on."

"What about the Americans who are listed as Missing in Action?"

"We need to account for every single one of them. We cannot forget their sacrifice. Or that of the veterans who came home wounded in many ways. As a nation, we still need to heal."

"And then there's Lisette Vo. What's next for you?"

"I'm happy covering Washington politics for now, but as for the future, I don't know. I've stayed in touch with some of the people who were with me in those difficult, final days. It's a comfort to know that they've been able to put those events behind them. For the most part, they've gone on with their lives. We all need to do that—move on, but never forget. What happened in Vietnam is part of history now, and perhaps future generations can learn something from that. At least, we can always hope they will."

Acknowledgments

T HE AUTHORS WOULD LIKE TO THANK numerous individuals who generously provided first-person accounts, historical insight, and technical details about the events and wartime activities recounted in this story. Among them are former Vietnam War correspondents George Lewis (NBC-TV), and the late George Esper (Associated Press Bureau Chief in Saigon), whose insights into the news-gathering technology of the time and the realities of reporting America's first television war were invaluable in helping us faithfully recreate the period setting. Our gratitude also goes to three former Central Intelligence Agency agents: Jack Devine, author of *Good Hunting*; Joseph T. Sampson, who was the CIA's Chief of Communications at the U.S. Embassy in Saigon as these events unfolded, and his son, Tim Sampson, for sharing personal letters and photos from his father's estate.

We were also aided in our research by former United States Air Force pilots Captain David Schwartz and Major Steven Dorian (Ret.), and U.S. Navy Captain Denis Faherty (Ret.), for their first-hand knowledge of fighter jet and air transport operations; and U.S. Army Captain Sean Kelly for military background details.

Others who added much-needed color and depth to our story include David Jacobson, proprietor of Saigon's renowned Q-Bar; Jean Marie Berton, hotel manager and French ex-patriate; and publishers Lisa Spivey (*Destination Vietnam*) and Albert Wen (*Things Asian Press*) for insights into the cultural life of Vietnam. Additional assistance was provided by Vu Thi Thien Thu, who studied at the University of Saigon in 1975, for researching individual and place names.

Thanks also to the Pan Am Historical Foundation, and to Robert Ruseckas, one of the many April 1975 heroes and rescuers.

The authors would especially like to thank Tuan Anh Nguyen, co-chairman of the Boston Global Forum, who supported our research and travel in Vietnam.

* * *

We also wish to acknowledge the following resources for invaluable historical information and first-person accounts of the April 1–30 time period covered in our story:

TimesMachine, the archives of *The New York Times*.

Vietnam Magazine, published by Weider History Group, Inc.

Vietnam Passages, Journeys from War to Peace, produced by Sandy Northrup and David Lamb, Public Broadcasting System (2002)

The Last Days of Saigon by Evan Thomas, Newsweek (2000)

Vietnam: The End, an academic work, by Major Thomas M. Bibby, United States Air Force (1985)

Eyewitness History of the Vietnam War by George Esper, Ballantine Books (1986)

War Torn: Stories of War from the Women Reporters Who Covered Vietnam by Tad Bartimus, Denby Fawcett, Jurate Kazickas, Edith Lederer, and Ann Mariano, Random House (2002)

Once Upon a Distant War: Reporting from Vietnam by William Prochnau, Mainstream Publishing Company, Ltd. (1996)

The Fall of Saigon: Scenes from the Sudden End of a Long War by David Butler, Simon & Schuster (1985)

Goodnight Saigon by Charles Henderson, Berkley Reprint Edition (2008)

Vietnam to Western Airlines, Bruce Cowee, Editor, Alive Books (2013)

Another Vietnam: Pictures of the War from the Other Side by Tim Page, National Geographic (2002)

Dispatches by Michael Herr, Everyman's Library (2009)

But This War Had Such Promise by Gary Trudeau, Henry Holt & Co. (1973)

* * *

Song lyrics from *Miss Saigon* by Claude-Michel Schönberg and Alain Boublil. Copyright 2016, Cameron Mackintosh Ltd.

* * *

For more about the history behind *Escape from Saigon* and information on book events and special promotions, or to leave your comments, please visit our website: www.escapefromsaigon.com.

Despite the war, Sunday strolls in one of Saigon's parks continued to be part of the city's lifestyle. Photo by Lt. Colonel Edward Walters, USAF (courtesy Michael Walters).

The Continental Palace Hotel, built by the French in 1880, was best known for its veranda, were press, politicians, diplomats and the well-to-do gathered for afternoon cocktails. Photo by Lt. Colonel Edward Walters, USAF (courtesy Michael Walters).

President Gerald Ford meets with National Security Advisor Brent Scowcroft, General Frederick Weyand, and Secretary of State Henry Kissinger, following General Weyand's return from his fact-finding mission in South Vietnam (courtesy President Gerald R. Ford Library and Museum).

Almost immedately after NVA tanks burst onto the grounds of the Presidential Palace, the edifice was renamed Reunification Palace, and Saigon became Ho Chi Minh City, named for the North Vietnam leader. Photo by the authors.

Refugee flights landed aboard U.S. Seventh Fleet ships in such numbers, and so rapidly, that crew members simply tossed the helicopters into the sea to make room for the continual wave of incoming aircraft. U.S. Marine Corps Photo.

A U.S. Marine helps refugees aboard one of the ships in the American flotilla during the final days of April, 1975. U.S Marine Corps Photo by PH3 Harold Brown, USN (Marine Corps Association).